Katrina Shelley

Embraced

AF204998

Katrina Shelley

Embraced

Beloved Trilogy - Book One

JustFiction Edition

Impressum / Imprint

Bibliografische Information der Deutschen Nationalbibliothek: Die Deutsche Nationalbibliothek verzeichnet diese Publikation in der Deutschen Nationalbibliografie; detaillierte bibliografische Daten sind im Internet über http://dnb.d-nb.de abrufbar.
Alle in diesem Buch genannten Marken und Produktnamen unterliegen warenzeichen-, marken- oder patentrechtlichem Schutz bzw. sind Warenzeichen oder eingetragene Warenzeichen der jeweiligen Inhaber. Die Wiedergabe von Marken, Produktnamen, Gebrauchsnamen, Handelsnamen, Warenbezeichnungen u.s.w. in diesem Werk berechtigt auch ohne besondere Kennzeichnung nicht zu der Annahme, dass solche Namen im Sinne der Warenzeichen- und Markenschutzgesetzgebung als frei zu betrachten wären und daher von jedermann benutzt werden dürften.

Bibliographic information published by the Deutsche Nationalbibliothek: The Deutsche Nationalbibliothek lists this publication in the Deutsche Nationalbibliografie; detailed bibliographic data are available in the Internet at http://dnb.d-nb.de.
Any brand names and product names mentioned in this book are subject to trademark, brand or patent protection and are trademarks or registered trademarks of their respective holders. The use of brand names, product names, common names, trade names, product descriptions etc. even without a particular marking in this works is in no way to be construed to mean that such names may be regarded as unrestricted in respect of trademark and brand protection legislation and could thus be used by anyone.

Coverbild / Cover image: www.ingimage.com

Verlag / Publisher:
JustFiction! Edition
ist ein Imprint der / is a trademark of
OmniScriptum GmbH & Co. KG
Heinrich-Böcking-Str. 6-8, 66121 Saarbrücken, Deutschland / Germany
Email: info@justfiction-edition.com

Herstellung: siehe letzte Seite /
Printed at: see last page
ISBN: 978-3-8454-4534-2

~~~~~~~~~~~

Embraced

~~~~~~~~~~~

~Katrina Shelley~

Contact Katrina Shelley:

authorkatrinashelley@yahoo.com
www.katrinashelley.webs.com
Twitter/@KatShelley
Become a Facebook Fan of Katrina "Kat" Shelley

To my husband, Michael ~
Your help, knowledge, and support with this project
were irreplaceable. My Love Always.

Mom, Ben and Peg ~
Thank you for not judging, and for helping me learn
while staying focused to make this story what I
wanted it to be . . . A different way to bring a lamp un-
to feet traveling a darkened path.

Melissa ~
My sweet, funny, vampire-loving friend, you would do
anything for anyone, so this one's for you!
"Team Embraced!"

Aunt Shari ~
Thanks for being so scary! ☺
(Just one of the ways you've inspired me to write!)
I love you!

The Holy Bible
2 Samuel 23:5 (NIV)

5 "Is not my house right with God?
   Has he not made with me an
      everlasting covenant, arranged and
      secured in every part?

   Will he not bring to fruition my salvation and
      grant me my every desire?

6 But evil men are all to be cast aside
   like thorns,
      which are not gathered with the hand.

7 Whoever touches thorns uses a
   tool of iron or the shaft of a spear;
      they are burned up where they lie."

~*Prologue*~

Abigail McBride liked her privacy and her world revolved around it. She had never been the kind of woman that needed a flock to use the restroom nor did she spend hours on the phone insuring that she and her friend's outfits would not clash—the truth was she had no friends with which to clash.

Professionally, Abigail's life followed the same vein; she was a disc jockey at WKOB, a local radio station where she opted to work the graveyard shift. Since East-Hager was a fairly small town—especially when compared to Baltimore or Washington, D.C. only seventy miles away—anonymity was easy to maintain.

Abigail assumed that many people would consider her night owl existence odd, but she had never been one to care what other people thought—she was her own person, for better or worse.

The few friends Abbey had ever interacted with usually drifted away after learning her preference of being alone and grew bored with her homebody ways. Still, through each year of middle and high school, Abbey was consistently approached by one or two peers who considered her natural beauty an asset to their "in" crowd.

Though not clairvoyant, Abbey had long had an uncanny ability to sense a persons feelings and as such, their sincere intentions as well—allowing her to realize how often people befriended her for her looks alone.

On the off-chance Abbey's inherited height, curves and—when it was set free—bubbly personality, were not blessing enough, her hair was a thick, red-blonde mass of spiraling curls, flowing to the middle of her back. The creamy perfection of her skin-tone enhanced the green-gold of her eyes, drawing on-lookers to stare boldly at her heart shaped face. Abigail McBride was beautiful in the most natural of manners; yet, not one of those attributes mattered to her.

Continuing the three-mile drive home from WKOB, Abigail squinted against the bright morning sun and felt a strange comfort as she watched the neighborhood awaken in weekday routines.

Cars, minivans, and school buses passed by conducting business as usual. Employees headed to work—some local, some commuters. Teens walked to school with backpacks strapped casually on a single shoulder, a few young couples held hands and stole unchaparoned kisses as they went. Others hid behind bushes, sharing puffs of a communal cigarette with their friends.

This was the way Abbey enjoyed socializing—she was a people watcher. From afar, everything remained anonymous, untouched, painless, and simple.

On Guilford Avenue, Abigail parallel parked her white Volkswagen Jetta in front of the small brick house where she resided all her life. Turning off the ignition, she glanced in the rearview mirror and watched two neighbors leave their houses to start the day. Diagonally across the street, a home daycare was already alive with the action of children.

Life was good, Abbey was content; now she would end her day with a cup of tea some lightly toasted bread, a few chapters of the latest Nora Roberts book and sleep the day away.

The very instant she opened her car door, Abbey's relaxed emotions fled. The skin on her arms and neck rippled and she felt a familiar sensation wash over her—the sensation of dread. Something dangerous was near.

Closing the car door again, she sat back and reviewed the area without her rose-colored glasses. Everything looked the same, as before, her instincts were the only thing that had changed.

Maybe she was loosing her touch with age; after all, the dreams she used to have had faded since her teens—maybe her ability to read feelings was slipping too.

After a few more minutes of scrutiny, the only danger Abbey saw was a housewife down the street, leave her home, glance up and down the row of houses nervously, before disappearing into a neighboring house—one where the wife commuted to D.C. daily and the husband had recently been laid off from his factory job. Instincts or no, it wasn't hard for Abbey to guess at the kind of comfort Mrs. Cameron was offering Mr. Smith.

With a sigh and rolling eyes directed at her overactive imagination—very likely due to the ghosts and demons Ms. Roberts so aptly detailed in her novels—Abbey looked around again. By this time, she was tired and hungry and wanted to get to bed. In a matter of steps, she would be safely inside her home.

Nerves still on the alert, Abbey grabbed her purse and slid from the car. Adrenaline pushed her hurriedly up the walkway and onto the front porch.

Her house key was ready and she slid it easily into the deadbolt and twisted.

Then she heard it—a soft rustling to her left, followed by a thumping sound and finally a low growl that declared a presence behind her.

Abigail turned just in time to see her attacker and instantly knew that she had not lost her gift and this was no ordinary assault or coincidence—this was real and dangerous and unbelievable.

This was her nightmare come true.

~ Chapter One ~

Abigail's eyes fluttered open and she squinted against the harsh hospital light glaring down on her. In a horrifying flash, the memories flooded her mind. Her worst fears were being realized—the visions had returned, more real than ever before.

The dreams—*hallucinations* as her childhood therapist had diagnosed them—had begun when Abigail was just three years old. In the two years since her parents' tragic deaths, Abigail's subconscious terrors had stopped—until now. Still, this was worse than any of those experiences—*this* was real.

Chills covered her body when she thought of the animal that had attacked her. The size of the dog alone was intimidating. Add to that the way its eyes had seemed more human than beast and how the deep sound emanating from it had changed from growl to snarl to a maniacal laugh—*how* was it possible that a dog could laugh?

Instinctively, Abbey knew the answer—it was possible because whatever it was that had been in her dreams and in her yard *wasn't* a dog and it *wasn't* human. It was evil and it was fear incarnate.

Most terrifying of all, it wanted her.

~~~~~~~~

Doctor Nicholas Adamouras looked at the patient chart in his hand, offered a preliminary knock on the hospital-room door, and then entered to check over the latest patient on his rounds. Without looking closely, he knew that this woman was blessed indeed. Her wounds were mainly superficial—something that rarely happened in an animal attack of this magnitude. Abigail McBride had indeed been fortunate to have a passerby who didn't hesitate to help her in her terrifying moment of need.

Turning to the task at hand, Dr. Adamouras stepped next to Abigail and with perfect bedside manner asked, "Miss McBride, how are you feeling?"

Abigail didn't respond; instead, her eyes scanned the doctor in memorizing detail—he was gorgeous. Uncharacteristically, Abigail McBride was speechless in response to a person's appearance. Her insides quivered as her gold-green eyes beheld the most handsome man she had ever seen.

The doctor's skin was olive-toned in a manner that would leave him looking tan even in the middle of winter. His black hair was thick and curly and kept at a length that didn't pass his neckline, but allowed the perfect curls full reign. The only thing darker than his hair was his onyx eyes and the lashes that rimmed them. As if that wasn't enough, he smiled and its brilliance warmed Abigail to her toes.

He was perfection—he even smelled good; he needed to bottle that scent and call it *Abigail's Aphrodisiac*. Somehow—and Abbey could pretty well guess how—Doctor Nicholas Adamouras managed to make the simple scent of vanilla-mint turn her insides to mush.

The hospitalized woman continued to stare openly at her doctor until he became concerned. Nicholas had found nothing to indicate head trauma, no great loss of blood—she should certainly be responsive. Leaning down so that their faces were on the same level, Nicholas spoke louder this time. "Abigail, can you hear me?"

Abbey blinked, shook her head, felt the pull of sore muscles, and so stopped the movement. "Truthfully, I'm not feeling like myself right now," she admitted with a grimace.

Reaching out, Nicholas pushed a button on one of the beeping machines by her bed and then looked back toward Abigail again. "Considering the jolting fall you took, I'm not surprised."

The attack flashed in her minds eye again and Abbey felt a new wave of fear wash over her. "That was the biggest dog I've ever seen."

"I'm amazed you didn't hear it coming."

"I had a feeling it was near, but I didn't know for certain until it was too late." Abbey could have smacked herself on the forehead—except she guessed how much that would hurt her already aching cranium. She never mentioned her attuned senses to strangers—surely, her doctor was not the place to start.

If Dr. Adamouras thought her comment was out of the ordinary, it wasn't obvious. "There is something to be said for intuitions."

"Yeah, sometimes they're a pain in the butt."

Doctor Adamouras smiled at her sense-of-humor and then turned back to business. Scribbling something on his clipboard, he inquired, "Just try to concentrate now. Is there pain or are you disoriented?"

Abbey concentrated all right--except for it was on the adorable way his slight accent caused his J's to sound more like Y's. She tried harder and admitted, "Disoriented more than anything."

"I expected as much; that dog was moving full force when it plowed into you."

Disoriented or not, Abigail caught that statement and it registered with something he had said earlier. "You were there?"

Nicholas smiled, "I was jogging and saw the animal dart across two lawns directly toward you. I'm only sorry I couldn't get to you sooner."

A new thought occurred to Abbey then. "Was it rabid?"

"There's no way of knowing that without a specimen and it ran off before anyone could subdue it."

"When will we know for sure? I mean, aside from me foaming at the mouth, that is." Her attempt at humor was nervous.

Flipping the chart up, Nicholas answered, "Honestly, we won't. After I get the results of your blood work and CAT scan, we can decide if you want to proceed with treatment or wait and see if any symptoms arise."

"What do you think?"

"I think it was a freak attack and you were lucky that someone was close by."

"I don't believe in luck, Dr. Adamouras." Abbey informed sincerely.

"Really?" The doctor seemed slightly amused.

"Yeah, my grandmother always said that luck lies in the hands of the Lord."

"And the Devil will take us all if he can." Nicholas finished promptly.

Abbey didn't hide her surprise. "I've never heard anyone outside my family use that phrase."

Clicking his pen closed, Nicholas returned it to his shirt pocket and informed, "I once knew a lady that was fond of the saying too."

"Wise woman," Abbey opinionated with a smile.

Nicholas returned the expression, "She was."

Not thinking beyond the way this man was making her feel, Abigail did something she hadn't in years—she flirted blatantly. "Doctor, I think I'd like to take you to dinner."

He chuckled and if he was surprised or Abbey's declaration made him at all uncomfortable, it didn't show. "Miss McBride, I'm flattered—"

"But you're married." Abigail finished for him.

The doctor shook his head. "No."

"Involved?"

The gentle shake again, this time causing a tempting curl to fall over his forehead and Abbey resisted the urge to reach out and touch it. "Not that either."

Biting her lip, Abbey stated, "Then that only leaves gay."

Now the doctor laughed loudly, "*Definitely* not that." Clearing his throat, Nicholas advised, "The truth is, I like my job and dating a patient is frowned upon."

Abbey smiled again, "Then discharge me."

A page sounded overhead for Doctor Adamouras—gallantly he replied without commitment, "Let's see about those test results first." Then he left the room to answer his call.

~~~

Abigail ended up spending the night in Washington County Hospital and to her further dismay, she hadn't seen or heard anymore from the handsome doctor by lunchtime the next day.

She cringed at how forward she had been—that was not her style at all. The fact was she could count on one hand the number of dates she had ever been on—proms included.

Her mother had worried, but Abbey had laughed at that concern. "You'll get grandchildren someday mom. It's just that these boys aren't anything like I want. When they start all that kissing and groping, it makes me sick—they smell like the trash that they are and I won't have my first memories of love tainted that way."

Even at sixteen, Abbey's reasoning had been valid—at least to her mother who had always been aware of her only child's over-sensitivity to other people's emotions. Whenever Abbey was near someone feeling an extreme sentiment, the child could literally *smell* that emotion. Kathleen McBride had studied her daughter after this current explanation. Ultimately, deciding that it was best to be grateful that her teenager was not sexually active, than to worry about her romantic future. "Well then, Pet, when you finally come across a guy that smells good to you, hold on to him because he'll probably be the perfect match for you."

Abbey smiled, "What does dad smell like to you?"

With a wink, Kathleen assured, "Mint Juleps and sunshine."

And had her mother been available to her now, Abigail would have loved to share the news with her that the greatest smell ever had come into her life and nothing—not even her normal tendency to be alone—would stop her from being part of Nicholas Adamouras' life.

On cue, the door to her hospital room opened and the fine doctor entered. "Got any good news for me doctor?"

Nicholas smiled. "Your results are all clear; as soon as the nurse comes in with the paperwork for you to sign, you are free to go." Holding a small slip of paper toward her, he added, "I have two prescriptions for you; one is an antibiotic to ward off possible infections, the other is my cell phone number."

Her eyes flashed up to meet his. "Follow up visit?"

He nodded and his shining black eyes danced, "If that's what you want to call it."

"What I *want* to call it is a date—six o'clock on Wednesday."

Pulling his Blackberry out of his pocket, Nicholas pressed some buttons, "Works for me; unless of course there is an emergency and I'm needed here."

Abigail nodded, "I'll take my chances."

With a new smile, Nicholas advised; "I'll pick you up." Then in a teasing tone added, "Just so I remember, it's the house with the Beware of Dog signs, right?"

Abbey laughed, "Yeah, that's the one."

~~~

Three days later, Abbey put the final touches on her appearance and walked down the steps from her bedroom toward the sound of knocking on her door. Swinging the divider open, she smiled, caught her breath, and maintained the welcoming expression. "Very prompt, I like that, but don't expect it in return."

Nicholas grinned and held a small bouquet of yellow daisies toward her. "I'm a doctor, how often do you know us to be on time?"

"So I shouldn't get used to it either?" She took the flowers, sniffed them lightly, before turning from the door and toward the kitchen.

From the open doorway, Nicholas replied, "Not unless you like disappointment."

"I don't." After sticking the flowers in a vase and filling it with water, Abbey placed the arrangement on her dining room table as she passed by. Grabbing her coral-colored handbag—perfectly matched to her sundress and heeled sandals—Abbey breezed to the door and offered, "Thanks for the flowers, they're beautiful."

Nicholas' eyes darkened noticeably and he smiled, "I knew you'd like them."

Despite her recent handling of the gift he'd brought, the scent of him--vanilla-mint, now hinting of the slightest bit of cologne--assulted Abigail's senses. "Maybe there *is* something to be said for instincts then, since yellow is my favorite color."

"Maybe I'm just lucky."

She loved the quick wit, possibly more than the great smell. Closing and locking the door behind her, Abigail grinned slyly. "As I said before, luck isn't something I count on."

"What *do* you count on then?"

"Myself," Abbey responded easily.

Taking her hand in his—with what seemed like the most natural motion in the world—Nicholas led Abigail down the three porch-steps and toward his car, informing, "I intend to change that."

"Good, then I have something else to count on." Abbey finished, allowing him to hold the car door open as she slid into the passenger seat of his silver Audi.

~~~

Though she had little to compare it to, Abigail was having the best date ever. The flowers, the man, and the restaurant—every part of it was perfect—and she didn't want it to end.

The place Nicholas had chosen wasn't far from her house and it was a local favorite, appreciated for its relaxed atmosphere and outstanding Maryland crab cakes. After two of those and as many strawberry daiquiris, Abigail was in a very happy place.

Across the booth-table, Nicholas had the distinct feeling that this beautiful woman was treating him to a side of herself that most people never had the opportunity to see. They were relaxed together and he hoped that the remainder of the evening would continue as such.

"What'cha thinkin', doc?" Abbey asked, stirring the last of the dark-pink slush around in the bottom of her glass.

"Just wondering what's next?"

Abbey smiled, "You mean you don't have a *plan*?"

Nicholas chuckled, "Not at the moment." The waiter came to collect the bill and the conversation lulled momentarily. When Nicholas turned back toward her again, he sensed the open invitation as clearly, as if she had spoken the words aloud.

Standing, he held his hand out toward Abbey and suggested, "Why don't you tell me what you'd like to do?"

The gold specks in her green eyes shimmered and the alcohol she was unaccustomed to ingesting supported Abbey's insinuation. "Because I think I'd rather show you."

Nicholas saw through her liquid courage and knew that she would quite possibly hate him in the morning if he took advantage of her now. "I'm not sure I believe you."

Abbey faltered slightly and Nicholas took the opportunity to lead her from the restaurant and toward his car. The fresh air of the fall evening was cool and the change in temperature heightened Abigail's awareness of the man with her. She waited until he held the car door open for her, but rather than slide in, she looked him in the eye and asked, "So you don't believe *me*, and I'm not clear on where you stand with luck—what *do* you believe in Doctor?"

His accented words were husky, "I believe in a great many things."

"But not my words?"

Involuntarily, Nicholas' eyes darted down to her full lips, then back to her eyes again. He wanted to look more, to peer at the teasing hint of cleavage that the scooped neckline of her coral dress allowed his hungry eyes. Nicholas wanted to continue lower over Abigail's curving waist and hips, bared legs with the shoes that allowed a peek at her perfect feet. However, every time he reached the pulse moving on the side of her graceful neck, he forced his dark eyes upward again. Abigail's excitement reminded him that it was better to wait—to be sure—than to rush forward and ruin what he prophesied to be a fantastic thing brewing between them.

Returning to their conversation and away from his errant thoughts, Nicholas assured, "I believe your words, I am just not certain you are really ready to speak them."

Stepping closer, she teased his lips with the breath passing over her own and whispered, "Then I won't speak." The kiss Abbey offered was slow and sensual, just as she had dreamed of kissing and being kissed—it was exactly as it should be.

The tender give and take, the test and reward was wonderful and for the first time in twenty-two years, Abigail knew what it was to want a man in the most basic of ways. True—many had wanted her, but not once had the feeling been reciprocated, until now.

Pulling back, she whispered, "Don't waste my time, Nicholas. I'm not a woman to second-guess my decisions and I don't make them lightly—no matter what it seems like at the moment."

"Then tell me what you want."

Raising her fingertips to the felt-but-unseen stubble on his cheek, Abigail stated plainly, "I want you." She kissed him again, though not as long this time. "Take me home." Then she sat down on the leather-covered car seat, Nicholas shut the door and moved around to the driver's side so that he could do her bidding.

~~~~~~~~

The next morning, Abigail woke to the bitter disappointment of loneliness.

Following their meal, from the time they left the restaurant parking lot until they completed the five-minute drive back to Abbey's house, Nicholas was paged twice and called once, —the hospital needed him.

Even with her understanding, Abbey still felt the slight sting of rejection. Moreover—in the bright light of day—*how* did one face a man whom they had so bluntly propositioned only to be rejected? With solid reasoning or not, the humiliation was certainly just as devastating.

It *must* be worse than actually completing the act and then having to face one another with such carnal awareness. But Abigail didn't know either way since she was a virgin.

Rolling from her bed and padding downstairs, through the living room and dining room—both filled with mismatched furnishings from purchases all generations of her family had made. Taking special note of the yellow flowers on the table, Abbey grinned, a goofy grin, and continued into the narrow kitchen.

Grabbing a mug from the cupboard, Abigail promptly began to fill it with the hot coffee her pre-programmed maker had ready.

The tiny kitchen was lit from one side, by a serving window, that opened into the dining room. A few green plants and herbs sat on its ledge—sunlight feeding them from the outside window opposite. Against the back wall, a small oak-laminate drop-leaf table and chairs waited invitingly—though if someone were to actually sit there, using the oven would be virtually impossible. A white range and re-frigerator stood at the far end of the room, butted against a line of cabinets and countertop that lined the rear wall.

The view from the over-sink window made Abigail feel at home. On a fall morning such as this, she loved to watch the morning start. The sound of the sturdiest birds, still remaining in the area before fly-ing south, the brightness of the changing leaves swirling to the ground in the cooling breeze—it was like a special greeting card, just for Abigail.

However, this morning, there was no evidence of blackbird caws or scurrying squirrels. Abbey did a quick re-survey of her yard—the gate centered in the chain link fence, separating her back lawn from the alley and neighboring lots, stood open. This was impossible—the bolt lock was rusted and immobile from disuse.

Then Abigail saw the motion.

The four-foot-high winter-sturdy greenery that lined the back of her quarter-acre lot shook lightly as the monstrous orange and black dog stepped out from behind its leafy screen.

Every move it made was deliberate. The space between Abbey and the snarling animal was closing at a taunting pace. The dark eyes watched its prey with concentrated hunger—its intent clearer with each step it took.

Before Abigail's horrified eyes, the animal changed—*misted* into the shape of a man. And aside from the obvious—Abbey knew this was no ordinary being. This was a predator, and the same one that had followed behind Abigail in dreams throughout much of her life.

She was not sleeping now though.

In an instant, it depleted the distance between them.

Abbey seared through a series of amazing and horrifying realizations, primarily that the man was scarier than she could have imagined. Not because he was hideous, but because he was beautiful with a physique, muscularly trim and taunt. Either the creature was of incredible height or had the ability to float since his upper body remained at Abbey's eyelevel, through a window positioned at least seven feet off the ground. The chiseled face and coloring reminded her of a statue, which made its lips dark-er—full red lips that seduced at a glance, promising pleasure that Abigail could scarcely fathom. Eyes the clearest crystal-blue, were specked with silver, and centered with a shimmering mercury pupil. The glistening pool slowly outlined with a golden circle.

It was beauty and beast.

Abigail couldn't move.

He spoke—his voice sounding like grating gravel and symphonic strings simultaneously and Abigail again felt her senses hover between horror and arousal.

His lips didn't move, but through the barrier of glass and screen, she heard the creature just as though he stood directly beside her. A smile, slow and dangerous lit his features and then his perfect expression morphed again—teeth glimmered like stars in a night sky, as canine fangs dropped down.

Won't you invite me in?

Abbey's nerves melded into full-on fear and her limbs began trembling. She didn't bother to still them. As much as she wished to hide her fear, she knew beyond doubt that he could smell it. Her silence was golden. The man/creature laughed, *Silly child, your silence won't save you. I could* The man/creature laughed. *Silly child, I could make you beg me to come in, to give you a million lifetimes to waste on your pathetic doctor.* The eyes turned colder still, the yellow ring glowing as the silver specks darkened. Drops of crimson seeped inward from the outer sphere, until the entire circumference filled with the red of blood. The music left his voice and only the grating continued, *Let me end your torment and show you what a lover of the night can do for your needing body, you diluted whore.*

Raising a hand—perfect except for the three-inch claws that capped the tips of long fingers—it lazily drew one of the razor-blade-like appendages down the screen, scoring as it went.

With every bit of her strength, Abigail broke the trance she was slipping into and ran to the next room to fumble for her cell phone.

Evil laughter followed on her heels—echoing through her mind and house in a way that seemed to have the noise clinging to the walls around Abbey. She hit the button and waited to hear the only person she knew to call on.

Nicholas' voice sounded, "Good morning."

A bloodcurdling scream of terror greeted him, as Abigail—feeling a strange empowerment the same instant Nicholas' voice crossed the lines—chanced a look back toward her kitchen.

The monster was gone—but in its place—irrevocably etched on the glass of her favorite view—was one terrifying word:

Soon.

~ Chapter Two ~

Abigail's sobbing had subdued to sniffles by the time Nicholas pounded on her front door. She wasn't sure how long it had taken him to get there, but it was certainly record time. She swung the door open and pulled him through the front entranceway. Then as though he had been part of her life forever, Abbey threw her arms around his neck for the support she so desperately needed.

He pushed the door closed behind them and immediately started speaking in a soothing manner as he slowly steered her wilted form toward the couch. Absently, Abbey guessed that he was speaking Greek, since she couldn't understand a single syllable he uttered. Still it was like a lullaby, and she could have listened to the smooth sound for hours—or at least until her heartbeat returned to its normal rhythm.

After a few moments, she looked up at him and wiped away the remaining tears on her cheeks. "I didn't know who else to call."

"I'm pleased to be the one you chose." Nicholas tucked a piece of hair behind her ear and met her frightened gaze with his steadier one, admitting, "Though, I must say you scared me a bit too."

She sniffled, "Sorry, but I've never known fear like that before. It was all so unbelievable."

"Are you *sure* it was the same dog?"

Nicholas' concern was sincere and Abbey hated to ruin the chemistry that was running between them, but she had to talk, to tell someone what she had seen. "You might think I'm crazy, but it was only a dog for the first few seconds."

"*It?*"

Abbey's eyes darted toward the kitchen window and her voice quivered as she spoke, "Aren't Greeks supposed to be superstitious?"

"Yes, some of us are *very* superstitious, but I think any culture is, depending on how many generations you go back." His smile was warm and calming. Squaring his shoulders in teasing preparation he asked, "Why, are my cultural beliefs going to be needed for the next face-off?"

Abbey closed her eyes—but the memory that met her in the darkness had her green orbs open instantly again.

"Why are we already assuming there will be another incident?" Abbey sighed silently accepting the certainty of that possibility, then continued, "And if so, I think it's going to take *several* different cultural beliefs to get us through."

Nicholas raised a dark brow and though his smile remained in place, he asked with a slightly teasing tone, "Abigail, do you have a werewolf chasing you?"

"Do not laugh at me. I don't know what it is except that it changed from a dog to a man to a . . . a . . . . demon."

All humor fled Nicholas' expression. "*Demon* is a fairly strong accusation in any culture." Taking her hand in his, he squeezed lightly, "Why don't you tell me what happened."

So, Abigail did as requested. She shared each horrific detail from the trembling flower bush to the etching on the window. When she had finished, Nicholas stood and walked into the kitchen. Abigail remained glued to the couch, watching him move.

Leaning against the counter, Nicholas searched the yard, then looked at the windowpane, reached his hand up, and wiped the glass with his fingertips. "Abbey, I don't see anything."

"I know; he disappeared when I called you."

"No, I mean, I don't see anything on the glass either."

"What?" Abigail walked into the kitchen and stood rigidly beside Nicholas. He was right—the glass was as clear as it had been the day before. "I don't understand."

Turning, Nicholas tilted her head up so that their eyes met. "How are you feeling?"

"Fine." She stepped back. Abbey knew that searching concerned look. She had seen it on countless other physicians during her childhood—each trying to determine why she had the plaguing dreams.

Nicholas sensed her emotional withdraw—her defenses were on the rise. "Abigail, I'm not saying that I don't believe you."

"You're not saying that you *do* either." She sighed, pulled out a kitchen chair, and sat heavily down upon it. "Nicholas, I know what I saw."

"Is there any other detail you can give me? Maybe something you left out?"

"You mean besides the bleeding eyes and gnashing teeth?" Abbey leaned her aching head against the upturned palms of her hands. Still not closing her eyes against the dull pain that throbbed through it for fear of the darkness, she replied, "I don't think so."

Nicholas wasn't convinced. "What else aren't you telling me?"

Abigail knew what he meant, what he wanted and that he was right—it was part of the gift she had carried since the first dream. "I've seen him before in visions."

"First werewolves, second demons—are you telling me now that you are a fortune teller?"

Her lips curved slowly upward and she stated dubiously, "Not if it's a turnoff." It was easier to grasp on to what was comfortable and for Abbey, comfort and humor were synonymous.

Nicholas laughed softly, happy that a bit of her fear finally slipped away so that the wonderful sense of humor peeked through. "Allow me to assure you that nothing at all about you is a turnoff for me, Abigail McBride."

She melted a little more. "I'm waiting for valid proof of that."

His laughter grew. "If you can see into the future, then you should know that is a great likelihood."

"It's not all futures I see; only those nightmares involving this beast and me."

"You've never seen others in these visions?"

"Other people or other demons?"

"Either." Nonchalantly, Nicholas looked out the window again, his eyes narrowed as he searched, then he turned back to await her answer.

"There is a man—two actually, though one is the same that I saw in my yard this morning, the other I don't know, but he seems connected to me in some way."

"Reincarnation?"

Abbey shook her head negatively, "That's even far fetched for me."

Nicholas chuckled. "Reincarnation or rebirth is too much, but you admit to believing in *vrykola-kas*?"

Abbey stared blankly at his Greek terminology, so Nicholas explained, "You believe in vampires. A creature that sleeps in his grave by day and roams the countryside by night, to drain the blood from the living, so that he might maintain his living-death?"

When her face turned an ashen hue, Nicholas realized she was no longer confused. "I never said the word *vampire*."

Nicholas was confident, "But you *thought* it, didn't you?"

Abbey considered that a rhetorical question, and so clarified, "So *I* have visions and *you* read minds." With a roll of her green eyes, she deduced, "We're a perfect pair of freaks."

Nicholas shook his head while correcting, "I can't read your mind Abigail. I am just patient and a good listener. Also, the description you gave me sounds like every vampire movie I've ever watched."

Abbey looked down at her hand and noticed that one of her fingernails was cracked and broken. Ignoring the need for a manicure, she whispered, "This is insane."

"Only because you don't have answers." Nicholas walked to her and brought her to a standing position within the gentle circle of his arms. "What's worse for me than the thought of real-life horror movies is the fact that you are in danger."

"Yeah, but how *much* danger? I mean, which horror movie are we dealing with here—just a little Fright Night or are we fighting off Salem's Lot?"

Leaning back to look down at her, Nicholas asked sincerely, "When's the last time you watched Fright Night? I don't think I'd want to face any of those creatures more than that thing knocking on the window in Salem's Lot."

Abbey cringed, "Apparently, I'm not to be given a choice."

"At least what you've described is, thankfully, no Nosferatu."

Both of Abbey's red-blonde eyebrows shot upward and her forehead crinkled with surprise. "Something tells me I should be glad about that, but right now I'm more curious as to your sudden knowledge on this dark topic."

He pointed a dark finger at his chest and grinned impishly, "Old world, Greek, remember?"

His playfulness helped her relax a bit. "I remember."

With a semi-guilty expression, he added, "Plus I'm a sucker for horror movies."

Abbey's eyes widened. "Seriously?"

"Completely."

"We'll have to have a movie night then."

"You like horror?"

She peeked toward her window and then at him once more. "Not so much in person, but I *love* movies."

Nicholas planned to run with this veering topic since he could tell it was beginning to clear her mind of the earlier events. "What's your favorite?"

"It's hard to pick one."

Nicholas was ready. "I'll take classics for five-hundred."

Abbey smiled easily and offered her clever reply, "What is *Gone with the Wind*?" Nicholas said nothing, which Abbey took for the typical male response. "I know, biggest of all chick flicks and you've not seen it before."

His smile grew confident. "No, I've seen it."

"Without falling asleep?" She accused curiously.

"From the first 'Fiddle dee dee', to the final 'After all, tomorrow is another day.'" He looked a little smug when he added, "I've read it from cover to cover too."

"I think I love you," Abbey said with forced awe.

"I'll settle for a second date."

Snuggling closer into the circle of his arms, Abbey questioned, "This doesn't count?"

"If you'd like." He kissed the top of her head. "I'm not going to bother keeping track."

She didn't move, but mumbled, "That's not very romantic of you. How else are you supposed to know when we've had our tenth date?"

"'Frankly, my dear, I don't give a damn.'"

"Cute," Abbey allowed, and then waited for more.

"The truth is I don't need to keep track of my time with you, Abigail. I'm so comfortable when you're around that it feels as though I've known you forever."

"Now *that's* romantic," Abbey sighed softly.

Nicholas couldn't resist moving in for a kiss. It was slow and warm, just what Abigail needed now. When he was finished with the tender caress, Nicholas punctuated it by stating, "No, *that's* the *truth*."

~~~

Nicholas had to leave. He assured Abbey that after he finished his remaining responsibilities at the hospital—which he had dropped for her instantaneously that morning—he would return to keep her safe from monsters.

She filled the time and her mind with the task of preparing an evening for them. Abbey hoped that the only scary entertainment they might have would be that coming from the flat-screen television hanging on her living room wall.

Nicholas was only gone two hours and, when he returned, Abbey noticed—with a tiny thrill—that he carried a small overnight bag with him.

He smiled at the scene Abbey had created in her small living room. There were about ten movies spread out on the coffee table, the smell of fresh popcorn filling the air and a divided basket with an array of snack foods—warm and cold—filling each section.

"Welcome to movie night."

Nicholas set his bag against the wall in the foyer and observed, "I don't think I've been doing it right."

Abbey chuckled. "This is special. It was sort of a family tradition with my parents. Every Friday night was movie and snack night."

Warm eyes turned toward her, "Thank you for sharing it with me."

"You are very welcome." Changing her tone to impatient she added, "Now go get into something more comfortable and hurry back so we can pick our first movie and eat." She paused, "What do you want to drink?"

"Whatever you're having is fine for me too," he supplied and took a moment to fully appreciate the adorable sight of her. Her mass of red-blonde curls were pulled back with a twist and held loosely with a hair clip. She wore dark-blue cotton pajama top and light-blue bottoms with fuzzy socks that sported horizontal strips of both shades. "I like this look," he complimented sincerely.

"Good, 'cause it took me hours," Abbey replied with mock weariness and then pointed toward the stairs. "The bathroom is the first door on the left."

"'I'll be back,'" Nicholas stated with a very bad impersonation.

"Yeah, that's not my style of movie."

"I'm okay with that," he called back, already at the bathroom door above.

~~~

Nicholas returned downstairs to find Abbey snuggled into the corner of the couch leaving the other side open for him. On the table in front of his empty space were a glass of iced soda and a small empty plate, waiting for him to fill with his choices of snack goodies.

"I think I could get used to this," he stated while coming around to sit beside her.

Abbey could tell from the wetness clinging to the curled ends of his dark hair that Nicholas had showered—a vision she tried not to dwell on for too long. He wore a clean set of light-green scrubs and a pair of flip-flop style slippers. "Do you use vanilla shower gel?"

Nicholas had just settled beside her and the unexpected question surprised him. "No, that doesn't seem very masculine to me." He looked at her in question, "Why, should I?" He sniffed as though checking to make sure he didn't stink.

Abbey laughed. "No, you're fine—*very* fine." Her additional words did not go unnoticed. "But I always smell vanilla when you are around."

He shrugged, "Maybe it's something in my fabric softener." Leaning forward, he looked at the array of movies she had out for them. "Are these all yours?"

She nodded and admitted, "Guilty pleasure. My parents figured as often as we did movie night, it was cheaper to buy our favorites than to rent them all the time."

"*Favorites*? How many do you *have*?"

"Eighty-nine."

"Because ninety is just a little too obsessive?"

Abbey smiled, "No, it just worked out that way."

"How?"

Abbey nodded and with smile bordering on shy, explained, "Since my parents . . ." she rerouted her words, " . . . I've stopped collecting. I usually get one through the mail-rental service. If I like it, I'll buy it. Mom had gotten into the habit of buying a movie before we even saw it. I never liked that plan since we got stuck with some pretty bad, low-budget films that way."

"I can imagine." Nicholas sympathized, while continuing to look over the titles.

A wide variety of choices were offered. Abbey must have planned it that way, so that he would have options from all genres. Romance: *While You Were Sleeping* and *10 Things I Hate About You*. Drama: *Rudy* and *Fried Green Tomatoes*. Action: *Righteous Kill* and *True Lies*. She also offered, *Dirty Dancing, Saw II, A Knight's Tale, Dead Silence, The Sound of Music,* and *The Phantom of the Opera*—the newest release of the film, with the Andrew Lloyd Webber music.

"What, no *Interview with the Vampire, Twilight* or *American Werewolf in London*?" Nicholas teased.

"Oh, I have each of those, but I wasn't quite in the mood tonight." She flipped her hand up absently, "Call me crazy."

"Crazy," he obliged.

Abbey stuck her tongue out playfully. "Just pick one."

Nicholas picked up *Righteous Kill*, looked at the back cover, and set it aside again. Next, he lifted *Saw II* from the pile and then *Dead Silence*. "I'm seeing a pattern here."

Abbey smiled, "My mom was a huge *New Kids on the Block* fan. I think we have every film Donnie Wahlberg was ever in—whether it was a big or small role."

Nicholas glanced at her briefly and then picked up *A Knight's Tale* while asking, "Is he related to Mark Wahlberg?"

Abbey could sense her mother rolling over in the grave. "Yes, Mark is Donnie's younger brother."

Nicholas didn't seem as impressed as Abigail's mother surely would have liked. Laying aside the three movies in discussion, he suggested, "Maybe we'll try one of his another time. Tonight I think we'll pay tribute to Heath."

Abbey took the movie from his hand, "Sounds great to me." Then she stood and put the DVD in the player.

Returning to her spot, she handed him a small plate and took one for herself. "If anything is too cold now, we can nuke it."

Nicholas nodded and followed her lead of putting a few different choices on his plate. Readjusting, they ate while the movie began. The silence between them didn't last long. "I'm breaking a family-movie-night-rule by interrupting the movie, but I have to ask you about something you said earlier to-day."

Nicholas easily took his attention from the screen to give it to Abigail, "Yes?"

With caution she questioned, "I've heard the word before and have a general idea, but do I want to *know* exactly what a Nasfo—" she tried again, "Nasforen—

"Nosferatu." Nicholas supplied.

"Yes," Abbey accepted, "do I want to know what *that* is?"

Nicholas' smiled faded. "No, you don't—but you're going to have to. In fact, we are going to have to learn about that kind of vampire and a lot more evil to keep you protected."

"You mean to keep *us* protected," Abigail corrected. "*Whatever* this thing is—considers you a threat for some reason too. I'm guessing it knows you want to help me and doesn't take too kindly to outsiders."

Nicholas shrugged, "I'm here either way."

Abbey looked into Nicholas' sincere dark eyes. "You're crazy if this doesn't scare you. You have to be at least a little concerned about getting involved in this situation which you can so easily walk away from, if you want to."

"But I *don't* want to." Appetite gone, Nicholas set his plate down on the table.

"Are you a glutton for punishment?"

He grinned, took her plate, set it aside, and pulled her close. "Not punishment." Nicholas kissed her lips softly and then pulled back to inform, "I'm a glutton for you."

Abbey kissed him this time—the caress lasting longer and going deeper than his had. "I'm thinking that's a good thing."

Nicholas responded with another kiss—passion equal to Abigail's now. "I'm thinking you're right."

And, for a while, the romance on the screen was forgotten for the one slowly unfolding between them.

~~~

The next afternoon, Nicholas and Abigail drove south. He wanted to get her out of the house for a while—not only would it be good for her, but for him it was much safer than the constant temptation she offered his old-fashioned ideals.

They stopped in Sharpstown and strolled through antique shops, making small talk and for a while, avoiding the burning topic.

Sitting on a bench outside an ice cream parlor just off Main Street, they each enjoyed their single-dips. The many patrons that lined up inside the establishment gave testimony to the quality and service of the family owned business. "Sometimes I wish I knew more of my family history. Maybe then my life wouldn't be such a mystery now." Abbey commented wistfully.

"You are an only child?" Nicholas questioned, catching a drip of strawberry-cheesecake ice cream just before it rolled over his fingers.

Abbey continued to work on her cup of peanut butter swirl. "Yes, and both of my parents are gone now too."

"They couldn't have been very old."

"They weren't." Suddenly the ice cream wasn't as tasty, so Abbey lowered the Styrofoam bowl to her lap before continuing; "It was an accident . . .." Her words faded and the look in her eye changed from reminiscent pain to dawning fear. "I hadn't thought of it until now."

"Hadn't thought of what?"

"The police report called my parent's death an accident, but now I wonder."

Nicholas lost interest in his treat too, "You think what happened could be linked?" Abbey nodded slowly, still thinking about the possibilities, so Nicholas prompted, "Why?"

"My parents had been hiking—they loved to do that on the weekends. I had a term paper due, so I had opted out on this trip at the last minute. The official report stated that one of my parents had slipped on loose gravel, fallen off the wooded trail and apparently disturbed a wild animal of some kind." Abbey swallowed over the imaginings, and then continued, "They were mauled beyond recognition. It had taken three grueling weeks and dental records to confirm what my heart already knew."

Nicholas took the container from her hand and tossed it and the remainder of his cone into a nearby trashcan. "Had you seen the accident before it happened, in your dreams I mean?"

"No." Abbey raised tear-filled eyes to his. "But I've envisioned it a million times since then."

There was a moment of silence before Nicholas asked the question on both of their minds, "It doesn't feel like an accident anymore does it?"

She allowed him to take her hand again—the feel of his warm flesh against her palm giving her an oddly natural feeling of comfort. "To be honest, it never really has. Now I just have a direction in which to speculate."

"If there is a connection, what do you think it might be?" Nicholas asked, spurring her mind into action.

"That's what I intend to find out," Abbey informed with mild determination.

Looking around at the growing crowd, Nicholas suggested, "Let's head back." Abbey nodded and together they walked hand-in-hand toward Main Street. "I know you've told me everything twice, but are you certain there was not some other detail to give us a hint?"

Abigail was feeling nervous. She glanced around, but saw nothing out of the ordinary. Looking back toward Nicholas, her feeling doubled and because of it, she dropped his hand—the feeling diminished. When he looked at her curiously, Abigail asked, "Why are you so emotional about this?"

"I just want to help you, Abigail."

"Your emotions are affecting me."

"What?" Nicholas didn't attempt to hide his surprise.

"Along with my dreams, sometimes when someone around me is anxious or sad, lonely, happy— whatever they are feeling, I can pick up on it as though it is my emotion too." Nicholas didn't speak and that made Abbey very uneasy. "Are you ready to bail now?"

He shook his head and took her hand again, "Is there something wrong with knowing how I feel? Do you want me to back off?"

Nicholas didn't realize he was holding his breath for her answer and when it came, he was relieved. "No, I don't want that. But I don't want you too involved either. The anger that thing spouted when he talked about you was dangerous."

"What about when he spoke of you, do you think—?"

"That's it." Abbey interrupted breathlessly, "I knew there was something, but I couldn't quite remember."

Nicholas looked to her expectantly, "Yes?"

"He called me a washed out whore."

Despite the seriousness of the situation, Nicholas chuckled, "That sounds like childish name calling to me."

"I know, but for some reason he seemed to believe the words."

"Are you sure that's what he said?"

"Yes." They reached Nicholas' parked car and when he let go of her hand, he casually rubbed his palm over her back. "No, that's wrong."

Reaching behind her, she grasped his hand again, brought it to her cheek and closed her eyes—the vision came clearly again. Though she knew it was only a memory, Abbey's brow puckered and chills covered her body as she recalled the gravel-hissed words: "'Won't you invite me in?'" Laughing uncomfortably, Abbey informed, "That's when I assured him: 'Not in a million lifetimes.'"

"What then?" Nicholas prompted, giving full attention to her details.

"First he laughed—it was a horrible sound and then he said: 'Silly child, I could make you beg me to come in, to give you a million lifetimes to waste on your pathetic doctor Let me end your torment and show you what a lover of the night can do for your needing body, you diluted whore.'" Abbey's eyes opened again; "That's when he scratched *soon* in the windowpane.

Her eyes rose to Nicholas' concerned ones and he spoke softly, "Abigail, are you okay?"

She nodded, "Yeah, believe it or not, it gets a little easier every time I go over it with you." Nicholas continued to study her silently, so Abbey questioned, "Why?"

"Because just now, when you spoke . . ."

Abbey's blood ran cold. "What Nicholas?"

His gaze collided and held with hers. "You sounded like a demon."

~ *Chapter Three* ~

Before going back to Abigail's house, they stopped at the public library and checked out nine different books on possession, reincarnation, and vampire lore. They decided that anything else they might need could certainly be found on the Internet.

With their information stash spread out on the dining room table, Abigail connected her laptop to the Internet and together they began to search.

Within the first ten minutes, they realized how daunting the task was actually going to be. The first thing Abigail did was phone WKOB, and take an indefinite leave of absence. There was no telling how long this mess was going to take to work out and she certainly didn't want to put anyone else in the line of danger.

With that chore done, Abbey leaned back in her chair and sighed, "I never would have guessed that there are so many ways for evil to overtake a human."

Nicholas looked up from the book he was skimming and grinned sympathetically. "The stress of your week probably doesn't help your research concentration either. Why don't you go take a hot bath? I'll order some food and stay here learning until you're ready to start again."

Abbey tilted her head to the side and studied Nicholas for a moment. "I'm beginning to think you're a fable too—but the good kind."

"I hope you'll always believe that." His expression turned serious for a moment, then he encouraged, "Go on. I promise not to leave the house until you want me to."

Abbey stood and walked around the table to him. Leaning down she whispered, "That's a mighty tempting offer, Doc. If spooks are what it takes, I might see if there's a zombie upstairs or maybe a few skeletons in my closet."

Nicholas accepted her light peck on his lips and replied, "They should all be afraid of what I might do to protect you."

Abbey smiled, "Why?"

His eyes met hers, "Just following my instincts."

"Good plan," she agreed and then moved up the steps toward temporary relief and relaxation.

~~~

Thirty minutes later, Abbey walked back down the steps with skin tingling from steam and smelling like raspberry bubble bath and lotion. Her wet hair was twisted and held up on the back of her head with a plastic clip. The wispy ends were sticking out in a myriad of directions. Instead of pajamas, she had slipped on a green tank top and white-cotton shorts that left every inch of her long legs bare, from the middle of her shapely thighs, right down to the tips of her manicured toes.

After a momentary falter, Nicholas managed not to stare by concentrating on the notes he had taken. Glancing up, he caught the natural sway of her hips in his gaze and somehow kept from groaning aloud. Clearing his throat he told her, "I think I may have found a few things."

"Hit me." Pulling out the chair closest to his, she sat on one hip, while bending her other knee so that her foot rested on the seat with her bottom. Nonchalantly reaching across the table, she grabbed the glass of water from in front of Nicholas, took a sip, and set it down again.

Nicholas didn't mind—in fact, he liked the familiarity—but he still couldn't help but smile at her absolute comfort in his presence. Looking down at his notes, he read aloud:

The notion of vampires, demons, or spirits is as old as the Mesopotamian, Hebrew, Ancient Greek, and Roman Cultures.

It is believed that vampires return to attack their relatives first.

Russians thought that vampires were created from humans who had been witches or rebelled against the Church while they were alive.

Abbey held her hands out to stop his flow of information. "Let me get this straight. If this thing *is* a vampire—and we seem to *unbelievably* be leaning in *that* direction—you're telling me it's an atheist, warlock ancestor of mine, which makes me its favorite target?"

Ignoring her flair for the dramatic, Nicholas questioned, "Can you think of any other reason this creature would choose to hunt you?"

"No, but right now I'm more concerned with stopping it than I am understanding *why* it's after me."

"That's understandable, but have you considered that the answer to all of this could be one in the same?"

"Yeah, *now* that you mention it and make it all sound so likely." Abbey stated in a fully disgruntled manner.

Nicholas chuckled, "I'm just trying to keep you thinking from all angles."

Leaning over and trying to read his notes upside-down—but failing miserably—Abbey questioned, "Well, while I'm thinking about it, do I have any options aside from garlic and crosses to keep me safe?"

"I didn't get that far."

"Why not? From all of the theories you've thrown my way in the last three minutes, I'd have thought you were spending all of your time thinking about this."

Nicholas nodded. "I am—or at least close to it." His resolve had been slipping since the moment she walked into the room—now it was gone. "But right now I'm thinking I need to tell you how incredible you are."

Abbey looked up startled by the unexpected compliment. "I can't imagine where in our short acquaintance you could have come up with that opinion. Was it when I was attacked in front of you, unconscious in the hospital or blatantly throwing myself at you," she blushed brightly, but continued talking, "practically begging for a date and more?"

Nicholas laughed, "Truthfully, it was *all* of those things, plus your great sense-of-humor and the bravery you are showing."

"Ha! You call this bravery?" Abbey shook her head, causing some of the reddish curls to spring free from the pinched hold of the hairclip and bounce around her bare neck. "Have you forgotten the way I screamed on the phone and collapsed into your arms like a blubbering mass when you got here?"

"I don't think I'll forget either of those things as long as I live." Nicholas stated honestly, and then added, "But I also consider that you are still here, you haven't deserted your home to this creature or your fears as an obvious act of bravery."

Abbey's green eyes grew serious. "That's not bravery, that's *you*." She had the impulse to avert her eyes, to find something on the table to fiddle with as she spoke, but she resisted and kept her gaze focused on his handsome face while she admitted, "I honestly feel like you are tied to me. It may be nothing more than wishful thinking, but considering the way my life has revolved around these dreams for so long," she took a deep breath, "and now this new theory on my parent's deaths and the fact that you just happened to be my rescuer . . .." Abigail's words trailed off and she shrugged, "Maybe I'm just becoming a firm believer in destiny."

"I don't care what reasoning you give it," Nicholas began, sliding his hand across the table to grasp her fingers in a now-familiar manner, "Just know that I am here because I want to be. I am here because you have allowed me to be your friend and—like you—I have no one else."

The food delivery person knocked on the front door—perfect timing. "I'll get that," Nicholas offered and patting her hand, stood to do so.

~~~~~~~~

During the following two weeks, Nicholas and Abigail fell into an easy routine. Abbey found herself—despite the demonic figure lurking in the shadows part—enjoying the feel of normalcy and hominess that came with their evolving schedule.

During the day, Abbey would research and Nicholas would call to check in from work for updates of anything interesting or important added to their growing stack of paperwork. Later, they would share supper and an evening of brainstorming investigation together.

It wasn't exactly the most romantic of settings, but for Abigail, Nicholas was more than stepping up to the role of hero. He was always a perfect gentleman—whether Abbey preferred it that way or not. He tried to keep her focused on the danger at hand, but for Abbey, being in the same room as Nicholas Adamouras was often a huge distraction in and of itself.

The biggest obstacle to their progress was Nicholas' work and the fact that at a page or call, he headed directly to the hospital—interrupting their learning at any point. Moreover, alone in her house at two in the morning was not the time that Abigail intended to face her fears.

The demon-silence of the last days was beginning to weigh on Abbey as heavily as the horrid visitation had. In waiting, it was more than just the memory of the occurrence that plagued her—it was the dread of the promised event and vague timeline as well. She always felt better when Nicholas was with her, as he was now.

They shared subs—or hoagies as Nicholas politely argued—crispy potato chips and some pickles on the side. Nicholas' plate was barely touched. He was busy concentrating on his nearly full legal pad and the notebook in which Abigail accumulated her research. Both made references that would have them back on the Internet for more bloodsucking detail.

"I'm thinking we should just royally review everything we've found so far." Nicholas suggested after about five minutes of back-and-forth skimming of pages.

Abbey's mouth was full of turkey and cheese, so she nodded. Taking a quick drink of her soda, she agreed verbally, "You're right and hopefully you won't be called away—it's very distracting." She offered a cute expression of frustration that brought a smile to Nicholas' features.

"I can't apologize for saving lives, Abigail."

"I know. It's just that all of this—with the note taking and the fear and the wondering—is very overwhelming. And, since you take your notes with you to find more when you can, I only have my own to fall back on, and so I don't really know where to start or stop during the day." Her brow crinkled and she added, "As odd as this sounds, it doesn't help that *it* has been so quiet lately."

Looking up from his scrawl on the yellow paper, Nicholas grinned, "You're right, that *does* sound odd."

Abbey shrugged. "You wouldn't know me if I were normal."

"There is that." Nicholas agreed easily, and then offered, "From now on, I'll leave my notes with you, this pad is nearly full anyway."

"That might help."

Glancing down at the documents in question, Nicholas offered, "I started by writing down what the creature said to you."

"Everything?" Abbey asked, with slight surprise lacing her tone.

"Probably verbatim—it's not everyday you get to see a beautiful lady speak like a demon."

"I'm betting there are lots of husbands that would argue that fact." Abbey interjected wryly.

Nicholas chuckled, and then continued with divulging his information. "I highlighted some words I thought would be key—the request for an invitation, his offer to end your suffering, the word soon—"

"You're a doctor and you don't know the definition of *soon*?"

"I'm just wondering if the monster uses it in the same context you or I would."

"As in Adam lived to be something like nine-hundred-thirty-years old in the Bible?"

Nicholas was impressed and looked it, "I'm not sure if that age is correct, but yes, that's *exactly* what I mean."

"So if we're going to believe in evil, we have to believe in the good too."

"I told you I believe in a lot of things—God and good is just the basis of them all."

Abigail looked doubtful, so Nicholas prompted, "You disagree?"

Abbey shrugged, "It's just that I haven't been to church since my parents died. Before that, we went regularly, dad and I sang in the choir and I was even getting involved in leading some of the youth programs."

"What stopped you?"

Abbey hesitated barely a second. "Anger is a powerful thing."

"So is grief," Nicholas reasoned evenly.

"There was more than just grief and anger though," Abbey offered briefly.

"Such as?" Nicholas pried carefully.

Her delay was longer this time before she opened this old wound. "The fact that I realized I hadn't been having my dreams anymore, I began to wonder why that happened *after* I cut off my relationship with God."

"I understand anger and grief, Abigail, but don't shut out the Creator. He is not to blame in all the bad that happens in the world."

Abbey sighed—Nicholas' reasoning reminded her of her father's wise manner. "In time I will return; I know that my heart will not be the same again until I do. But for now, returning to that church is just too painful without my parents beside me." Clearing her throat of the heavy emotion there, Abbey reverted to their original track, "So we are considering *soon* in Biblical time?"

"Maybe." For a moment, Nicholas contemplated staying with the topic of Abbey's wavering faith. However, as the tears began to fade from her shining green eyes, he chose to give her some space.

Running his finger down the page of his notes, Nicholas flipped the top sheet over and skimmed halfway down the second one before responding further. "During my online search, I found the oldest known myths surrounding vampires."

"Are they believable?"

Nicholas shrugged, "I think at this point in your life, questioning the existence of vampires is not really a possibility, Abigail, and what was once taboo is fact."

"Point taken." Abbey agreed, and then asked, "So, what did you learn?"

"If nothing else, they are interesting tales and give us a basic idea of what we are fighting."

"Read on, good sir," Abbey invited dramatically.

With much less flair than Abigail, Nicholas began, "The first story is of Lamia—a beautiful Libyan queen who was loved by Zeus. After Zeus and Lamia had a child, another woman—Hera—became jealous and stole the child away. In grief, Lamia fled to live in a cave by the sea where her form changed from beauty to match her inner hideousness. She roamed at night and stole babies, eating them until her tastes grew to thirst for young men. She was able to return to her previous beauty on a whim and using this gift of seduction to her advantage, Lamia would kill her lovers either by physical exhaustion, drinking their blood or both."

"How can one story be sad, disgusting and erotic all at once?"

"Much in folklore is," Nicholas reminded her, before continuing with his findings. "The second story is of a woman named Lilith. She is said to have been the first wife of Adam in the Bible—created at the same time and from the same clay as he. As such, she expected to be his equal in all things. Refusing to be subservient to him, Lilith grew wings and flew away from Adam and the Garden of Eden where they lived."

"I don't get how people never realize that you can't hide from God."

Nicholas merely shrugged and refrained from pointing out that Abigail was doing just that in her own right. "When the angels found Lilith hiding, they said that her punishment for leaving Adam would be that all children born to her would die."

"How is that fair?" Abigail demanded, as though the punishment was hers to bear.

"Nothing in life—especially God—has ever claimed to be fair. Though I think He has proven Himself to be sufficiently so at other times."

Abbey thought about that for a second, "Yeah, you're right about that."

"And the angels *did* take pity on Lilith. Seeing the depths of her despair, they gave her guardianship over all babies for the first week of their lives." With a punctuated point in Abbey's direction, Nicholas questioned, "And how did Lilith repay them? She allowed her anger to overtake her, killing and drinking the blood of the newborns she was to watch over."

Abbey gasped and covered her mouth with both hands. "What was her punishment for *that*?"

"She was cast into Hell where she became Satan's wife—seducing young men and capturing their souls for eternity."

Abbey was instantly skeptical. "Is this in the Bible?"

Nicholas' answer was definite, "No."

"So, only Eve is mentioned as Adam's wife there, right?" Abbey sounded as though she was desperate to prove this story false.

Nicholas grinned, "Correct." Giving her another second to contemplate that portion of information, he offered cautiously, "There's a little more, if you're up to hearing it."

Abigail waved her hand toward him—an obvious shun of his concern. "What's one more, scary story?"

Nicholas smiled comically at her open-minded reaction, before continuing, "This one comes from the Book of Nod, or what some people consider the vampire bible." Nicholas paused, thought, and then added, "Then again, it comes from the Holy Bible a bit too."

"This sounds conflicting." Abbey said sincerely.

"And a little more real?" Nicholas didn't push for more faith-declaration than that.

Abbey's only offering was an unfooled, "Hmm."

"It involves Cain."

"Like, he killed his brother Able, Cain?"

"That's the one."

"At least it's not another woman."

Nicholas chuckled and then informed, "The verses from the Bible are," he glanced down at the page of notes, *"Genesis 4:8-16."* Looking up at Abbey again, he asked, "Do you have a Bible?"

"I said I haven't been to church in a while, not that I'm a heathen." Moving from her chair toward the living room, Abbey returned moments later with a brown-leather-covered Bible in hand.

Nicholas took the offered book, observing, "This is old."

"It's my family Bible." Plopping back down in her seat, she added smartly, "Don't bother looking, I already checked, but nobody marked *vampire* after their entry."

With a false scowl, Nicholas flipped open the thin pages and stated, "That really would have made our job so much easier."

"I *know*." Abbey replied with forced enthusiasm.

Rolling his dark eyes, Nicholas read the referenced passage:

8"Now Cain said to his brother Abel, "Let's go out to the field." And while they were in the field, Cain attacked his brother Abel and killed him.

9Then the LORD said to Cain, "Where is your brother Abel?"

"I don't know," he replied. "Am I my brother's keeper?"

10The LORD said, "What have you done? Listen! Your brother's blood cries out to me from the ground.

11Now you are under a curse and driven from the ground which opened its mouth to receive your brother's blood from your hand. 12When you work the ground, it will no longer yield its crops for you. You will be a restless wanderer on the earth."

13Cain said to the LORD, "My punishment is more than I can bear. 14Today you are driving me from the land, and I will be hidden from your presence; I will be a restless wanderer on the earth, and who ever finds me will kill me."

15But the LORD said to him, "Not so; if anyone kills Cain, he will suffer vengeance seven times over." Then the LORD put a mark on Cain so that no one who found him would kill him. 16So Cain went out from the LORD'S presence and lived in the land of Nod, east of Eden.

"Wow," Abbey breathed, leaning back heavily on the wooden seat supporting her. "God doesn't play around, does He?"

"Nope." Nicholas reached for the paper and pen in front of him. "Let's go over this passage by passage and take notes."

"Good idea," Abbey agreed. "First, we know that Cain lied to God about killing his brother and then mouthed off to Him about it."

Nicholas smiled as he wrote Abbey's layman terms to Cain's interaction with God on his notepad. "The statement God makes here," running his finger on the tissue-thin Bible page, Nicholas read aloud, "Listen! Your brother's blood cries out to me from the ground, indicates that God recognizes blood as powerful enough to "cry out" from the ground—whether in the literal sense or not."

"And here," Abbey, pointed to the words and read as Nicholas had, "I will be a restless wanderer on the earth, and whoever finds me will kill me."

Nicholas wrote *God made Cain indestructible. Even to this day, he may be living on earth.*

"Do you *really* believe that?" Abbey tapped the place on the legal pad in front of Nicholas, where he had written that completely incomprehensible, overly terrifying note. "Even *more*, do you want *me* to believe that? I don't know if I buy into the possibility that *today* Cain is still out there—somewhere—wandering around the earth."

With a sigh, Nicholas laid his pen aside and turned toward her to instruct, "Abigail, none of what I say or find out will ever be what I *want* or *expect* you to believe. You should come up with your own conclusions in all of this. I am just trying to offer options—no matter which one either of us chooses to follow, it's obvious that *one* of them is real."

"Which one do *you* think it is?" Abbey asked, still mulling over the details of the tales Nicholas had just shared with her.

He shrugged, "I lean toward the Bible base. Cain is certainly a theory I will keep in mind."

"And what about Lilith?"

There was no hesitation, "She wasn't written in the Word of God."

With relief in her tone, Abbey admitted, "To be honest, that was my first instinct too." Skimming over the remaining Genesis passage, she questioned, "What about this mark or the land of Nod—have you found more detail about either?"

Nicholas shook his head negatively. "I have not."

They conducted a quick second-search. The land of Nod turned up only offers for an array of books or lullaby's.

"Apparently God was quite secretive about the place to which he ostracized Cain." Abigail grumbled with frustration.

"Well, at least we have our basics for vampire beginnings," Nicholas optimized. "On with the research. Is there anything else I missed in your attacker's threats?"

Abbey looked over the paper and added, "Diluted whore; that one is really a mystery."

"Why?" Nicholas had looked down at the paper, picked up his pen again, and prepared to write her answer.

"First of all, I am about as far from being a whore that a woman can be."

Unintentionally, the pen slipped from Nicholas' fingers, his dark eyes darted to hers, and an overly happy grin lit his features. *"Really?"*

Abbey rolled her eyes and she purposefully tapped the paper between them, "Can we focus, please?"

"As long as you don't give me anymore thoughts like that one—otherwise, I make no promises."

She laughed lightly and then suggested, "The word diluted makes no sense to me whatsoever. How can someone be a *diluted* whore? Washed out, I've heard of, but not diluted."

"That I may have an answer to." Using the pen as a place marker, Nicholas scanned the paper with his eyes and stopped about halfway down the page. "If one believes in such things—and at this point, I don't see that we have much choice—there are different social aspects of vampires. Different personality types flocking to separate clans, some that live together in harmony and some that don't."

"Okay." Abigail approved, letting him know she was paying attention.

"The older or hierarchy clans and vampires see themselves as supreme beings over each other and especially humans."

"But how does that explain diluted?"

His dark eyes looked seriously into hers. "How well do you know your family tree?"

Abbey studied Nicholas with a seriously curious expression for a moment before his suggestion dawned on her. "You've got to be kidding; we're back to this again?" She laughed, before adding, "I like my steak rare, but not running and screaming in the opposite direction."

Nicholas didn't laugh. "Let's keep to the essentials for now. We have a possibility for *diluted* and we can gladly throw whore out as a common insult toward women." Abbey nodded, so he continued, "Your parents were killed by some kind of wild animal in the same style of threat you were given."

"Yes." Abbey's answer was quick. She was always eager to shove that topic to the side and this time was no different, so she added her own opinions, "I think the invitation part makes some sense. I've seen enough vampire movies and read enough books to know that a vampire can't enter your home without an invitation."

Nicholas rolled his eyes, "I don't think this is the time to start believing *everything* you see in the movies, Abigail."

"Normally, I would agree with you, but under the circumstances, I don't have much else to base my theories on. At least that one will let me sleep a little better tonight." Closing her eyes, she rubbed the back of her neck with her hand.

"You're tired." Nicholas closed the laptop and watched her eyes open lazily.

"Yeah, I am."

"Let's give this a break; we can pick it up again whenever you're ready."

Abbey's hand dropped from her neck to his hand on the table. "I'm afraid to take too much time learning. What if it comes back before I know enough?"

"Considering the beast, does it matter what you know?"

Abbey sat back heavily in the chair. "I'm not sure that makes me feel any better about resting."

Nicholas grinned. "Will it make you feel better if I stay here tonight?"

"Well now, doctor, we've recently established that I'm not qualified to answer that question, haven't we?"

Her flirtatious manner made Nicholas chuckle. "We have." Clearing his throat lightly, he added, "But let me clarify, that I plan to sleep on the couch."

Abbey pouted cutely—the expression not entirely false. "Spoil sport."

"Not at all." He guaranteed, "I'm just postponing the sport, not spoiling it."

Abbey leaned toward him and kissed Nicholas lingeringly on the lips, "Okay, Doc, but if you decide to *change* your plans, I'm at the top of the steps on the left, just past the bathroom." Turning, Abbey walked through the living room and up the stairs without looking back.

~ *Chapter Four* ~

The next morning Abbey woke to find her couch vacant. Nicholas' bag was gone and, as promised, the notes he had been taking remained on the research pile.

Deciding to make the most of her quiet time, Abbey settled in to watch the tower grow. Guessing that it would be faster if she used the same website Nicholas had taken his information from the night before, she clicked the drop-down bar for search histories. With a groan, she cursed technology—for some reason the sites had not been book marked, so she would have to start from scratch.

Typing in the word `vampire`, a list of choices appeared, including the clan names that Nicholas had told her of already. Choosing one on a whim, she found a description of typical behaviors of the group including feeding and hunting techniques, preferred prey characteristics, and certain gifts that the group carried.

Next Abbey clicked on a link entitled:

```
Vampires:
Myth or Legend, Fact or Fantasy?
```

The home screen stated:

```
Belief in the vampire legend was once so pervasive that mass hyste-
ria was caused and public executions were held for those accused of
Vampirism.
```

"Sounds like the Salem Witch Trials," Abbey mumbled and then she continued reading.

Apparently, there were numerous methods of discovering if one, in fact, was a vampire or merely *seemed* to be a vampire.

One way was to find the suspected creature's grave by gathering one virgin boy and one virgin stallion—black or white in color depending on the region in which the search was taking place. Once the appropriate materials were located, the virgin boy was seated on the virgin horse and led through a graveyard. When the stallion was spooked, the nearest plot contained a sleeping vampire and it could then be killed to avoid the demon doing any damage.

"No problem," Abbey stated aloud. "I'll just run over to the high school and search out a virgin— *that* should be easy. Then we'll hit the equestrian center and randomly pick a cemetery to figure out where this thing's grave is."

With a roll of her eyes and a click of her finger on the mouse, Abbey moved on in her reading.

```
It was thought that a vampire was present in a specific village if
```

cattle, sheep, relatives, or their neighbors began dying at around the same time.

"Welcome to germs, folks." Scrolling downward, Abbey remarked, "What would these people think of the Swine Flu?" With a sarcastic chuckle, she answered her own question, "Probably that the pigs had fangs."

Another way for vampires to be suspected was through the occurrence of individuals hurling stones at one another, household objects being moved or misplaced or people being smothered or pressed to or near death in their sleep.

Abbey disregarded each theory as it came, with a rational one of her own. "Throwing things—anger or mental instability, losing things—absentminded people that can't or *won't* take responsibility for their faults, smothering—don't piss off your spouse and then go to sleep."
The next passage caught her attention with a bit more seriousness:

In 1746, prominent French theologian and scholar, Don Augustine Calmet wrote on his belief in the existence of vampires:

These vampires were corpses who went out of their graves at night, to suck the blood of the living, either at their throats or stomachs, after which they returned to their cemeteries. The persons so sucked waned, grew pale, and fell into consumption while the sucking corpses grew fat, got rosy, and enjoyed an excellent appetite.

The cold chills on Abbey's neck indicated this was the closest she had gotten to the truth that she had seen first hand. Her monster may not have been fat or rosy, but he was in exceptionally good health—especially considering the possibility that he was a walking corpse.
It was time for a new topic—for instance, figuring out how to avoid or kill this damned creature.
Abbey clicked on Protection From Vampires—a nervous laugh slipped from between her lips—"Why does that sound like an oxymoron?" She read on anyway—hope trying desperately to find a way to break through the terror waiting to overwhelm her.
Abbey jotted some notes, but since she found little more than items from the produce aisle of the grocery store to offer protection from the menace threatening her, Abigail didn't feel any better. She was still virtually clueless about warding off the demonic thing that had stood ominously at her window days earlier.
The section on how to prevent a vampire from being "born" or wandering the earth didn't seem much use to Abbey at this point, though it *was* entertaining. The degree to which people would go with their superstitions was amazing.

To prevent the recently deceased from turning into one of the "undead," many cultures have resorted to burying a corpse upside down in the grave. Another precaution was to place scythes or sickles near the fresh grave as a sacrifice of sorts to any demon tempted to possess the deceased, soulless-body or appease the deceased and keep them from wanting to leave their coffin.

The next entry was of particular interest to Abigail in consideration of Nicholas' heritage.

Ancient Greeks would sometimes place an obolus [money] in a corpse's mouth so that they could pay a toll for crossing the River Styx in the underworld.

The coin is also said to have been a payment of sacrifice to ward off evil spirits wishing to enter the body.

Further European precautionary beliefs were severing corpses' knee-tendons to keep them from walking around later. Abbey leaned more toward the less gruesome and easier method of spreading poppy seeds, millet, or sand around the gravesite of a suspected vampire. Still, she found the idea that the demon would rather count the fallen grains than feast on blood, humorous.

"Yeah, that sounds like it would work—*Rainman the Vampire.*" Abbey rolled her eyes and kept reading.

An archaeologist discovered and documented a sixteenth-century Italian burial site where a brick had been forced into the mouth of the corpse. All professional studies led to the conclusion that this was a prevention of vampirism; for Abigail, it led to the knowledge that the description would remain forever engrained upon her imagination.

Next, she read how—if one was unsuccessful in stopping a vampire's birth or roaming—it was possible to keep the creature from entering a person's home.

The degree to which families went was astounding. Some bore the trouble of removing part of the masonry of a wall to have a deceased loved ones body taken from the house. They thought this would keep vampires from being able to return to their home since they are able to come into a home when invited—and then only continuously if that invitation is given at the homes main threshold.

"You'd think finding them standing dead at the front door would have been a clue to close it and not welcome them home," Abbey mocked dryly.

Another click of the mouse and Abbey sighed in relief. "Ah, finally something that might *actually* help me."

This section was entitled:

Vampire Destruction:

If one was actually discovered to be a vampire, the corpse was usually disinterred during daylight hours and had one or more of the following rituals performed upon it.

➤ The body was dismembered.
➤ The body/pieces were burned, mixed with water, and administered as drink to the family members. The belief was that the lost soul wouldn't possess the non-demon.

Abbey's stomach rolled, "Gross."

➤ A lemon was placed in the mouth of the deceased.

➤ The corpse's heart was removed and destroyed—usually by spearing or burning.

Abigail was frustrated, she was scared and she was getting absolutely nowhere with this—it was time to choose a different route.

Abbey typed her father's name, displaying several choices—some living, some deceased. She clicked on the name that shared the same birth date as her father.

Birth certificate, death certificate, and censuses from different years, high school classmates, and public records were the choices listed. Abbey went for one she didn't know all details of—Death Certificate. This linked her to a genealogy search website. After keying in her credit card information, a banner welcomed her to her past and the community of HeritageFamilyTree.com.

She had to reenter her father's information, but was glad she had chosen this website when it displayed, Michael James McBride born May fourth nineteen-sixty-three to Jacob E. McBride and Emmaline C. Lowery. At least that was a start—even if she barely remembered her grandparents, she was sure of their names.

Abbey moved the cursor to the search space again and typed in Jacob E. McBride. Her new choices were, Jacob Elijah, Jacob Edmond, or J. E. Jacob Elijah and J.E. were born around the same time her grandfather would have been. She chose the listed order, Jacob Elijah born December 31, 1942 to Martha and Alexander McBride.

There was no marriage information and only two census records, both for Harrisburg, Pennsylvania. With a disappointed sigh, she moved on.

J.E. McBride born April 17, 1942 to Malcolm and Rebecca Standish McBride, there was no death information for J.E. or Malcolm. However, Rebecca's death certificate listed her date of death as April 17, 1942—a sadly interesting coincidence in its own right. Abbey clicked on the link to learn more about Rebecca McBride—nothing showed.

The phone rang and Abbey absently picked it up while still reading the information on the computer screen. "How is your day going?" Nicholas asked immediately.

Abbey smiled, "So far, so good; no creepy visitations, which is always a plus. I've started some research, but haven't gotten too far—I just know that my mom's recipe for spaghetti would knock the creature out cold and that I should invest in a crucifix necklace."

Nicholas laughed lightly. "Keep looking, maybe we'll find some clue or better options for protection later." Abbey took a mille-second to enjoy the fact that Nicholas had said *we*, encouraging her even more than he'd expected. "If I'm too late to cook tonight, do you have a preference as to what I bring to eat?"

"Are you planning on being late already?" Abbey teased.

"Not planning, preparing." Nicholas corrected.

"Just don't be after dark, please."

"I promise."

"And don't worry about supper; I've got it under control."

"Are you sure?"

"I'm positive." Abbey guaranteed

"I'll see you around five or six then."

"I'll be here," she promised and the call ended with Abigail smiling like a goofball. So, the guy had called to check on her—why was that so special?

It was special because it was something she had seen her dad do for her mom a thousand times during her childhood. It was special because Abbey realized that Nicholas was a busy doctor and his time was precious—still he had managed to share some with her. It was special because it was exactly what

Abigail wanted him to do—how she wanted to be treated—and Nicholas once again showed his knack for instinct and it pleased Abbey thoroughly.

~~~

Tapping laptop keys greeted Nicholas as he walked into the room. He had knocked five times and after gaining no response, started to worry. He opened the unlocked front door—another issue he intended to discuss with her—and walked freely into her home.

When Abbey looked up, startled, he reprimanded, "That serves you right, you scared me when you didn't answer the door."

"Sorry." Abbey offered, suitably chagrined.

"And why isn't your door locked?"

Abbey smiled, "Sorry again."

"And why are you smiling?" His already thin gruffness was wearing off.

"Because I like that you worry about me."

"Well, *I don't like* worrying," he huffed, and then stood behind her chair, looking over her shoulder at the computer screen and the notes she had added to his. "What did you find?"

Abbey sighed with weariness, reached her arms overhead, and stretched. "Not a lot about demonic details, but a fair bit about my family."

"Anything juicy?" Nicholas questioned, leaning in closer to look at her handwriting.

Abbey swiveled on her seat, rose to her knees, and slipped her arms around his neck. "Not enough to sink my teeth into." She leaned back so that she could see his expression better; "Get it; *sink my teeth into?*"

Nicholas grinned and rolled his eyes, "Yeah—ha, ha—I get it." He leaned forward and kissed her offered lips. "So, honey, what's for supper?"

Abbey couldn't resist another kiss—one with a little more depth—before replying, "Well, I'd planned on hot dogs and macaroni 'n' cheese."

"My favorite," Nicholas responded insincerely.

"But since I didn't drag myself away from the computer long enough to start the food, I ordered pizza from this seat about thirty minutes ago."

Running his hands down her shapely sides, Nicholas chuckled, "If you keep up this lifestyle, your figure is going to gain a few curves that might not be so tempting."

Abbey pouted, "Are you saying you don't love me for my intelligence?"

His hands slipped around to cup her backside lightly, "Not even close to the truth, I'm just warning you since I hear women complain daily about the way they look."

"Then neither of us has a thing to worry about. I've always been an accidental exerciser and eat what I want when I want with nothing to show for it in weight gain or loss." In her best Popeye voice, she finished, "I'yam what I'yam and dat's all that I'yam."

Nicholas chuckled, "I have no idea what that means, but you're really cute with your face scrunched up like that."

Abbey laughed and tried to remind herself that his family interests had probably been far different than hers had been growing up. "Suffice it to say that I'm not gonna change."

"So long as you don't go away, I'll keep you no matter what you look like."

Changing to her best Scarlett O'Hara, she flirted, "Why sir, how you do go on."

"Now *that* one I know." Nicholas informed proudly.

"I know, and it's a good thing, 'cause that one's a deal breaker." Another peck on the lips and she moved around him. Grabbed her wallet and headed for the door.

A knock sounded from her destination point.

"Do you do that often?" Nicholas questioned from behind her.

"Do what?" Abbey inquired, still moving toward the arrival of supper.

"Answer the door *before* someone knocks?"

Abbey shrugged, and kept moving, "Since I'm usually alone, I don't really know."

He waited until the delivery boy was paid and Abbey returned to the table before asking, "What do you want to drink?"

"Water; glasses are in the—" Abbey stopped her directions when she looked up and saw that Nicholas already had the full glasses at the table with him. With a self-satisfied grin, he held out her ice water.

Abbey chuckled, took her glass, a sip, and a seat, and then reversed his previous question. "Do *you* do that often?"

Nicholas winked a dark-lashed eye in a way that made Abbey feel like she did when she watched her favorite rock star, and then replied, "Since you're my first soul-mate, I don't really know."

"*Nice.*" Abbey complimented, then opened the pizza box, "I got double cheese, double mushroom for me; supreme for you."

"Perfect."

"I considered extra garlic to make sure our unwanted visitor didn't come back, but since my research never founded that wives tale about garlic keeping vampires away to be true, I skipped it on the preliminary basis of tasty kisses later."

"I'll do my best not to disappoint," Nicholas promised.

"What makes you think I was talking about you?" Abbey teased smartly.

"Kismet."

"I see." Pulling a slice of pizza with the works out of Nicholas' half of the pie, Abbey laid it on a paper towel in front of him. "Be careful not to chip the fine china."

"I'm flattered you went to all this trouble for me," Nicholas returned playfully.

"You can thank me later."

"I'm planning on it." Abbey's mouth was conveniently full of mozzarella cheese, so Nicholas took the opportunity to continue, "For now, why don't you fill me in on what you learned about your family."

Abbey swallowed her bite and then told Nicholas what she had read and the blocks therein. "Now I just need to start over with the McBride's to see if I missed something."

Nicholas looked at her notes, then at his and remarked, "Did you find out more about the shape shifters?"

Abbey looked lost, "The *what?*"

He tapped the list of notes he had written. "The breed of vampires that are able to change forms— they're called shape shifters."

"Sorry, after I got freaked out researching the plain, old, *regular* vampire, I opted to check out my family tree instead." Wiping her mouth with a paper towel she stated, "Which did not reveal a bloody past yet—shape shifting or not." Sliding the ever-present laptop in front of her, Abbey clicked a few keys and was back at the now-familiar website. "Let's see what we can find now." It took only seconds for the information to load and Abbey paraphrased it to Nicholas. "This defines shape shifting as a *being* transforming in a purposeful way that is not related to a curse or a spell." Looking up Abbey stated, "Not very helpful."

Nicholas encouraged with a grin, "Keep reading."

She did as requested. "Here it says that every time a shape shifter transforms it becomes harder for them to revert to their original form." Abbey paused, reading ahead silently, "huh."

"What?" Nicholas prompted.

"Oh, sorry. It says that they can only change into a person or animal that they have actually *seen* before."

"Like a copy machine." Nicholas suggested.

"For hideous creatures," Abbey deduced, without missing a beat. "Just what we need—more than one and after reading this, I'd venture a fair guess that my new friend is a shape shifter for sure."

Nicholas nodded, "It certainly seems that way, which makes him even more dangerous than we'd thought."

Abbey contemplated a moment longer and dread filled her eyes and words as she realized, "Because they can assume different shapes, they can obtain an invitation easier too."

Her fear was palpable and Nicholas wanted to lessen it for her. "Just be careful, on guard and you'll be fine."

"Easy for you to say, you're not the one being stalked," Abbey remarked. Looking into his eyes, she saw the genuine concern there and added, "At least I'm not usually trusting of people."

"Forgive me if I find that hard to believe," Nicholas teased with a smile.

Abbey's features relaxed and leaning toward him, she whispered, "You're just special."

Nicholas closed the distance and kissed her lightly while pulling her around the table-corner, bringing her to sit on his lap. Continuing to seduce with his kiss, he whispered sincerely, "I missed you today."

Abbey laughed lightly. "Isn't that strange since we've only known each other for a few weeks?" She kissed his chin and felt the stubble there scratch at her lips.

"Are you telling me I'm strange or are you looking for validation of *your* feelings too?"

Abbey smiled, "Both."

The kiss deepened and Abbey's hands gripped his muscled shoulders as Nicholas' touch began to roam freely over her back and sides. The movements were still slow, but the ease was fading with every heartbeat. His lips left hers and moved over her neck, down to her collarbone and his fingers pulled the straps of her tank-top lower on her shoulders.

Abbey leaned back, bracing herself against the table edge, allowing Nicholas full access to her wanting body. Her top slipped lower and his mouth continued to introduce Abigail to new pleasures. The heat of his mouth coursed through her limbs, brought chills to her skin and made her moan deeply. Nicholas stood, pushed her back to lie on the table—pizza box and papers giving way for their need—and their lips met again.

His breath trailed over her cheek and he nipped at her ear, whispering, "You are delicious." Nicholas' words were added pleasure. Not sure what to expect or give, Abigail did as she always had—she followed her instincts. She raised enough to completely remove her top, slid back down to the table, and watched Nicholas' eyes as they darkened to an onyx that reminded her of a shimmering black pearl.

"Is this how you want to remember us?" He asked, watching the rise and fall of her breathing, the pulse pounding on the side of her graceful neck, the change in her eyes as desire enhanced them.

"Oh yeah, I'm fine with this," Abbey mumbled. Then she pulled him in for another kiss.

Nicholas caught the band of her shorts with his fingers and began pulling them down over her legs. Abigail's hips rose in accommodation and he smiled at her eagerness. "I will be as gentle as I can, but you are intoxicating."

"Good." Abbey kicked her foot to the side so that the remainder of her clothing fell to the floor behind him.

Nicholas had never felt such a loss of control with a woman—this was more than lust or desire, this was a need that went to the core of him. His hands found her, touched her and the sounds that he brought forth nearly sent him over the edge. Abbey reached for him, pushed against his clothing, doing away with any barrier between them. Then her hand found him and the pleasure that seared through Nicholas was insane—it was indescribable.

Abbey opened her eyes to watch his face and without conscious thought said, "I think I've always known you would be mine."

Nicholas looked down at her—hair tousled in their passion, lips full from kisses and eyes burning with an unquenched need. "And do you know that you'll never be rid of me?"

"I can't even grasp the possibility of *without* you."

Nicholas leaned down to kiss her again, and then whispered against her lips, "Abigail, are you sure about this? I hear your words and I believe you, but this moment cannot be relived for you."

"I can't think of a better way to live it than *with* you Nicholas."

He moaned and moved their bodies closer together—with the slightest of movements, he would bring them together. Abbey could not deny herself the satisfaction of watching his face as he fought between his need for her, his own pleasure and his determination to go slowly.

"Abigail."

His lips hadn't moved.

"Abigail."

It wasn't his voice—Nicholas' expression proved that he had heard the whispers too.

~ Chapter Five ~

The motions of the entwined couple ceased instantly.

Abbey's voice shook as she focused her gaze on Nicholas' strained features. "I can't look, tell me if he's there."

"Nicholas," the name came out in a hiss, "tell me, does she taste as good as she looks?"

Nicholas bounded to his feet, stunning Abigail with his fluency, and with no hesitation, he strode into the kitchen. His body was bare and his muscles bunched so tightly that Abigail could see them quiver when he walked. Her eyes slid to the window and the tormenter whose face hovered there.

The monster stuck out his tongue and vulgarly lapped it against the window. "Let me in and I'll have my own sample."

Abbey scrambled to her feet, grabbed her clothes, and pulled them on quickly—all while watching in amazement as Nicholas faced-off with the demon. "Go to hell."

The thing laughed, "One day, but first I'll finish my business here."

Abbey forced the words to clear her lips. "What business do you have with me? What is it about me that you want?"

Those terrifying blood rimmed eyes slid her way again and lust of a different kind filled them. In a hiss he explained, "I want to feel the life drain from your body."

Her one word was a barely audible whisper, "Why?"

If the monster responded, Abbey didn't hear. At that moment, Nicholas took an insanely threatening step closer to the window—seemingly completely oblivious to the fact that he was facing one of the darkest creatures imaginable. His voice was deep and menacing as he spouted, "Do not be like Cain, who belonged to the evil one and murdered his brother."

The evil visage smirked amid the madness Abigail was witnessing. "And *why* did he murder him?"

Nicholas' answer was ready, "Because his own actions were evil and his brother's were righteous."

Its eyes began to darken, the yellow ring glowing in the midst of blood red. "And in *your* righteousness, are *you* challenging *me*?"

Nicholas responded in no way other than to stand his ground in stubborn silence.

The demon laughed—a taunting humor that reached its hellish eyes and wrapped around its words. "I think I'd enjoy it if you would. Shall I give you incentive?"

"I've more than enough reason already," Nicholas informed blatantly.

With patronizing promise the monster assured, "You've had *nothing* in comparison to what I'll show you soon."

Abigail came up behind Nicholas and felt her terror give way to anger. "Soon, soon, what is your *soon*?"

The thing's eyes changed directions, and its voice sounded exactly like Abbey's when she had ridiculed Nicholas before; *"You don't know the definition of* soon?*"*

The sound of her voice, coming from her worst fear, knocked air and reason from Abigail. In her loss, Nicholas responded, "You blood sucking bastard, leave us." Nicholas' voice was harsh—*demanding.*

My name is Remington.

Abigail heard him speak in her mind, but just as in his first visit, his lips didn't move. When she looked toward the source, he smiled and this was worse than any time she had looked at him before. This time, in Remington's smile, she saw her father.

Then, she heard his voice—her *father's* voice; "That's right *Pet*, keep searching." Remington evaporated on a hideous laugh and Abbey felt the tears slide down her cheeks.

Turning immediately toward Nicholas she whimpered, "I have wished so many times to hear my father's voice again, but not like this." She sobbed, "Dear God, not like this."

Nicholas gathered her tight against his bare chest. *"That* was not your father." He pulled back and with his fingertips, tilted her face so that their gazes held, "Do you hear me, Abigail?"

The green eyes that looked up at Nicholas clouded with doubt and fear. "I hear you, but I also hear the echo of Remington's words." Her voice cracked; "What's worse is that I could see my father in his smile."

"What do you mean?"

"I mean that I think you may be right about my family tree and it's time to do some more research." Nicholas nodded, "Let me just get dressed again and we can get started right away."

Nicholas would have moved, but Abbey's grip on his arm tightened. "Hey?" He turned to look toward her again and she questioned, "Do you think you can stay again?"

He smiled, kissed her lips lightly, and assured, "I'll be with you until you wish otherwise."

~~~

Abigail felt something brush against her forehead and she inhaled the sweet scent of Nicholas. Opening her eyes she greeted, "Good morning; I don't remember falling asleep."

She was nestled in her bed, the covers tucked tightly around her and Nicholas sat on the edge beside her. "That's because it was only four hours ago and you nodded off at the table. I carried you up here and tucked you in."

She looked mildly disappointed. "You should have woken me creatively."

Nicholas laughed softly. "You need to sleep."

"Did you?"

He shrugged, "No; but I'm a doctor, we're expected to run on adrenaline. I kept researching instead." Turning to the dresser, he produced a tray, with a plate of food on top. *"And,* I made you breakfast."

Abbey grinned, straightened to a sitting position, and accepted his offering of scrambled eggs and toast. "Thank you."

"You are most welcome." Nicholas sat quietly, watched as she took her first bite, then suggested, "I'll tell you what I've learned while you were sleeping." Abbey nodded her approval, took a sip of perfectly hot coffee and listened to Nicholas speak. "Unfortunately, what I learned only adds to my belief that you are related to vampires."

"I'm listening."

"The term *Diluted* is used by the *Pure Bloods* or *Embraced* vampires. Meaning those who became an undead by the regular means—a bite to one of the main arteries on the body, through which the venom infects the human."

"Okay," Abbey sipped her coffee, processed that information, and then stated, "Embraced sounds so romantic, not at all like the tissue tearing experience I think Remington has in mind. Do you have any idea why he is drawn to me?"

"Yes, but first I want to tell you that I've learned that diluted refers to one that is sired by a vampire and a human."

"Details?"

"With each new generation, the offspring's blood runs thinner with the inherited vampire gene, so where as the second generation may still require the intake of blood, the next may require only animal blood, the next only occasional cravings and so on."

"How many generations until all traces are gone?" Abbey asked, unable to hide the hopefulness from her question.

"I don't know."

"Any guesses?"

"A few, but I also think that with the cons, there are pros. While you don't need blood to survive and the sunlight has no affect on you—"

"About *that*," Abbey interrupted, "what happened to the instant liquidation of the vampire in sunlight?"

A vision of Abigail dressed as Dorothy from The Wizard of Oz and brandishing the melted witches broom in her hand came to Nicholas' mind. He couldn't stop the small grin that graced his lips as his next explanation began. "Apparently—and this one took an abundant amount of time to learn—Vampire's grow stronger with age."

"Okay?" Abbey prompted.

"The older and stronger a vampire is, the greater their ability to function in daylight."

"So they don't melt, they grow weak."

Nicholas nodded his dark head. "Exactly. If a young or ungifted vampire ventures into the sun—especially what they consider the Brightest Hour, then their waning strength can even be fatal."

"And so the myth is born."

"Partially." Nicholas seemed to be remembering something he had read and then continued, "They can survive this loss of strength if they feed immediately."

Abbey deliberated this and then questioned, "When is the Brightest Hour?"

"There was no exact time to be found," Nicholas explained. "The best I could figure is between the hours of eleven in the morning and two in the afternoon—the same time humans consider it most dangerous to go out without sun block."

Abbey couldn't hold back her laughter at this humorous analogy. "So why don't the sun-weakened vampires just feed? Not that I'm anxious for that remedy, mind you."

"I'm guessing it has something to do with the mass hysteria chewing on a human in broad daylight might cause."

Abbey nodded, "I see your point."

Nicholas took her momentary processing silence to continue with his teachings. "Back to our discussion of Diluted's—in addition to them having little or no need for blood and the sunlight having no effect on them, some powers of the vampire-genetics have been known to remain."

Abigail spoke on a whisper, "My dreams."

Nicholas nodded, "Yes, your dreams. I also think there is something to your sensibilities; the fact that you are so untrusting of people and that you automatically knew that I could be trusted and how deeply I desire you."

A slow seductive grin covered Abbey's face, "How deeply *do* you desire me, Doctor Adamouras?"

Nicholas clicked his tongue at her in reprimand, "Well, since you're gifted with the ability to read my feelings, I don't need to tell you."

Abbey pouted cutely.

"But maybe when I come back, I can show you."

"Come back from where?" Abbey was immediately on edge.

"I have to check in at the hospital and I want to pick up some more books from the library."

There was nothing remotely romantic about his comment, but Abigail felt like she had just been given the best Valentine ever. This man had no real reason to help her—but he was anyway.

Abbey put the nearly empty tray aside, pushed the covers away, and invited, "Do you really have to leave? Maybe we could finish what we've started a few times now."

Nicholas hesitated—that was all the possibility Abbey needed and she pounced on him, rolling his unresisting body beneath hers and in a seductively sweet voice promised, "You don't have to take your time with me; I'm tired of waiting."

Nicholas accepted her kiss, and then laughed softly. "I'm afraid, my impatient love, you'll have to wait at least a while longer."

Abbey was ready to do battle when she raised her blazing eyes to meet his. "Why?"

He lifted his hand with his vibrating cell phone in it. "Because duty calls and I'm needed elsewhere."

Flopping dramatically to the side of the bed, Abbey sighed and proclaimed, "I've waited all my life; what's a few more hours?"

"That's the spirit." Nicholas coaxed in a teasing tone and then left the room before she could convince him to stay—an event that was not impossible in the least.

~~~~~~~~

Abbey wanted to focus on the research she was trying to complete, but all she could think about was how desperately she wanted Nicholas. It was embarrassing. She had never felt like this about a person before—tonight had to be the night. The only way to get over this distraction was to get what she wanted. Then she would be able to concentrate on the rest of her life—like the monster stalking her in the shadows and waiting to attack her and suck her blood and eat her flesh.

Since she had no experience with the sort of seduction she was planning and no one she could turn to for advice, Abigail flipped through the television channels. She watched a few minutes of talk shows, Soap Operas, checked out a few web sites and then finally went shopping at an eye-opening store that would have her blushing for the next three hours. Still, the outfit—if one could even consider the small amount of material in the bag, an outfit—was what the sales clerk assured Abbey was guaranteed seduction.

"We'll see," Abbey said with a nervous sigh. Glancing at the clock in her living room, she headed up the stairs toward her shower and preparations for her eventful evening to come.

~~~~~~~~

Nicholas entered the silent house and called out from the dim entranceway. "Abbey?"

"Up here."

He hadn't anticipated her answer to come from above or to be so soft. He hadn't expected the first floor of the house to be so faint, either. Nicholas presumed to find her diligently bent over the computer screen, as usual.

The instant he looked up the steps, he understood her change of location.

Only the backlight from her bedroom lit the hallway where she stood and the filmy white, thigh-length gown was sheer enough that he could see every curve and shadow beneath its scarce barrier.

"How was your day?" Her voice was fairly deeper than usual and raspy with emotion.

Nicholas closed the door and locked it without moving his eyes from her. "It's getting better." She smiled. "Hurry along then."

How he moved so quickly—Abigail could not fathom, but she was eternally grateful that he did and in the next second she was in the warmth of his arms, moving into her bedroom with no hesitation at all. "I've thought of nothing but this all day." Abbey breathed softly against his ear.

Even as Nicholas shuddered sensuously at her admission, he pressed her onto the bed, pinning her beneath him. "Be careful what you wish for Abigail."

"I'm careful about everything else, lately; I don't want to hold back from you." She kissed him hotly and further assured, "I have no fear with you, Nicholas. You are my safety, you are an answered prayer."

Every movement, every sound, everything around and about Nicholas stopped with her words.

Harshly he pushed away and stood up from the bed. "I am *no* answered prayer, Abigail." Disgust laced his self-accusing words. "Look at how I treat you now, with such little respect. I can't even seem to consider the fact that you are a virgin." Looking her tempting form over again, he questioned, "Do you realize what a prize you are in that Abigail?"

In complete confusion, Abbey pushed herself up to a sitting position and adjusted the drooping straps on her negligee. "Nicholas, I'm willing, so what's the problem?"

"This is wrong." He couldn't concentrate when he was looking at her, so he turned away. "You are in danger and all I can think about is getting you into bed. There are much more important matters at hand. Get dressed, I'll be waiting downstairs."

He started to leave the bedroom, but Abbey's words halted him. "Don't bother. I won't be down." She was horrified—but in an altogether different way than she had been in the past days. "If you don't want me, then you should just tell me, Nicholas. Go home, let me sleep this embarrassment off and I'll call you if and when I'm ready to see you again."

He didn't turn toward her, but his entire form stiffened. "*If?*"

Abbey sighed, there was no point trying to lie to either of them, so she admitted, "I'll call you tomorrow." She blinked, her shining green eyes forcing back the tears of humiliation that wanted to overflow from them.

Nicholas still didn't move and Abbey said no more. The silence only lasted seconds, but to each of them, it seemed to last an hour. Finally, he admitted, "Abigail, I *do* want you. In fact I want you in so many ways that it's *beyond* sinful."

Her tone was scathing. "Forgive me if I find that hard to believe."

He still didn't face her. "I won't make you mine in the midst of this horror. However, I will promise you this. Soon you will be mine, in body and name and I will never let you go again as long as you live."

Abbey swallowed hard over the lump his passionate words caused in her throat, "No more *soon*, I want *now*, Nicholas. I want *you*."

The powerful determination in Abbey's voice broke Nicholas' resolve and with a growled curse, he hurled himself back at the bed and her waiting form. Abigail had no time to respond before Nicholas was perched over her, not touching her, but waiting for her response.

"Abigail, look at me."

Abbey did as he requested and her breath caught in her throat. He was tense with the strain of holding back the passion coursing through him—all of it evident in his dark eyes.

The proof of it only made Abigail want him more. "Please, Nicholas, don't wait."

"I have been too free with you already. I have not treated you with the respect you deserve, but I've pawed at you like the animal that I am."

His self-disgust was palpable in the small space between them and Abbey recoiled at the intensity of it. "You have done nothing that I didn't want you to."

"You are a lady; you don't know the way a man's mind works in this. You have no real say in the matter."

For a moment, Abbey was speechless. Who was this man over her spouting this caveman drivel? "What in the world are you talking about?" With an uneasy giggle, Abbey added, "I am certain all the blood has left your brain."

Nicholas didn't share her humor. "Do you have any idea how close to the truth you are?"

Abbey fought the anxiousness spilling into her gut. "What truth?"

"The truth of knowing me."

Abbey's instincts were screaming, but none came through clearly enough to give her the answer she needed. "I know your heart."

"And what of my soul?" Nicholas pressed.

With the emotions flying between them and Nicholas' body fully against hers, Abigail could scarcely breathe enough to make her declaration. "I think that it is one to be shared by both of us."

Nicholas closed his eyes, called on his restraint, and urged in a firm voice, "Use what is yours, Abigail. Pay attention to what your gifts are telling you."

"I don't understand." She looked confused, frustrated, and frightened—Nicholas wanted no more of it.

Without words he begged, *Know what I am.*

Abbey's green gaze widened in realization and with clear purpose, she lifted her lips to his as her mind replied, *I don't care what you are. Damned or not, you are mine and I am yours.*

Then Abbey kissed him with all of the soaring, climatic emotions she was feeling. She brought every joy, every sorrow, every hope, every desire, and every love and forced it to him for she knew now what he wanted her to know—they were the same.

Nicholas understood her better than anyone ever had or would again.

When the kiss ended, tears streamed from both of their eyes. Nicholas was first to speak and he softly declared, "Abigail, I love you."

She blinked to ward away surprise and her tears so that she could see this special moment more clearly, but when her eyes opened again, Nicholas was gone.

~~~

Twenty minutes later, Abigail still lay in bed, looking at the white ceiling and wondering how her simple life had turned completely around in just a matter of weeks.

She was angry that he had not told her the truth, no matter that she wouldn't have accepted it. She was terrified that she was in love with him and what that might mean for her future—*their* future, but most of all—now more than ever—she wanted answers.

Abbey sighed, sat up, and put her legs over the side of the bed, the pads of her feet resting lightly on the coolness of the hardwood floor. Lying in bed looking at the ceiling, wallowing in amazement and fighting off fury that the man she loved was a vampire, was not the place to get her truths.

Moreover, what would discovery bring with it?

Even with all she and Nicholas had shared, did she really want this for her future? Did she want to build her life with a *monster*?

But, Abbey knew she would never be able to think of Nicholas that way. He was good and kind. He was caring, loving, and gentle. Her Nicholas was no monster.

Nicholas was the one she wanted and to keep him she would need knowledge.

She kept on just her tee shirt and panties while traipsing down the stairs to the workspace she and Nicholas had set up in the dining room. Bringing up the search engine, she typed in Vampire. Now that a new light spread upon the situation, she needed to go back over some of what she had learned and hash out what was real and what was fantasy.

Resisting the insane laugh that was tempting its way up her throat, Abbey focused on the screen in front of her. Skimming over the now-familiar information, Abbey felt bored and a little angry about the time she had wasted researching already. Nicholas was quite likely a wealth of knowledge on the subject at hand.

Clicking on a link, she had yet to try, Abbey hoped for something different. As soon as the site opened, she realized it was more of a pop-culture site than a research one—but at least it *was* different. The heading declared:

```
Vampire Evolution ~
   From Demon to Delicious
```

Visions of Bella Lagosse as the infamous Count Dracula topped the column headed `Delicious`. Following the original seducing vampire, were the likes of Gerard Butler as *Dracula 2000*, Brad Pitt as Louis and Tom Cruise as Lestat in the movie version of Anne Rice's *Interview with a Vampire*.

In addition, who—at least in her generation—would soon forget *any* of the irresistible Cullen family? The list of Stephenie Meyer's creations, followed with a movie-version picture of each character listed in alphabetical order. Abbey personally thought that would have been a good spot to add hot werewolves to the mix as well.

The next column—Demon—showed drawings of the original cover picture of an eighteen-forty-six *Penny Dreadful* story depicting a—apparently at its time—well-known vampire called *Varney*. Next were *Nosferatu* and a similar creature from Stephen King's *Salem's Lot*—the original and the remake. Keifer Sutherland and his band of bad-boy-vampires in *The Lost Boys* filled the lists center.

Abbey scrolled down past the remaining pictures of some of *Buffy the Vampire Slayers* conquests and found pictures of the Cullen enemies. Next, Lestat in his less desirable form and countless other vamps from movies even Abigail hadn't seen.

It was the picture of the *Nosferatu* that kept drawing her attention back. Remington was far more beautiful than that creature, but the hunger in their eyes was the same. The only thing that made it worse was the fact that the picture before her was just an actor—Remington wanted her blood in life-size reality.

Abbey scrolled down past a very nice picture of Emmett Cullen and read the site creator's entry.

```
In the research I have done, it seems that good vampire equals
beauty and bad vampire equals ugly or scary. The only changes I
have seen in this are when "bad" vampires use their beauty to suc-
ceed in their ultimate goal of feeding or killing a human.

Even the most recent vampires created for entertainment have ten-
dencies toward scary features when they are hungry and their evil
counterparts are still lovely to behold in their own right.

All of this is accounted for by the Bait-and-Trap theory. What
woman—or man—would allow themselves to be seduced by creatures like
a Nosferatu or the wall scaling Dracula from Bram Stoker's famous
novel-turned-movie?

Early descriptions of vampires, handed down through centuries from
the beginning cultures of our world claim that vampires are bloated
```

in appearance with ruddy, dark purplish skin. The darkness—
attributed to the blood it drank was often described as "seeping
from the mouth, nose and eyes" of the vampire. Also, it was usually agreed that the vampire was clothed only in its burial shroud;
giving reason for Dracula's infamous cape. As time passed and the
dead began being buried in their best attire, so to, recent cine-
matic vampires are depicted in the most fashionable of styles.

The biggest difference in the "original" vampires and ours (aside
from pop-cultures current favorites) is that originally vampires
were never described as having fangs.

"Probably because by the time someone got that close, they weren't going to be spreading that particular detail around." Abbey grumbled aloud, recalling the shiny, fierce canines she had seen Remington drop down first-hand.

Leaving this fun—but not-very-helpful site, Abbey turned her thoughts toward her maternal ancestors. Pressing the keys, Abigail typed in the name she had found in the family Bible and on this site before—her great-grandmother, Rebecca Standish.

Ten choices lined the screen—one jumped out at her as though it were the only one visible: Rebecca Standish, date of death April 17, 1942.

That had been as simple as she could have hoped. Abbey clicked on the name and read the known
list of relatives for her great-grandmother.

Listed were parents for Rebecca Standish, Nathaniel E. Standish and Rebecca L.
Remington Standish.

Abbey's hand began to shake as one primary part of that display jumped to her attention. Quickly,
she moved down to Rebecca's listed siblings.

Born in Atlanta, Georgia
  May 4, 1910, Nathaniel
Born in Atlanta, Georgia
  December 7, 1912, William
Born in Atlanta, Georgia
  February 27, 1915, Jonathan
Born in Atlanta, Georgia
  October 28, 1917, Twins
  Remington and Rebecca

~ *Chapter Six* ~

The breath rushed from Abigail.

Nicholas had been right all along—she was related to that monster. Remington was her great-uncle.

So, you've finally solved one of our little mysteries. If you like, I can give you some more clues. I hold all of the answers.

Abbey looked to the window, but it was vacant save the overcast day that dimmed the house. She chose to ignore the voice.

Childbirth at best was difficult—with twins and a turn for the worse, a mother stood little chance. Our father named us appropriately don't you agree?

Still Abbey made the choice to ignore.

Remington would have none of it.

If you are not brave enough to allow me into your home, then allow me into your mind. Let me end your pitiful search for knowledge.

"You speak to me of bravery, yet you hide your face."

You'll not see my face again niece until I wish it. This game is no fun unless I make the rules. It's time I up the ante—just as you have.

"I've done nothing." Abigail continued to speak aloud, though she knew by now that there was no need.

You have given your heart to the devil.

Abigail thought back through her eventful morning. "Nicholas is not the devil."

Not to you, but what about to those he has Embraced?

"He would never."

Only light laughter followed.

Hatred filled Abbey—at Remington for spouting such words, at her for allowing his misleading thoughts to taint her mind.

The sound of humor was deep and rich as it filled her senses. *Yes, think about the darkness of this great secret he has kept from you and wonder how many more there are. Think about how you have allowed him to damn your soul right alongside his own.*

"If I am damned already, then why do you continue haunting me? The end result will be the same; go away and leave me in peace."

I have a vow to keep.

"What vow?"

Laughter ensued. *I am not the fool in this, Abigail; I will not give you the answers so easily. Like everyone, I have a price.*

"Are you suggesting that *I* am fool enough to pay that price?"

You are no fool. So long as you don't let your lust for one interfere with your talents, you will have all the answers—all the desires—you could ever fathom.

Abbey ignored his temptations and focused on his insults toward her love. "Nicholas is no fool."
He lied to you; where is the wisdom in that?
"A lie and an omission are two different matters."
Are you convincing yourself or me? The laugh sounded again. *To be fair, you are right, Nicholas is not a fool either—he's played this role of protector long enough to have learned much.*
"Protector of what?"
Silence.
"Remington, protector of what?" The silence continued; it was deafening and Abbey felt the emptiness—Remington was gone.

~~~~~~~~

Nicholas called twice, but Abigail didn't answer. She would talk to him tonight and he could use his ability to read her for that information. After her conversation with Remington—confusing as it ended—she didn't want further interruption as she began the new part of her searches.

She left her family—for now, she had enough information there. Clicking on the address bar of her Internet service, Abigail went to the vampire page. She didn't bother reading through the choices, but went straight to the search and typed in Sexuality.

A two-page description on each clan, and how they chose to reproduce, was her reward. First was the Embrace—for a vampire the creation of another vampire was a pleasure above and beyond that which humans found in sex. "I guess I'd like that too—or at least I imagine I would," Abbey said to herself.

She kept on with her scanning of the page until something relevant caught her attention—Fertility.

Apparently vampires still enjoyed the sins of the flesh too and used it as a means to procreate—and often did so as a way to create offspring that were not always born as vampires.

Abbey took a breath and continued.

Vampires were also—male and female alike—extremely fertile beings. The more emotionally connected they were to their mate the more likelihood pregnancy was to occur.

Imagined or not, she heard Remington's laughter.

The next paragraph contained the highlighted words: Vampire Pregnancy.

Unexpectedly the lid to her laptop closed and Nicholas' hand remained firmly in place. "There is no need for that, especially not before we talk."

Abbey screamed, slapped at Nicholas with her shaking hand and demanded, "Don't come in without an invitation again."

Nicholas smirked despite her sincere anger. "My love, I've already received *my* invitation."

"Well the next time you get here early *knock* instead of just walking right into my house anytime you choose," Abigail returned in a tone that showed Nicholas she had nearly reached the end of her rope with him—or at least by being terrorized by his kind.

He eased up a bit. "What makes you think I walked?"

It wasn't enough for Abbey and she tossed back, "I liked you better before the fangs."

Nicholas' hand did move then—to her chin and he gently tilted her head so that their eyes met. "If memory serves, you liked me just fine, fangs and all this morning."

Completely without intention, Abigail opened to him, he filled her mind, — his senses' melding with hers, and the invasion of desire was unbelievable. She could feel his hands on her already, his mouth caressing her—she could feel the heat of him against her and neither of them had moved. Abbey's breath hitched, coming out on a gasp that made Nicholas smile in aggravating arrogance.

"Maybe I should just let you embrace me, then at least I would have an excuse for these gifts and deep desires you bring out in *me*."

"First, if I *wanted* to Embrace you, there would be no stopping me. Don't ever think that it is a decision that you will make." Before she could argue, he added, "Second, it would please me tremendously if you would tell me more about these *deep desires* you have for me, Abigail."

Her eyes narrowed, "Use your imagination."

He smiled. "I want to marry you."

Completely surprised by his change of subject, Abbey responded with her usual dry wit. "Well, that definitely sounds like a plan." Then—amid her laughter—she realized he was entirely serious. "Nicholas, these matters usually take time and, I might add, a *proper* proposal." With a noticeable step back and arms crossed over her chest, Abbey added, "Not to mention, I'm just a little perturbed with the fact that you dropped a bomb on me then disappeared this morning."

"I know that, and under normal circumstances, everything would have been different. But you must admit we are anything but normal."

Abbey wasn't ready to give in to his excuses, but she was too curious to resist asking, "Exactly when are you planning for the joyous event to take place?"

"This afternoon."

Abbey laughed shortly. "What's the hurry?"

"Because as I told you, every instinct within me wants you."

Abbey considered his reasoning in silence, accepted its validity, and then moved on. "And?"

"And I'll not make love to you until you are my wife."

She stared blankly, as if waiting for a punch line—none came, so she spoke to his serious expression. "Nicholas, don't you think you're being a little ridiculous?"

With a sigh, he explained, "Abigail, I've spent most of my existence trying to live as God wants me to. I have very few options left to me in my current state of being and after our recent close calls; I don't intend to take anymore chances with my lust for you." He paused, tilted his head to the side so that a dark curl dropped across his forehead, before he added, "Plus, I love you more than anything in this world and want you to be my wife."

Tears sprung to Abbey's eyes. "Now *that's* a *much* better proposal." With a wavering smile she added, "I have many questions I want answered about you first though."

"We'll talk on the way," Nicholas offered, pulling her into the circle of his arms.

Slowly a sincere smile spread over Abbey's face, and lit her green eyes. "Well, then of course I'll marry you—every day of forever if you want me to." She then sealed her answer with a kiss.

~~~

Nicholas and Abigail were changed and headed down Interstate-81 within thirty minutes of his proposal.

They had not even turned off Guilford Avenue, before Abigail adjusted in her seat and stated, "Now, about those questions."

Nicholas reached a hand over and grasped hers with it. "Yes?"

"Do you know what our connection is?"

"Yes."

Abbey closed her eyes, swallowed and inhaled deeply through her nose, exhaled slowly and replied, "I am going to do my best not to let the fact that you have been allowing me to waste precious time searching for an answer you already have, ruin our wedding day."

He squeezed her fingers lightly, "I would appreciate that."

"And *I* would appreciate those answers now."

"Malcolm McBride was the dearest friend I've ever known."

Abbey was silent.

After a minute, Nicholas glanced away from the road toward her to make sure she was still conscious. "Abigail?"

"Processing, here."

Nicholas grinned at her response, and waited a few more seconds until she was ready to continue. With a shaky voice, Abbey clarified, "You were *friends* with my great-grandfather."

"He was my mentor."

Her voice raised an octave, though the volume stayed the same. "As in the vampire in my family tree I've been searching for mentor?"

"Yes."

Another deep breath with closed eyes, "Tell me."

In a tone that suggested his mind was drifting with his words, Nicholas began, "I was born and Embraced in Greece and eventually my travels brought me to America." He cleared his throat lightly, "The year must have been around nineteen-thirty . . .."

~~~~~~~~

Malcolm McBride was not a man that blended easily into a crowd. At six-feet-four-inches, he towered over his co-workers. He was muscular due to his willingness for hard labor and his thick hair was wavy and deep auburn. He had an easy smile and most times a quick laugh, which endeared him to those he chose to interact with – which, were few and far between.

For this chapter of his journey, Malcolm was working on the docks in Fell's Point, Maryland. The pay was miserable – but then the pay anywhere in America was paltry during nineteen-thirty. Still, finances were not an issue with which Malcolm McBride worried. His primary residence was the Admiral Inn – though where he laid his head during the day could change at his whim.

This area was perfect for one such as Malcolm. There was easy feasting and any delight of the flesh that a man could desire was at his disposal. When he tired of this – be it through discovery of his curse, a woman that hounded him for a commitment or the need for different scenery – he would seek out a new home. That was how Malcolm had conducted his existence since his Embrace in seventeen hundred seventy-four. That was how he would continue to exist until someone blessedly had the nerve and the strength to drive a stake through his heart or decapitate him in sleep.

So far, none had succeeded.

He worked through the night, fed on the way "home" and day was for sleeping. Sunrise was impending and so was his hunger. When his need to eat rose, concentration became more difficult and Malcolm avoided all the men he worked with as much as possible. There was no need to torment his senses with something of which he would not partake.

From across the dock, he saw the overhead wave of the supervisor that indicated time was up and the men were free to leave their duties until the next night. With a returning wave, Malcolm headed from the docks and the temptations there.

The alleyways were bare during this early morning hour, but Malcolm wasn't hunting for people. He had given into frenzy feeding only a few times in his existence – never did he feel that the satisfaction was worth the death he caused.

At times he fed off rats, cats, dogs – disgusting but much preferable to taking a human life. On days when he was released from work early enough, he would move out toward the edge of Baltimore's harbor and catch fish, using them to feed his hunger.

Sleep was nearly as necessary as feeding for Malcolm today and so he would scavenge what he could on his walk back to the inn. Moving into the third alley, he heard the telltale scuffle of a small animal from behind a stack of crates.

Instantly Malcolm's movements slowed, changing to stealth like in the blink of an eye. He felt the shift in his demeanor – man to predator. His senses heightened and he stepped around the wooden boxes to pounce on his prey.

Instead, he came face to face with one of his own.

The dark man growled over the animal he was draining of blood. His eyes glowed in the dim light. Blood dripping over his chin, the vampire hissed, "Go away."

Malcolm was so stunned at seeing another vampire that he stared in momentary shock.

The other man bared his fangs, clearly challenging Malcolm for the space they now shared. "Go away before I kill you."

Malcolm snickered. "Like you, I'm walking dead already."

The man's features changed, the meal gripped in his hand forgotten, his heavily accented voice laced with an equal mix of doubt and hope. "When was your Embrace?"

"Long enough ago to know that you are going to need to give in to the frenzy soon or become so weak that you won't be able to function."

"I became like this against my will. I trust that God will accept me into paradise if I withstand the desire until that day."

Malcolm studied the man before asking, "What's your name, lad?"

After barely a moment's hesitation, the man answered, "Nicholas Adamouras." He wiped his mouth against the back of his shirtsleeve, stood, and extended his hand as though they were meeting in the highest quality environment.

"Well, young Nick, I'm Malcolm McBride and pleased to meet you." Malcolm offered the smile that he befriended many with, before questioning, "Do you have a place to rest yourself today?"

"I don't plan that far ahead." Nicholas admitted sullenly.

"Then come along. I've a safe haven until you move on."

Nicholas studied the large Scotsman warily. "What will you want in return?"

Malcolm didn't have to wonder far to guess at Nicholas' insinuation. Shaking his head negatively, Malcolm assured, "Nothing of that kind. It's just that I'm a man for company and in the state I find myself that is a luxury sorely lacking."

Nicholas' voice was husky from feeding fatigue and loneliness. It was easier to give in and possibly die than to waste time worrying about the outcome. "Can you show me where the best hunts are?"

"Aye, but for now, this will sustain you." With lightening speed, Malcolm snatched a pair of pigeons that had roosted too near. Holding one tightly outward for Nicholas, the Scot informed, "As soon as I've fed, we'll have rest and then you can work with me until it's time to move on."

Nicholas nodded, "I accept your generosity with thankfulness." Then he turned and fed on the pigeon, leaving Malcolm privacy to do the same.

~~~

Abigail was not one to listen to a story in silence—she never had been. "Baltimore isn't far. Is that where Rebecca lived?"

"No."

"Were you with Malcolm when he met Rebecca?"

"Yes and no."

"Are you going to give me details?"

Nicholas chuckled at her impatience. "I think that's what I was doing, but you couldn't keep from commenting."

"It would be best if you just get used to that," Abbey suggested sincerely.

With his laughter growing, Nicholas agreed, "I've guessed as much already."

Abbey chose to ignore his taunting and instead questioned, "When did they meet?"

"Not until ten years after Malcolm and I became friends."

"That long?"

With a patient expression, Nicholas reminded, "To a vampire, ten years is nothing."

Pondering that thought briefly, Abbey commented, "I suppose not. Will you tell me more now?"

"Will you listen without interrupting?"

"Probably not," Abbey replied honestly.

"Try, *aatria mou*," Nicholas prompted with a smile. Then he slowly began to focus on the picture in his mind again.

~~~

Malcolm and Nicholas were the closest of friends – over the nearly ten-year span of their relationship, they became like brothers. Malcolm helped Nicholas find healthier feeds than the rats he had relied upon for so many years and Nicholas persuaded Malcolm to aspire to greater things professionally – primarily real estate.

Now Malcolm was the proud – and exceedingly wealthy – owner of three nightclubs, six apartment complexes, and four hotels.

They had moved through many of the east coast's biggest cities during their friendship and now they resided in Atlanta, Georgia. This move had been fairly recent, and Nicholas' idea. He wanted to be among the guests at Loews's Theater for the debut of the great film created from Margaret Mitchell's novel, Gone With the Wind.

Watching his friend primp – though by memory alone since reflections were a thing of the past for him – Malcolm laughed. Nicholas threw him a silencing glare, but that only brought the man laughing harder. "I just can't believe that you've brought us to the south for a movie."

Adjusting his bowtie for the last time, Nicholas slipped on his coat and tails and replied, "Mark my words, Malcolm; this will not be just any motion picture. This will be history in the making and since I find myself entrapped in this predicament of half-life, I will always be in the places to be remembered."

"You Greeks are a traditional lot, aren't you?"

"Be thankful we are loyal to our friends as well or you would have a problem on your hands."

Malcolm laughed; "You have never been a problem for me, Nicholas. Perhaps like a son is to his father, but no more than that."

Nicholas smiled, stood by the door, and waited for the only true friend he had known in the years since his Embrace and encouraged. "Then let's go Papa, before all the best sights are already seen."

~~~

"Wait—you were actually *at* the *premiere* of *Gone with the Wind*? No wonder you were so smug that night we talked about our favorite movies. All along I just figured it was because you watched all three-and-a-half hours when most men don't even get to the barbecue at Twelve Oaks."

Nicholas smiled at her rambling, mini-tirade and then let go of the laugh behind his expression. "Yes, but aren't you missing the point of my story?"

"No," Abbey stated and then explained, "As far as I'm concerned, there are *two* points to *this* story."

Nicholas' laugh grew, "Then ask away, *aatria mou.*"

"Where to begin . . . was it as grand as all the literature says?"

Nicholas winked—the sight causing insane butterflies to alight in Abbey's stomach. "It was far grander than any words can adequately describe."

Abbey's green eyes narrowed, "I think I'm jealous enough right now to revoke my marriage agreement."

"Even if you were '*pea green with envy*' you wouldn't back out on me, Abigail McBride." Nicholas assured with a slight smirk toward her already wounded *Gone with the Wind* pride.

Raising a very Scarlett-like brow, Abbey questioned, "What makes you so sure?"

"Because the premiere of *Gone with the Wind* is not the *only* thing that words do not adequately describe."

His meaning was quick to take root and Abbey blushed cutely and laughed despite her best intentions of dramatic irritation. "Well then, I guess you *are* right and I will *have* to settle for your best account."

A dark brow rose over an equally dark eye, "Of?"

It was Abbey's turn to wink, "For now, the premiere."

Nicholas laughed again, and allowed his mind to revert to the story Abigail had requested.

~ *Chapter Seven* ~

At nineteen years old, Rebecca Standish was breathtakingly beautiful and spoiled rotten. As the youngest girl-child of one of Atlanta's oldest families, most people in her social circle considered it her right to be so though. Whatever her father didn't give to her, one of her three older brothers did. The only one to ever stand up to her wishes was her twin brother – Remington.

However, tonight, even he had easily given in to her request and they now waited arm-in-arm on the red carpet outside Loews's Theater. For days Atlanta's Mayor – and close friend of Rebecca and Remington's father – William B. Hartsfield, hosted an array of special festivities leading to this particular occasion.

Along with grand welcomes for the movie stars and production staff, Confederate flags flew – even more than normal – and false antebellum fronts had been placed on many homes and stores lining the drive to the theater.

A few of the epic film's production staff had made their way into Loews's for seating already, but most people still waited outside to see Clark Gable and Vivian Leigh make their entrance. Rebecca was just as excited as everyone else in attendance to see the headlining stars, despite the actress she had met already.

As a shining member of the Young Daughters of Confederates, Rebecca had been part of an elected group to greet Ann Rutherford, the lady playing Careen O'Hara – Scarlett's younger sister. Rebecca had chatted and guided Ann with enough refined southern hospitality to make Varina Davis proud. Her efforts were rewarded when Miss Rutherford personally invited Rebecca to join in a group luncheon after her arrival at the Terrace Hotel. The other Young Daughters nearly fumed as Rebecca graciously accepted and was allowed entry into the elite hotel where any part of Hollywood visiting the Gateway City of the South would be residing during their stay.

The only downfall to the unexpected plan was that Rebecca was unable to rush off from the lady-filled luncheon in time to reach Chandler Field and greet the other stars arriving for the Gone with the Wind events.

Fortunately for her – Rebecca thought with silent sarcasm – one of her Y.D.C. "sisters" had, and Sally would now – and forevermore – gloriously reiterate each detail of what Vivien Leigh, Olivia de Havilland and David Selznick's wife wore during their Eastern Air Lines flight and arrival to Atlanta.

One small satisfaction for Rebecca was the fact that Governor Rivers had declared a three-day holiday for this grand event. As such, Sally had been forced to wear Civil War Era clothing during the reception of the movies biggest stars and the typically spoiled-southern-fashion-plate gave off the appearance of mere decoration.

Yesterday – Thursday – while on her way to help prepare for the premiere party that the Y.D.C. was *hosting, Rebecca had again seen Ann Rutherford as the actress visited with Confederate Veterans. There was only enough time for a cursory wave however.*

Scanning the crowd around her now – even as her mind raced, replaying the excitement of her last few days – Rebecca recalled with mild irritation how, yet again, she was the Y.D.C. left behind while others lined Peachtree Street to watch the motorcade bringing Clark Gable and his wife, Carole Lombard to the Terrace Hotel.

This arrival was a particular relief to many planning to attend the movie. Upon hearing of Hattie McDaniel – who played Mammy – and all other black actors in Gone With The Wind being barred from the premiere due to Georgia's Jim Crow Laws, Mr. Gable had threatened to boycott the entire event. It was only through Ms. McDaniel's gracious persuasion of Clark Gable that he attended despite the public humiliation this caused his friend and co-stars.

The crowd around Rebecca and Remington picked up a definite buzz. A car pulled up and the people – fine southerners the lot of them – pressed forward so that the only thing Rebecca could see – if she looked down at the ground and between the feet of the gentleman in front of her – were the shoes of Carole Lombard and Clark Gable as they passed by into the theater.

Looking down at his twin, Remington smiled and in his most charming southern manner reminded, "Don't fret, Becca, our name has guaranteed us a seat inside and an invitation to the best celebrations after." Tapping her lightly on the nose, Remington added, "You'll get to see the color of her eyes and every shiny piece of jewelry before the night is over."

Focusing only on her teasing brother, Rebecca forgot all of the decorum she had maintained throughout the earlier week and stuck her tongue out at him.

Remington laughed loudly, drawing a few odd glances, but he didn't care as he steered his sister toward the red carpet entrance for the theater premiere.

~~~

The press was everywhere within the throng of people. Malcolm was uncomfortable with the constant flash of bulbs, but the excitement around him was contagious, so he bore the minor problem silently.

Nicholas had wondered off in search of his own entertainment for the night – Atlanta's finest were present and he usually enjoyed rubbing elbows with the elite. He had the assumption that it was the best way to remain part of his accustomed lifestyle. Malcolm remained on the edge of the crowd – until he saw her.

The lights glaring down from atop the theater caught the flash of her silver gown as she turned to comment to the man at her side and Malcolm was overcome with a need that went beyond lust and hunger. His eyes maintaining their goal, he moved effortlessly through the crowd – an amendable feat considering his size.

When he stopped beside her, he made eye contact with only her and boldly announced, "I am Malcolm McBride and until I know your name, my existence means nothing."

Rebecca turned in the direction of his voice, the chestnut hair hanging down from its side-up sweep fell over her shoulder gracefully and her blue eyes scoured over Malcolm in an attempt to notice some flaw aside from his boldness. She flitted her eyes, back toward her brother and suggested, "Remington, perhaps you could make a proper introduction?"

Remington had also spent the last moment gathering a first opinion of the man before them and the only feeling that came to his refined southern mind was danger. The interested look in Rebecca's glim-

mering emerald eyes helped in no way. Remington could imagine – had seen firsthand on several occasions in fact – the fit she would throw if she did not get her way in this.

Rather than chance such a scene, Remington tipped his head slightly forward and offered, "Mr. McBride, I am Remington Standish and this is my lovely sister, Rebecca."

Malcolm took her hand without waiting for it to be offered and lifted it to his lips. "Lovely is indeed an understatement, Mr. Standish."

"Since she is my twin, to say more would be conceit." Remington justified in a tone broaching little friendliness.

Rebecca said nothing. From the instant Malcolm touched her hand, it was as though a fire lit and seared through every inch of her body. She was overwhelmed with heat and the scent of peaches warmed in the sun – her favorite smell in the world.

"Mr. McBride, I cannot lie, it is a distinct pleasure to meet you." With a single glance in her brother's direction, Rebecca looked back to Malcolm, got lost in his green eyes, and offered, "Would you care to be my guest for the film this evening?"

"Rebecca?" Remington questioned in a one-word reminder of all that they had learned during their lives – propriety, etiquette, and caution. It was obvious his sister was remembering none of those lessons.

Already allowing Malcolm to lead her toward the entrance way for the privileged guests, Rebecca called back, "Do not fret, Rem, find yourself a pretty girl to escort; there are plenty available."

Then she gave the rest of her attention to Malcolm McBride – her intense view never again faltering.

~~~

True to her warning, Abigail began a new barrage of questions—afraid she might forget one if she didn't spout them out quickly. "Did Remington leave? Did he follow them alone? Did he meet someone? What happened inside the theater?"

He smiled, "You mean did they get to meet Clark Gable and Vivian Leigh?"

Abigail's expression faltered momentarily, "Well, I'll want to know that too, but when did Malcolm and Rebecca fall in love? Was it romantically instantaneous or did they drag it out for the approval of her family?"

Nicholas offered Abbey an expression that reminded her very much of Clark Gable as the sardonic Rhett Butler. "You'll recall your great uncle and the lengths to which he is currently going so that he might destroy Rebecca and Malcolm's offspring?"

"Yes."

"Allow that to be your answer."

"Okay, but then did they marry at all? Is that why I wasn't able to find a marriage certificate?"

"Perhaps you should tell me what you have learned *already* and save me at least some of the task of enlightenment."

Abbey laughed, "Do you realize that since I've learned the truth, you speak like you are from another time. How are you able to guard the obvious so well?"

"Years of practice," Nicholas informed honestly.

"Well, for what it's worth, I'm impressed."

Nicholas nodded in polite acceptance before questioning, "Shall I continue?"

Abbey's silent nod was his awaited answer.

~~~

The romance between Rebecca and Malcolm came fast and easy. Nicholas enjoyed seeing his friend so happy. Rebecca's father liked Malcolm well enough. Any uneasiness he did have was overlooked on behalf of Malcolm's self-made fortune. Her older brothers accepted him grudgingly per their father's example. Nevertheless, Remington didn't trust the man at all.

The way his twin sister became instantaneously obsessed with McBride was unusual to say the least. Normally, Rebecca was the most fickle of any young woman Remington encountered – now she flitted around with a constant smile on her face. Of course, Remington wanted to see his sister happy and settled. However, the issue remained that there was just something about Malcolm McBride, which made the older brother uneasy. As yet, Remington couldn't figure out the cause, but it was there, sure and strong none-the-less.

This evening Rebecca was again planning to go out with Malcolm, but before she left, Remington intended to have a talk with her. Making his way to her bedroom door, Remington knocked and waited for her singsong call of admission.

When he entered, Rebecca greeted him with a smile that made her lovely face – all peaches and cream – glow with happiness. "Rem, are you going out this evening?"

Remington moved fully into the room, taking the chair by the fireplace and watching as the servant worked her fingers through his sister's hair. "I've not decided yet."

"You should." *Turning to look in her brother's direction, Rebecca added,* "You've been a bit gloomy lately; a fun time out would surely do you some good."

"What would do me well is for Malcolm McBride to either disappear or make his intentions known."

Rebecca's laugh was carefree. "Since his intentions are toward me, don't you think that concern should be mine and not yours?"

"You are my twin sister, my dearest relative and as such, you are my care."

The female servant finished arranging Rebecca's chestnut curls into a French twist and moved out of the room nearly unnoticed. Swiveling in her seat, Rebecca replied, "Your dedication is touching. Do not fret though; Malcolm intends to speak with father before the week is out."

"About what?" *Remington demanded, his words a bit more harsh than he'd meant them to be.*

"About my hand in marriage."

"It's improper that you should know that before your family does." *Remington informed stubbornly.*

"Why, Remington? Do you think that whatever the high and mighty Standish men decide will sway me?" *With a short laugh, nearly void of sincere humor, Rebecca finalized,* "I'll marry Malcolm McBride because it is the greatest desire I've ever known."

Remington scoffed, "That's because you are young and innocent."

"No more than you." *Rebecca returned pointedly.*

"I highly doubt that," *Remington informed with certainty.*

Rebecca's eyes narrowed. "Don't be crude."

Remington rolled his sky-blue eyes at her sudden turn toward propriety.

"You know that life and social etiquette are different for a gentleman than it is a lady." *His tone was patronizing and Rebecca despised the fact.*

"Only because a gentleman is free to expand upon his . . . emotions and a lady is stifled by the propriety of which you speak."

"These rules were made for a reason."

"Don't worry your fine southern sensibilities, Remington. I'm not breaking any rules. I don't in-

tend to either. But I am in love and will not give that up for any bit of propriety or masculine Standish acceptance such a choice might offer me."

Remington's cool blue eyes narrowed and a glint that Rebecca was as familiar with as her own reflection lit them. "I'll fight this every step to the altar, Rebecca."

The ferocity with which he made his vow was shocking to Rebecca and her sapphire eyes flashed to match his similar ones. "Then I'll see to it that there is no fight to be had." Without further explanation, she slammed out of her room to meet the man she loved and leave behind the brother that was breaking her heart with his stubborn prejudices.

~~~

They had crossed the boarder into northern Virginia nearly an hour earlier. After silence reined in the car for three straight minutes, Abbey asked, "Why did you stop talking?"

"Because I don't know much about the details of their falling in love; only that they did and deeply." Nicholas rubbed his thumb against the back of her hand as he continued speaking. "Malcolm was open with me because we were the closest of friends, but with good reason, some aspects of Rebecca were off limits even to me."

Abbey couldn't hide her disappointment—Nicholas tried to compensate for it. "However, I *can* tell you that they would have been insanely proud of you."

"Why?"

"Because you are their first female." With a soft chuckle, he reminisced, "Rebecca would have been beside herself having a girl to spoil and care for."

"Will you tell me another story of them? Anything is okay; I just want to know them better—as my ancestors and as your friends." Nicholas smiled, her words filling him with a new pride.

In a manner that begged a short respite, Nicholas stated, *"Eventually,* I will tell you everything I know."

Accepting his unspoken request, Abbey looked out the window to the back road scenery passing by. "We've been driving a while. Do you have an actual destination in mind?"

Amusement filled Nicholas' onyx eyes. "Yes."

"Do you know where it *is?"*

Nicholas smiled fully now, but rather than reply directly, he asked, "Are you hungry? Should we stop?"

Abbey smiled at his concern—even if it was a diversion. "I can wait if you promise me a special meal after our wedding."

Nicholas glanced toward her to respond—his smile warming—but the expression on Abigail's face turned horrified.

She tried to speak, but couldn't. Nicholas followed the line of her gaze and saw Remington—in full vampire mode—flashing through the woods beside them. He kept perfect pace with the car despite the fact that he was on foot. Nicholas took Abbey's hand, forced her eyes to meet his, and stated, "What would our wedding be without some fireworks?"

"This is the kind I could have done without." Her throat was tight and so were her words.

"Don't worry; we'll be rid of him before long."

Abbey continued to stare out the window at Remington who began new antics by throwing small wounded woodland animals toward the car. Nicholas never swerved and no thud sounded, alerting Abigail to the fact that it was all a farce for her mental benefit only, but the sight of the gore was sickening just the same.

Nicholas rounded a bend in the road and informed, "We're here." Reaching over to squeeze Abbey's hand, Nicholas added, "Remington will have to leave now, he cannot walk on hallowed ground."

While Abbey took note of the dark blue Honda parked alongside the road in front of where Nicholas stopped his silver Audi, she wondered who this stranger awaiting their arrival was. Nicholas opened Abigail's car door for her and a shrill evil screech sounded from her enraged great-uncle the moment her foot touched the ground.

The unknown man moved from his vehicle as Abigail and Nicholas walked toward him. With a warm smile and outstretched hand he introduced, "Good afternoon, I'm Pastor Gustafson."

Nicholas nodded as though completely expecting this declaration. "This is my fiancée, Abigail McBride and I am Nicholas Adamouras."

With the preliminaries over, the pastor turned to lead them into the overgrowth that contained the remnants of a stone wall. "I must admit that I've never had such a request as this, Doctor, may I ask why you've chosen this sight to be wed?"

Nicholas replied to the preacher, but looked at Abbey when he spoke. "Abigail wanted to be wed at the same place her great-grandparents were."

Abbey's steps faltered. "Nicholas?" She threw her arms around his neck and pummeled him with chaste kisses, "You are fantastic."

The preacher cleared his throat. "Let's save that for later, Miss McBride." With shared laughter, the threesome agreed and continued the fifty-yard walk to where the men halted.

Light from the afternoon sun spread through the leafless trees. The chilled fall air stirred around them as Nicholas and Abigail turned to face one another in the remnants of the tiny church. The still-standing archway-entrance served as the altar and on the same grounds where Malcolm and Rebecca had been wed decades before, Nicholas took Abigail as his wife.

~~~~~~~~

Rebecca Elizabeth Standish was a bundle of nerves – excitement, nervousness, and fear. The only constant was happiness since she and her beloved Malcolm would be married before the night was through. Dozens of men had courted Rebecca – boys they were better considered.

Now, it would seem, as promised, Remington was swaying her other brothers and father to his way of thinking and Nathaniel Standish was "giving some serious thought" to his discussion with Malcolm rather than immediately giving his blessing.

Rebecca would stand no more than the month wait he had already put them through and had convinced Malcolm of her plan too. Now, she waited in the car in which Malcolm had swept her away from the gala.

With any luck, her brothers would only now be missing her and since she and Malcolm had departed more than two hours earlier, Rebecca would be wed and consummated to Malcolm, before the Standish men were able to track the newlyweds down.

Her father would be saddened – his only daughter was taking away his right to give her away properly, but with the resistance she had been feeling between her men folk and Malcolm, Rebecca would take no chances.

Just then, Malcolm emerged from the tiny country church they had happened upon and with a beaming smile on his features; he opened the door and helped Rebecca out. "He's agreed to the ceremony?"

Malcolm nodded, "Aye, there's the Scottish connection to be considered. Still, we must be gone before your brothers' catch up with us. He wants no knowledge of where we are going or your brother's names."

"Then we'd best hurry." Rebecca suggested.

Malcolm laughed and followed his non-blushing bride's hasty steps into the stone church. Glancing back over his shoulder, Malcolm nodded into the darkness where he knew his friend stood watch over the happenings. Nicholas would not allow Rebecca's family to interrupt early – all would be well within the quarter-hour.

~ Chapter Eight ~

It was not difficult to find a properly romantic Bed and Breakfast in northern Virginia. It was an area cluttered with history and inviting homes, encouraging guests to visit a while longer. After booking a room, Nicholas arranged for a candlelight meal on their room's private verandah and in the waning afternoon sunlight, they shared a wedding meal that Abigail decided was perfect.

"What did she wear?"

"Who?"

"Rebecca, when she married Malcolm. Was their wedding anything like ours?"

Nicholas bubbled with laughter. Pushing aside the amazement he felt, whenever she so closely followed his thoughts, to reply, "When you ask such questions, you sound very much like her." Clearing his throat of the humor, he answered, "If I recall correctly, it was a light blue gown and her hair was upswept."

With a sardonic smile, Abbey teased, "You *would* remember the state of her neck."

Nicholas shrugged, "I never had any such inclinations toward Rebecca."

"You really *are* loyal, aren't you?"

"I'll be spending the rest of my existence proving as much to you."

"Good."

"As for the similarities in our ceremonies—I think Rebecca would have liked more of a show, but she wanted Malcolm as her husband enough to give that up." Looking closely at his new wife's expression, Nicholas supplied, "I assumed you never wanted the pomp and circumstance of a wedding that most young girls dream of—especially the kind Southern Belle Rebecca Standish would have had if her father had gotten his way." Nicholas waited patiently as Abigail enjoyed her taste of beef Wellington.

"You are very right about that. Besides, what friends would I invite? I've never felt a connection to anyone save my parents and you."

"In that you seem more like Malcolm."

"He was quiet?"

Nicholas smiled and the expression of reminiscence Abbey was coming to recognize covering his handsome face. "At times. He was friendly, but leery of others. I often wondered if that were the case before his Embrace. He rarely talked about that life, though. Malcolm was a man for the here-and-now, not wallowing in self-pity or the past. He played the cards life dealt him."

"And Rebecca?"

With a laugh, Nicholas offered, "Suffice it to say they were polar opposites."

"Not a chance of me sufficing," Abbey grinned cutely, and Nicholas felt her unseen hold on him grow stronger. "More please," she persuaded.

Not hesitating to grant her wish, Nicholas explained, "Like *that*—Rebecca was never quite satisfied with what she was given. Not *ungrateful*, just always hoping for a bit more."

"Even with Malcolm?"

"No, Malcolm was her perfection and that was why she gave all to be with him."

"Then you are my perfection, too, for I will never be parted from you so long as there is breath in my body."

Nicholas studied her silently. He made no move to gain more from her, merely took what she said and the feeling with which she declared it. Allowing the loving warmth of her declaration to warm his cold body, he stood and as he moved around the table, keeping his dark eyes on hers, he offered his hand.

Abbey accepted and without words, they moved into the room. This was the time where Abigail knew that she should feel nervous or shy. The awkwardness remained at bay, however. Abigail was never more comfortable than when Nicholas was near.

There was no sound as they stopped in the center of the room. Nicholas placed her on the bed with him and in a matter of seconds, the casual sage skirt, and taupe blouse Abbey had worn for their wedding was no more than a memory.

Naked beneath his touch, Abigail savored the heat of his bare form pressing her into the mattress. She could feel every pulse within him racing with hers. He tormented with his hands, his lips, and—with extreme care—his teeth. When Abigail was ready, he braced over her, kissed her, and slowly eased them together.

At last, Abbey witnessed this new dimension of passion with Nicholas. She watched in pleasure-filled horror as her lover's eyes changed from the smooth onyx that had lulled her in, to silver-speckled orbs that declared the monster within. Refusing to allow the feeling of terror screaming for release to find any—Abbey concentrated on her body and the way Nicholas' lovemaking tantalized her.

There was pain—some of which remained—but the pleasure outweighed it. Abbey's desire for Nicholas pushed aside the reality of what she now saw—of what they truly shared.

She climbed an unseen mountain until—pulling Nicholas' lips to hers—Abbey tumbled over the edge. It was a bittersweet release, tormenting Abigail with what she knew was to come—what they would have to face when this pleasure ended. Her kiss deepened and she tasted the metallic result of her split lip less than a second before her husband reacted.

Nicholas jerked away from her. His breathing turned sharp and his eyes closed. When they opened again, Abbey forced her self not to recoil.

Nicholas sensed her fear just the same.

His eyes remained speckled with the metallic on onyx as they had been in passion, but now blood-lust joined his desire. The outer edge was changed to red, the iris rimmed with gold—just as Remington's had been.

"And now you learn what it is to play with fire. Remember that my emotion for you is threefold what I feel for others, *aatria mou*." Nicholas ran a fingertip gently over Abigail's collarbone as he added, "It doesn't matter if that attachment is love, lust or hunger. You are never entirely safe with me."

Wiping the back of his hand roughly against his lips, Nicholas tried in vein to rid his senses of the taste of her blood.

Abbey's thoughts raced and—so connected to her now, body and soul—Nicholas could read every one of them. He laughed—more cruelly than he intended—and replied to her thoughts. "Yes, I *am* a monster, just like Remington."

Abbey didn't move—aside from the heavy rise and fall of her chest and the pounding of her heart she was completely still as she whispered, "You are *not* like *him*."

Nicholas' eyes filled with hard truth and he used his mind to speak to her. *I am exactly like him.*

"Get out of my head," she demanded in a hoarse whisper. "I've let you into my body, my heart and my soul. I've taken your name—you'll leave my mind to *me*."

Instantly, Abbey turned to the side of her bed and vomited into the small trashcan there. When she turned back, Nicholas was standing by the bed, looking toward her with the same kind eyes she had fallen in love with. All traces of the terrifying truth were gone for the moment.

Softly he apologized, "I'm sorry. I hate what I am and I was wrong to take it out on you."

Abbey's green eyes were the pair to be feared now, and her demanding tone proved it. "Don't do it again. I know what you are and I've accepted it." Nicholas nodded and Abigail invited—though her tone was just barely forgiving, "Now come back to bed and answer more of my questions."

"Not now." Nicholas moved slowly—*carefully*—back toward Abbey and the bed. He was pale and Abbey could *feel* his fatigue.

Despite the anger and fear she had known minutes before, her love for him won out. Moving toward him—careful not to touch him yet, Abbey asked, "Nicholas, what's wrong?"

He lifted his head and demanded, "Stop moving, Abigail."

She looked bewildered, "What?"

"Every time you move, your heartbeat quickens and the small bit of blood you are letting surrounds my senses with the smell of you."

She looked stunned, "My lip is dry already. You still smell it?"

Nicholas looked her over from top to bottom and for the briefest instant she wondered if he were going to make love to her again. He didn't touch her, but his eyes made her shiver in anticipation—the smirk that graced his lips proved that he knew it too. "Abigail, you bleed from your lost innocence."

Abbey held her breath, but couldn't resist asking, "What do I smell like?"

His expression deepened. Even in the sparse light of the setting sun, Abbey could see the grin lifting the corners of his full red lips—lips that looked darker either from the pallor of his skin or the fact that Abigail was so very much aware of his vampire state now. His answer came honest, "You smell like my favorite meal."

Abbey's eyes narrowed, "You don't frighten me."

"I don't intend to; but I *do* want you to know what is foremost in my mind when I'm with you."

Abigail smirked with clear meaning. "*Not* the emotion I would have guessed."

Nicholas' humor was currently lacking. "Believe it and remember it. It won't matter how long or how much I come to love you, Abigail, my priority will *always* be the feast. Even as I find pleasure from your body, I will be resisting my hunger for your blood."

"Then Embrace me." The solution seemed so simple to Abbey. Nicholas—considering his emotional state of the moment—couldn't even fully broach the subject. His reply was final, "No."

Abbey merely nodded, indicating that she made a mental note of his decision, but planned to revisit the subject again. Instead, she requested, "Then tell me this; after the primal scent of food, what do I smell like to you?"

There was no hesitancy in his description. "You smell like autumn—when the leaves are crisp and falling to the ground. You remind me of fireplaces warming homes from within, making the air heavy with smoke. You smell like warm bread baking in the oven."

"Wow," Abbey breathed, overwhelmingly flattered. "Is that the truth?"

His eyes, fierce and weak at the same time, gazed boldly into hers. "The truth is all you shall ever hear from me again, Abigail."

"This could come in handy."

Nicholas' grin was weak, "Really?"

Tapping her chin with the tip of her index finger, Abbey mulled playfully before asking, "Why are you warm when I touch you?" She reached out, touched his bare arm, and was encouraged when he didn't shirk from her hand. "You should be cold—at least by all aspects of research and entertainment I've ever come across—but you are warm against my skin."

"And only yours," Nicholas replied.

"How can that be?" Abbey questioned in amazement.

"Because when a vampire discovers or chooses their Beloved, the desire they have for that person—in love or passion—warms them to the recipient's touch only."

"That is wild." Abbey stated showing the generational gap between them once more.

Nicholas chuckled at her description, adding, "Yes, but it also makes much sense too. Think about this—how enticing would you find me if I were cold and stone-like under your touch?"

Abbey smiled, moved to her knees behind him, and wrapping her arms over his shoulders ran her fingertip downward along the centerline of his chest. "I cannot even imagine such a thing."

"And I assume you find my scent alluring too?"

Automatically, Abbey sniffed against the curve of his neck, "You could say that. In fact, it was the first thing I noticed about you—aside from your handsome face and smile."

Nicholas turned to offer her that same expression now. "Naturally, *aatria mou.*"

"And what does *that* mean?" Abbey asked as though the curiosity could be contained no more.

"It is Greek and it means *my adored.*"

All breath left Abbey for a moment and the instant she regained it she declared, "Nicholas Adamouras, I love you." Leaning around his shoulders to kiss her husband's lips, Abigail allowed them to forget her questions, his stories, and both of their fears for the time being.

~~~

Abbey needed air. She woke to a dark room. Sweat drenched her and every muscle in her body was shaking with exertion as though she had just finished a triathlon. Nicholas was next to her—resting peacefully if not sleeping. Carefully, she slid from the bed, donned her thin robe, and padded out onto the balcony.

Leaving the door ajar, she sat on the ornate black-iron chair closest to her, allowing the coolness of the metal to chill her skin. Resting her head in her hands and her elbows on her knees, Abbey took three deep breaths and slowly exhaled them. The heat left, but the shaking muscles remained. Chills joined the feeling and a slow nausea seeped into her system.

Too late, she smelled magnolia—normally a pleasant scent—but this was mixed with sulfer and so strong that it made her eyes and nose burn with the strength of it. She didn't look up, didn't have the energy. Instead, she weakly thought, *Will you kill me now?*

The laughter was audible inwardly and outwardly, but the words came unspoken. *I expected far more of a challenge from my sister's child.*

"Just as I am sure Rebecca would have expected your protection of her offspring rather than the torment you are offering me." Abbey looked up then and saw the man that Remington must have been the night Rebecca and Malcolm met. The only exception was that he was hovering in the air, just an inch above the railing of the balcony on which Abigail stood.

You are the spawn of Malcolm McBride as well as Rebecca's. He took my sister from me, so I shall take life from you.

"I think that you would have hated *any* man that loved and married your sister." Abbey informed her demonic ancestor disdainfully.

Any man? No. Heat filled Remington's eyes. *However, we both know that Malcolm was no man. He was a monster and he seduced my sister. Rebecca was so lovely, she could have been so happy, but he took her away from all of those who loved her.*

"Malcolm loved her, Remington."

Not enough to spare her the pain of the truth.

Abbey felt as though she needed to defend her great-grandparents. "You mean that he was a vampire?" Remington was blank. "Rebecca stayed with him even after learning that."

Yes, but she had no idea what lie ahead, what she would endure. He smiled then and his teeth slowly grew. *Just as you do not.*

Though her body trembled with unexplained weakness, Abbey held her ground and Remington's gaze. "Then be fast about it so that I no longer have to hide." *I'll do nothing.* The hand he held out toward her was long-nailed now. *There is no need; it will be done for me.*

A bravado Abbey hadn't expected filled her and she stood. Though Remington remained five feet away, she wouldn't have cowered if he'd been directly in front of her. "I'm tired of your riddles." *No, you are tired from giving your body to that seducer. You are weary from the chase I am giving you.*

"Do not correct me." Frustrated beyond control, Abbey flared, "I know what I mean. *My* words are not puzzles. Nicholas is my husband, he is my love, and he is my life. He did not seduce me; none of what we have done was without my consent. I gave myself to him willingly and I intend to do so again. I will never regret my love for Nicholas."

Disgust oozed from every bit of Remington's being. *You cannot give vows to God for a soulless creature, you stupid diluted whore.*

Mad for even trying to explain her feelings to this unfeeling monster, Abbey finally dismissed, "Just do something or go."

Expecting a remark, Abbey was stunned when Remington presented a courteous bow and then back flipped out of sight without another sound. The spot Remington had occupied was clear, the scent of magnolia-sulfur fading.

Abbey's chills subsided, though the shaking remained. She forced her legs to carry her back into the room and the relative safety of Nicholas' presence.

~~~

Nicholas walked through the door with warm Danish and coffee and found Abbey sitting on the middle of the four-poster bed they had shared. Flipping through the pages of notes she had brought with them, Abbey glanced up as he announced in greeting, "I brought breakfast."

Reaching toward the offering, she questioned, "Why didn't you wake me?"

"I don't like to wake you when you are resting."

"Really?" Abbey grinned in a manner that left no question as to the direction of her thoughts.

Sitting beside her, Nicholas pecked her on the lips, cheek, and neck before responding, "More than three times."

"Thanks for the clarification." She laughed lightly, took a sip of her coffee, and then informed, "Well, I don't like to wake with you gone. Especially with Remington around."

Removing the notes from her hand, he looked her in the eye and stated, "You're worrying too much today. We haven't seen him since before the wedding."

Looking sheepish she informed, "No, *you* haven't seen him since before the wedding."

"What?" Concern was instantaneous.

"He paid me a late night visit and it *wasn't* to congratulate or wish us well."

Nicholas easily ignored her attempt to lighten the mood as his concern gave way to anger. "He was *here* and you didn't wake me?"

"He was *here*, I was five feet away from him, and *you* never woke." Somewhat calmer, Abigail reasoned, "Nicholas, he did me no harm."

"Do not be so confident. His control has nothing to do with you; it's all a game to him." Cursing, Nicholas looked toward the daylight streaming through the window and back to Abbey's stubbornly confident expression. "He is defiantly preparing for something we don't know about. He presented you no danger, *that's* why I wasn't alerted, and why you remained safe. Now we need to figure out *why*."

"It won't change anything; not really." Abbey responded with calm.

Nicholas wasn't feeling the same. "This is a world of which you know little, Abigail. You would be wise not to second guess my advice."

Being confident was one thing, but arrogance was something else. "Do not spout high and mighty to me, Nicholas Adamouras. You'd best remember that I would know far more if you'd been honest with me from the beginning and not allowed me to waste precious time scanning books and websites on a wild goose chase you already held most of the answers to."

Forcing calm into the moment, Nicholas asked, "What did he say?"

"We talked of Rebecca and his reasons for hunting me."

"Are they different than we would have guessed?"

Abbey shook her head negatively. "Not different, but definitely deeper. It was almost as if he resents Malcolm for entrapping his sister and Rebecca for her stupidity of falling in love. He has no care for the fact that they loved each other dearly."

Nicholas looked sad. "*Aatria mou*, that's because all he has known for so long is hatred and revenge. It is all he will ever feel again."

Suddenly, Abbey felt cold and empty. "Nicholas, I want to go home."

"Then we will," he replied without hesitation.

~~~

With Nicholas in the driver's seat, the newlyweds were home before noon. Throughout the entire ride, Abbey was unusually quiet which put Nicholas on edge. He didn't want their first full day as husband and wife strained by an argument—no matter what the cause.

The moment they stopped in front of the house, Nicholas swept her from the car, into his arms, and—ignoring their small amount of luggage—carried her over the threshold into the house.

After accepting her husband's kiss, Abbey remarked, "Until I met you, I never realized how important my threshold is."

Nicholas held her in his arms a moment longer, then sliding her slowly down the length of him, asked, "Why were you so quiet coming home?"

"Did I worry you?" He nodded. "I didn't mean to," Abbey supplied as an apology. "It's only that I have so many questions still unanswered that I don't know which to ask first."

"You've never had a problem with that before," Nicholas teased.

Abbey wiggled her eyebrows playfully, "But after last night, I have so much more to fill my mind with."

Nicholas chuckled, "Then we should combine your two *problems*."

Not entirely agreeing yet, Abbey prompted, "I'm listening."

"Give me a kiss and I'll answer a question."

Abbey studied him a moment, not sure if she could trust him—or herself. "How will I *ever* get my answers that way?"

He shrugged, "That's a chance you'll just have to take."

They both knew that he would have her either way, so Abbey made it easy by deciding she might as well play along with his game and enjoy the fun of newly wedded bliss with him.

Abbey kissed Nicholas, very lightly—knowing it wasn't anything near what he had in mind, but she intended to learn something. Pulling back, she asked, "Are you related to me?"

"That's disgusting—no."

"You drink blood—don't be a hypocrite."

Nicholas merely smiled, and moved in for another kiss. This time he took more than she would have given.

Abbey pulled back, *"Tease*—did you make Remington what he is?"

"No."

Nicholas kissed her again and she felt the tenderness of her injured lip. "How old are you?"

"That might be a turnoff and I'd rather not have that happen right now."

Abigail smiled. "It's only a number Nicholas." She kissed him this time, meeting him in the middle and giving him a taste of her truth. "I'll want you even if you're six hundred years old."

He sighed dramatically before offering, "I'm young compared to that, but I think I get another kiss first."

"Nope, you haven't answered my last question yet." She dodged his lips and laughed—the playfulness taking over them was far better than the strain they had been feeling throughout the day.

"I am one hundred and ten years old."

Abbey was silent for a moment, then smiled, "You don't look a day over seventy-three."

"Really?" Nicholas grinned, and then swooped in for a rewarding kiss. "Shall I show you what this old man can do?"

"Not just yet; I like this method of getting my questions answered."

Nicholas playfully growled, stole another kiss, and stated, "One more answer and then I'll give nothing until I get my reward."

"What's your hurry?" Abbey touched the side of his face delicately—he was warm to her touch and she tried not to focus on the life she felt pulsing through him—it was an illusion. With whispered words she added, "We've got my lifetime."

Nicholas' eyes grew serious and soft. "And I thank you for allowing me that."

"Do you kill people?"

"Never."

"Then how—"

Nicholas put his finger to her lips and whispered, "It's my turn now." He took her mouth before she could offer more resistance and then he took her body—each either unaware or uncaring that a silent observer witnessed every touch, whimper and whispered promise that they shared in the shelter of their home.

~ *Chapter Nine* ~

During the next several hours, Nicholas' insatiable desire for Abigail thwarted her planned onslaught of questions. Occasionally, he allowed her rest, then he would look at her, his eyes telling all and she had no means of defense.

When she woke from a nap of necessity—Nicholas was not there. On his pillow was a note:

I'll be back at 7:00.
Please stay where you are.

Love, Nicholas

Abbey smiled and wondered if it would always be like this between them, with this feeling of new love and intense desire. Looking at the clock, she saw that it was four-thirty—she wanted to do something for him.

Rising quickly, she pulled on her clothes and went downstairs to her computer. Keying in some words, she found what she wanted, jotted down a list and grabbed her car keys.

As she headed to the door, she glanced out the front window—the sun was lowering. It was still full enough in the sky for her to get to the store and back safely, before Nicholas knew she was gone or Remington had darkness.

~~~

The child is a simpleton of the largest kind.
Remington was close enough to smell Abigail's blood the entire time she walked from her house to her car. He could feel her warmth while she drove to the grocery store, while she loaded her items and returned home. Her only saving grace was that she had chosen a busy time of day to shop. Others were just leaving work, rushing home and stopping at the store to grab something to make for supper. Even Remington wouldn't be so bold as to attack her with this many witnesses around.

He was also weak. It had been too long since he had feasted on a human and now—surrounded by the fast-paced motion of so many, the temptation was too great for Remington to stay long.

Disappearing in search of suitable prey—one he had in mind and had been stalking already—Remington felt a small victory in the knowledge that his niece was brave and idiotic enough to leave her house as she pleased.

In the very near future, that would be his greatest asset.

~~~~~~~

Nicholas was at the hospital; he had fed already—the blood bank was a wonderful thing for him. Now he was finishing his rounds and eager to return to Abigail and the tempting state he had left her in.

Walking to the nurse's station, Nicholas leaned over the desk to grab the clipboard holding the list of patients he was to care for on this floor. A red-nailed hand slipped over his and Nicholas looked up into the eyes of an attractive brunette. "You've been out a lot lately Dr. Adamouras; is everything alright?"

Nicholas had dodged Jennifer for months now—though in the weeks before Abigail's attack, Jennifer's attentions had become more obvious. "Everything's fine."

"Good." With a sidelong glance she added, "I've missed seeing your handsome face."

There was nothing about the woman that should turn Nicholas away, she simply made him uncomfortable. In addition, with Abigail as part of his world, he would allow no such distractions. "I am flattered." Nicholas started to tell her about Abigail then, but Jennifer's next move—even with his powers—took Nicholas by surprise in its boldness.

"Flattery is not *all* I'm offering, Doctor," Jennifer purred. She then proceeded to lean closer, so that Nicholas had an open view down the top of her blouse.

Nicholas chuckled, trying to remain friendly, "Well, with Abigail in my life, *flattery* is all I'm accepting." Since he didn't care what comment she had for his revelation, Nicholas promptly turned and left Jennifer and the temptation she thought she offered behind him.

In reality, she was nothing compared to his Abigail.

~~~~~~~~

Abbey was in the kitchen cooking when she felt Nicholas. Glancing over her shoulder, she watched through the front window as he moved up the walk toward the front door and pure joy filled her. Laying her wooden spoon aside, she moved through the house to welcome him.

He knocked on the door just as she reached it and opening the barrier, she smiled, "This time you could have walked in." She took his hand and pulled him through the doorway, closing it behind him.

"I was afraid of what you might do if I did," he responded in a teasing tone.

Abigail slid her arms around his neck and offered him a chaste kiss. "You don't need to be afraid. This is your home now too."

Nicholas kissed her this time and very likely would have headed directly up the stairs except a timer in the kitchen sounded. "Are you *cooking*?"

Abbey smiled, "Don't you smell it?" She offered a cute wink, adding, "Maybe it's *too* cooked for you."

Nicholas rolled his warm dark eyes and allowed her to lead him into the brightest room in the house. "It smells like home."

Dipping the spoon into the stainless steel pan on the stovetop, she held it out for him to sample. "That was my plan."

Nicholas sipped and sighed, "Avgolemono is my favorite."

"I hope you like lamb and spanakopita too."

"Spanakopita?" Nicholas questioned with awe in his voice.

Abbey misread his emotion. "I've whipped together a Greek salad that should be okay."

"Where's the Ouzo?" Nicholas asked looking around with feigned interest.

Abbey laughed. "I want to keep you conscious."

Waving as though in greeting, Nicholas announced, "Greek vampire here, not likely that I'll pass out." Laughing with Abbey, he looked at the array of ingredients on the countertop. "Abigail, thank you. These are my very favorite foods." He kissed her sweetly, "You know me better than you even realize."

Abbey loved his appreciation, but she didn't want her work wasted and so ignored the feelings welling between them. "I've got wine too; red, of course. Which reminds me, have you already had your *other* favorite meal? I really don't want you to leave tonight."

"I have." Nicholas popped a black Calamata olive in his mouth. "And I don't intend to go anywhere for the next two days."

"Then it's a good thing I got enough for leftovers." Abbey smiled and turned to pull some plates down from the cupboard. "I learned today that some vampires don't like or cannot stomach human foods. Why can you?"

Nicholas helped her remove the lamb from the oven and answered, "We receive different traits depending on the clan we are sired into and those gifts that our Embracer has."

"Like vampire genetics?" Abbey asked, slicing down the meat and placing the rare pieces on their plates.

"Exactly." Nicholas confirmed, then dished up steaming squares of spanakopita, grabbed the bottle of wine, and walked to the dining room. "Any other questions for me?"

Abbey laughed lightly. "Maybe a *couple*." She brought in two glasses for their wine and bowls full of lemon-egg-chicken soup. "Who Embraced you?"

Nicholas helped Abbey arrange the plates and sat across from her before answering. "I'm not really sure." He sipped his wine and relaxed into the story—Abbey could see that he was thinking back—remembering a time he'd rather have never experienced.

"I was twenty-four at the time. My father's family was third generation landowners just outside of Athens."

"Did you have siblings?"

A flash of loneliness passed over Nicholas' face, but then he gazed at Abigail and it was gone as quickly as it came. "Yes, an older sister, Olga. Then I was born to my parents, Constantine and Zoë. Three years later, they finished our family with my younger brother, Peter."

"Were you close?"

Nicholas looked momentarily surprised. "They were my family," he said as if that explained everything. Then remembering the time and place in which he currently lived, he readjusted his statement. "Yes, they were my world."

For a moment, Abigail sat in silence absorbing what he had just said and realizing how that now translated to her. A slow smile spread across Nicholas' handsome dark features and she crinkled up her nose playfully. "Just finish the story, know-it-all."

Dipping his head slightly in her direction, Nicholas silently agreed to her wish, though the smug smile of knowledge remained in place a few moments longer. "It was tradition to have an annual festival that would celebrate the return of the dead."

"Is that something you're *supposed* to celebrate?"

Nicholas smiled at her reaction. "If you're Greek and your parents tell you to do it, you generally obey."

"I see."

"These festivals would last three days. Families would leave gifts outside their homes to welcome the dead. This was always important because my people thought that death would not change the character of a person. The gifts would keep the kindhearted spirits happy and appease the malevolent ones."

"I think I understand why you took so easily to helping me with my unusual situation."

Nicholas grinned, "Do you?"

Abbey's eyes narrowed with forced irritation. "Yes, and you *know* you could have given a little more information while we were doing our research."

Nicholas looked shocked. "Everything I told you or wrote down was from memory as it is. What *more* would you like me to store in my brain?"

Amazement replaced her disdain. *"That* explains why I could never use the drop down bar and bring up the same sight you had gotten your info from."

His wife's deductions thoroughly entertained Nicholas. "Yes, I imagine it does."

Abbey switched gears again, "But that's not exactly what I mean."

"What *do* you mean?" Nicholas patiently waited without silently delving into her mind.

Her attempt to appear irritated fell extremely short of its mark. "I *mean* you could have given me more clues as to what you were—*are.*"

Abbey's fumble only caused a bigger grin. Tapping into her feelings, he assured. "I understand what you are trying to say, but the truth is I am bound to secrecy. Just as any of our kind." He paused and pondered briefly before adding, "I'm assuming you are held to the same regulations now too."

Full curiosity washed over Abbey. *"What* are you talking about?"

"The Vampirial Constitution." He made this announcement as though explaining something of which Abbey should already be aware.

Abigail laughed.

Nicholas remained straight-faced.

Abbey's laughter ceased. "You're not *kidding,* are you?"

With a negative shake of his head, Nicholas guaranteed, "Not in the least."

Abbey's mind reeled at the idea of enough vampires in the world to justify an established government of their own. "Do you have a President?"

Nicholas smiled, loving the way his wife's mind worked. "Not exactly." Thinking quickly through the details of what he was about to explain, Nicholas began with, "There are vampire rulers—*Sovereigns* they are called. These are the most powerful of our kind and they create and uphold certain *guidelines*—if you will—for our world."

Abigail knew that when he said *our* world, he was including her into this new and dark-realm—dark beyond her thoughts of Nicholas at least. "Need I ask how these rules are enforced?"

Nicholas met her gaze head on. "You are an intelligent woman, Abigail."

Abbey closed her eyes, inhaled, and slowly opened them again to face her husband. "I guess that makes your reasoning for secrecy understandable."

Nicholas smiled and waited for more.

Once again, Abbey did not disappoint him.

"But *you told* me the truth," Abbey whispered, as though anticipating a sudden assault from this regime she had just learned about.

Nicholas shook his head, "You *guessed,* —I just gave you the clues."

"That's allowed?" Abigail sounded doubtful.

With a slight shrug, Nicholas admitted, "I wasn't sure, but I couldn't continue to live without you knowing everything about me."

The fear coursing through every part of Abigail as she envisioned a group such as Remington hunting someone down, overrode her reaction to Nicholas' touching words. "Would they have reacted immediately, had they disagreed with your hinting?"

Nicholas' answer was sure. "Their enforcement is almost instantaneous."

"Then they know about me." Abbey stated as much as questioned, and then poured forth, "How is this instant knowledge possible? Where is their base? How many are there?"

Nicholas waited until the inquisition was finished before replying, "The Sovereigns have many talents among them. The Visionaries span the gifts of seeing Past, Present, and Future events. The Ambiancers can influence any being to feel different emotions with a glance, touch, or thought. Then there are the Trackers and the Enforcers. Of all the Sovereigns, these are the most visible. The Trackers are used to hunt down rebellious vampires or sympathizers, while the Enforcers follow close behind to—"

"Uphold the laws." Abbey finished, not yet wanting more detail on that particular branch.

Nichols nodded in affirmation, and then continued his description of vampire-politics. "Each gift is used to assure that our kind remain a secret beyond myth and legend."

"How many rulers are there?" Abbey was starting to feel as though she were claustrophobic.

Nicholas waited for some of her color to return before replying, "There are always fifteen that govern together. Three, rule over all and the remaining twelve are dispersed around the world, also in groups of three."

"Why three?"

"For rulings that require a tie-breaker."

Nicholas could see Abigail's struggle to grasp just one of the questions rolling through her mind and speak it—he helped by continuing with the details she would most want or need to hear. "There are five seats of rule. The three Sovereigns that rule over all are in Italy, just outside Rome. They are the oldest of the governing clans and have the most power and knowledge over all."

"No Democracy then?" Abbey stated with a tension-breaking smile.

Nicholas chuckled, "I'm afraid not."

"Where are the other seats?"

"There is one in Athens and then London, Romania and The United States."

"The United States?" Abbey's surprise was evident. "We are so young compared to the other countries you mentioned."

Nicholas nodded. "True, but also the fastest growing clan there is."

"Let me guess," Abbey winked at her husband, "Washington State?"

Nicholas laughed outright at Abbey's thought direction, before correcting, "Wrong book."

"One can dream." Abigail teased.

"Am I not vampire enough for you?" Nicholas returned with mock offense.

"What makes you think it's the *vampire* I'm interested in?"

Nicholas bared his teeth with a low snarl.

Abbey rolled her eyes and waved a dismissing hand in the air, "Enough of that. If it makes you feel better to hear it, then yes dear, you are all the vampire I need." With a playful laugh, she then prompted, "Tell me more."

His smile still in place and pride intact, Nicholas continued his tutorial. "Until Hurricane Katrina, the American Clan Leaders were in New Orleans; but living underground became a problem with the widespread devastation of that natural disaster."

"So where are they now?"

"They are somewhat nomadic, looking for the best place to settle."

Only partially wanting an answer, Abigail asked, "What are their requirements?"

"As I've told you, the first thought on any vampires mind is the feast. There must be good hunting."

"I'm guessing they aren't as particular about killing humans as you are."

"You are correct."

"So a metropolis with a large population is the most likely answer." Abbey considered this a moment then her mind registered another possibility. "Have they always been a part of my world too?"

"You must be a Pure-Blood to be held entirely accountable for your actions."

With sincere curiosity, Abbey inquired, "What if I were to announce on the radio the existence of vampire's?"

Nicholas' smile faded. "Beyond being considered insane by the human world, your new connections to the Sovereign would bring immediate repercussions."

"Such as?"

Nicholas knew better than to hold back. "Death or Embrace." Abbey's breath caught and her eyes met Nicholas' and, even without the ability to read her mind, Nicholas would have known her thoughts.

"However, *I* would be punished for not controlling you better."

That slowed her planning, but she still wondered in a barely audible whisper, "How?"

"Death or banishment from my clan—My Beloved in particular." He reached out to touch her face lightly and promised, "I would choose death."

"I'll keep the secret," Abbey pledged with as much sincerity as she had given in her wedding vows. "And I stand corrected."

Nicholas' complete interest was evident in his tone, "About what?"

"You are *far* more informative than *any* website could be."

Nicholas smiled, "And the knowledge is yours for the asking . . . *now.*"

"Yeah," Abbey chuckled lightly, "for the all-time-low price of wedding vows and learning that the man I love is a vampire."

Nicholas looked sorrowful. "Do you have regrets so soon?"

Abbey was immediately repentant for her flip comment. "Not for all eternity, Nicholas."

Knowing her need for humor, Nicholas lightened the mood by stating, "If you ever change your mind, just splash some tar across the doors and windows."

He didn't make her laugh, but her spiked curiosity eased the previous tension, just the same. "That really works? The tar or pitch crosses?"

"It doesn't have to be a cross. The scent of the fresh tar is so intense that it's blinding."

"Why didn't you tell me that sooner? I could have taken that precaution against Remington already."

"Because, just like different things cause headaches or sickness in humans, different things repulse vampires, as well."

"I should have guessed it wouldn't be that easy." Then another thought occurred to Abbey, "What do you do when a street is being repaved?"

Nicholas smiled, loving the way her mind worked. "I call in sick, of course."

"Remind me to call the roads department about that pothole down the street." He laughed loudly at her antics, and then listened as she rolled directly into her next question, and returned them to their original topic. "If your family left the gifts for the dead, why were you attacked?"

Nicholas glanced toward Abbey and offered the same answer he had given himself for decades. "Either the monster didn't care or didn't pass by our home."

"How did it happen?" Abbey spoke her question softly, knowing that Nicholas had no difficulty hearing her words.

Nicholas was silent, watching Abigail's face, feeling her emotions as clearly as if they were his own—and indeed they were.

Carefully he began his tale.

"Let me tell you this first. One of our beliefs was that before the dead departed again for the hereafter, the more *unsavory* ones might try to take a fresh soul along. I no longer doubt this, but consider it in a different light than I used to." Abbey only nodded, waiting for his story to continue. "It was thought that if we heard our name called out in the middle of the night, we should never answer until it was called three times because the spirits were only able to call for us once. The legend said that if one *did* answer the first summons, he was found dead the next morning."

"Did it call *your* name?"

Nicholas made a noise that should have been a laugh but was so void of humor, and full of disgust and sorrow, that it could not truly be classified in that way. "The creature never made a sound. It was late as I left the celebration at my older sister's house—a distance of less than two miles from my family home. My head was aching from the amount of alcohol I had subjected it to; but I somehow managed to stay upright. I took a shortcut path through the grape fields, and when I was a distance of only three hundred yards from my house, it stepped from the shadows and knocked me to the ground."

Nicholas took another drink of his wine, then continued, "When I woke in the morning—or at least I assume it was the following morning—I felt indescribable pain and nausea. The noise of the party was gone and I was entangled in the grapevine of my family's vineyard." His voice grew soft—longing, "The very future that awaited me held me in. I was a healthy man, strong and in a matter of minutes, I had been taken down by darkness and awakened to vines that held me tighter than the strongest bonds. I stayed there for three more days."

"What about the workers? No one noticed you injured in the fields?"

Nicholas shook his head negatively. "*Anthesteria* as the festival is called in Greece, is very serious business—but so is the clean-up after. Every Greek household would have an exorcism ceremony to make sure no souls were hiding, waiting behind to take possession of family members or cause chaos in some other way. Following the exorcism, a blessing was set upon the house and family to see them safely through the following year."

"So the workers were busy in their homes. But what about your parents, your family—where did they think you were?"

Nicholas smiled, shrugged, and said, "I was a virile Greek man, probably off making fine Greek babies with some fine Greek virgin I had met at the festival."

Abbey looked at him for a second and then stated. "I would laugh, but I'm guessing that you are entirely serious."

"Only a little," he conceded and then added, "My father was also busy with other cleansing duties. As the specifically purified head of household, he had to walk backward through each room of our house—one of the biggest in the area—while throwing black beans over his shoulder and saying," Nicholas started to speak in Greek and then corrected himself for Abbey's sake, "With these beans I ransom this household."

Abbey was quiet for so long Nicholas began to worry. "I can't believe *you* have nothing to say." She smiled. "Black beans? I would have thought black olives or grapes or orzo—but black beans?"

Nicholas shrugged. "I did not come up with the tradition."

"What year was it?" Abigail held her breath. Nicholas had told her his adjusted age already and she now knew that he was forever frozen at twenty-four, but her head hurt too badly for math problems.

"July 13, 1883."

"What did you do when you were able to move?"

Nicholas' eyes shaded over again. "I took my plan from the Bible and like Joseph's brothers; I left my bloody and torn clothes in the field. Then I snuck into my home, took only enough clothing to cover me and enough money to see me through a long journey and I left."

"How did you know what had happened, what you had become?"

Dark eyes rising to hers, Nicholas vowed, "Because the one thing I remembered from that night was the look in its eyes. The teeth that it bared and the growl that it made just before feeding on me will never leave my memory. As you know, Greeks are superstitious people. There had been rumors of nearby village slayings and speculations as to what had left the bodies bloodless and broken." Another deep breathe and Nicholas continued, "To my misfortune, *my* Embracer did not finish the job and instead created a new monster to join his clan."

Abbey looked at the food in front of them, wishing she had asked her questions after they had eaten the meal she'd prepared. It was obvious neither of them had any appetite left. Quietly she offered, "I don't know what to say."

Nicholas' grin lacked humor. "There is no need for you to say anything, *aatria mou*."

"But you seem so emotionally drained, I want to comfort you."

"You do comfort me, Abigail. In fact, I've not known such comfort since Malcolm and Rebecca were part of my world.'

"Truly?"

His smile was heartfelt now, "Truly."

"There's something I've been meaning to ask you—about when you met Malcolm."

"Yes?"

"Why did you hunt for scavengers when human blood would have strengthened you so much more?"

"Because from the first time I felt a taste for blood, I fought the urge and swore that I would never kill humans or create more vampires. I lived off the scavengers and injured animals in the forest instead."

"Why not the healthier choices?"

"I didn't deserve health."

Tears sprung to her eyes. "Oh, Nicholas, you didn't *ask* for this."

"I pray that God has your same mercy when one day I stand before him."

"And what will He think of me for loving one like you?"

"I do not presume to know God's ways or wisdom, yet I cannot imagine that he would damn a creature as loving and good as you. You are a victim in this just as I am."

"Even so, I could not *stop* loving you—you are a part of me which I cannot live without."

"Your honesty is wonderful. I've never known a woman to speak so openly of her feelings."

Nicholas' comment brought another question to Abigail's mind. "Nicholas, are you or *were* you married?"

Enjoying the way she asked the question with obvious dread and just a hint of jealously, Nicholas replied, "Nearly, but I was dragging my feet. In my heart I knew the girl my father had chosen was not the love I desperately wanted."

"So you were engaged?"

"Just three months after my Embrace, I would have been married."

"Then no children." Abbey stated as much as questioned.

Nicholas smiled, "Not that I'm aware of."

"So *that's* the kind of Greek boy you were."

"If you consider me a boy, then I've been doing something wrong." When Abbey playfully offered no verbal confirmation either way, Nicholas continued, "Perhaps I'll spend the next two days revising your opinion. And let me tell you something that you *won't* find in those books and notes and websites of yours." He leaned close—the vanilla-mint stronger than ever—even with the table separating them. "Once I've tasted of my greatest desire, the need for it grows stronger." His eyes slid over her face, over her neck and shoulders, and slowly back up, to her eyes again. "Can you imagine how badly I want you now, *aatria mou*?"

Abbey's gaze remained steady, "My *blood* or my *body*?"

"*Both.*"

~ Chapter Ten ~

Abbey narrowed her green eyes and wagged her index finger admonishingly in Nicholas' direction. "Just stay where you are. I have more questions to be answered before you distract me like that again." Nicholas' intense stare turned self-assured. "I could stay here and *still* convince you." In the next instant, she felt him slipping into her mind with well-planned seduction.

Abbey amazed them both by immediately shutting him out. "Oh, no you don't."

The prospect of physical pleasure flew from Nicholas' mind, replaced with the shock of Abigail's powerful and unexpected accomplishment. "*How* did you do that?"

Abbey shrugged. "I just focused on what I wanted and you were gone." With a flirtatious grin she added, "*Not* that I'm *opposed* to trying that interesting tactic at a more appropriate time."

Her newfound ability distracted Nicholas past the point of playfulness, and so he missed her comment. "You've never been able to do that before have you?"

"I've never tried."

Nicholas was near frantic. "*Think* Abigail; are there other gifts you seem to have picked up since I took your innocence?"

Abbey smiled, liking the way he sounded of chivalry and kindness even when he was tense. "Nothing that stands out—aside from the fact that I've never really had the urge to cook before. But since we've not had a bite, I can't say if that was successful or not."

Nicholas promptly sampled a bite of each item she had prepared for him and replied, "It's perfect."

"Thanks," Abbey dryly accepted his systematic complement of her efforts.

Again, if he noticed her underlying emotion, it went unmentioned amidst his interrogation. "When you went out to the store—which, by the way, I'm not happy that you did—was there any sign of Remington?"

"No." Abbey studied his expression closely, wondering what direction he was going with all these questions. Carefully she tried to channel into his mind, but Nicholas merely looked at her with a mixture of amusement and confidence. "Compared to me, you are still a novice, *aatria mou*. You'll not gain any information from me that I don't want you to."

"That doesn't seem fair." Abbey pouted, then demanded, "Just tell me what you want me to know." Silently she added, *The rest I'll get from research.*

Nicholas chuckled, "It'll take longer that way."

"Just answer the damned question show-off."

His smirk faded. "I'm uncomfortable with Remington's silence and with your increased power."

"Obviously, but *what* does it mean?"

"It could mean a few things, none of which is rather appealing."

"Tell me anyway."

With only the slightest indecision Nicholas stated, "Either you have gained some of my gifts in giving yourself to me or Remington is preparing for an attack and your heightened gifts are a way for you to subconsciously defend yourself against him."

Abbey's eyes narrowed in concentration. "Are you saying I could have gifts I don't even *know* about?"

"Possibly, but it's more likely that gifts you know about are much more powerful than we guessed."

Abigail's mind raced at the idea Nicholas presented. "What did you mean about *your* power transferring to me?"

"When a vampire discovers his Beloved—which in most cases it is another *vampire*—the strongest of their powers are shared. I've always been able to read the feelings of others, but never to the degree I can since we've married."

"Just like I've been able to hear and speak telepathically, but now I can push others out."

"Indicating that your abnormal human ability is from me," Nicholas deduced with heavy guilt.

Abbey smiled at Nicholas' train of thoughts and turned the familiar words of endearment back on him in an attempt to comfort and console. "*Aatria mou*, it came from *us*."

Her plan worked and Nicholas silently stepped to her side and offered Abbey his hand. The meal completely forgotten, with fingers entwined, they walked toward the stairs.

Midway up, Nicholas turned to kiss her, soft and slow and seductive and Abbey leaned into him with acceptance. Opening her mind to his senses, she allowed Nicholas to pull her emotions in and grant them each a new pleasure.

"Abigail," he placed one hand on either side of her face and stared intently into her green eyes. "Even before I met Malcolm, I dreamed of you." He chuckled, but it sounded more like a shaky breath. "I am fairly certain I dreamed of you even before my Embrace."

Abbey couldn't resist initiating another kiss before replying, "I don't doubt anything now, Nicholas. Surely there must be some reason that I have never desired another man—could not stand the thought of touching one—until you."

Nicholas slid his hand up her arm and down again, bringing it to rest on the curve of her hip. "You are the one thing that makes me grateful for this curse I live with."

They kissed again and Nicholas lifted her in his arms, and carried Abbey to their bedroom. She watched as he removed his clothing, did the same for her and then they made love—their souls touching as much as their bodies.

In the sated aftermath, Abigail whispered, "Make me like you so that we can be together forever."

Nicholas was quiet for so long that Abbey thought he would not reply. Finally, in the stillness he whispered, "I will be with you for the forever that is yours. I promised God that I would never add to these demons; I am certainly not going to start with you."

"So I am to grow old, weary and withered while you remain young. Am I to watch while you find passion with someone in the next generation?"

"Is that all you believe of my love for you? Do you think I love you for our passion alone?" Before Abbey could answer, Nicholas added, "For if it is, I will never touch you again and love you from afar as I have done for years."

Abbey pushed up to her elbow and looked down into Nicholas' face, her green eyes narrowed, and her words softly demanding. "*What* did you just say?"

Nicholas adjusted to a sitting position, and spoke in a resigned tone, rather than the defensive one Abbey anticipated. "As I said earlier, there is still much I need to tell you. It will take a long time with the details and your endless questions."

Abbey didn't rise to the bait of his teasing or his charming smile. Instead, she positioned herself comfortably and stated stubbornly, "Then it's a good thing you've promised me forever."

"Yes," Nicholas said smoothly, "I believe it is." Then his eyes grew distant, as he spoke of another time.

~~~~~~~~

Nicholas didn't have to look at Malcolm to know that the large Scot was but a shell of his former self. His happiness was gone – his Beloved dead because of the love they shared and now, he had given the last reminder of her to the care of strangers.

They had watched the family for weeks – seen how the adorable young woman yearned for a child. The petite blonde-haired woman, reminded both men of Rebecca in stature and energy. Malcolm and Nicholas' combined powers had shown them that she and her husband tried in vain to bear their own children, but God had not seen to their wishes.

Malcolm chose to intervene.

In the cover of darkness, he slipped into their home. He had perfected this skill long before, though for reasons entirely different from the plans he had this particular night.

While Malcolm worked, Nicholas stood guard outside – his senses attuned to anything within miles that would alert him to Remington – the newborn vampire that stalked them constantly these days.

In minutes, Malcolm was in and out of the small town house. Surrounded on all sides by neighbors, streetlights, and servants constantly coming and going this was a safe location for his arrangement to unfold. It was evident the young couple was loved and befriended by many, offering more witnesses to help keep the baby safe.

With a brief glance in Nicholas' direction, Malcolm indicated his work was finished and together they moved into the shadows as stealthy as they had come from less than a quarter-hour earlier.

The only indication that they had been in the area at all was the small cry of an infant within the house, already waking the startled couple that would love and raise him as their own.

Malcolm's only request – made in the note he had left with the babe – was that they allow occasional visits from his "Uncle" Nicholas – a man who spent entirely too much time abroad to raise a child – and that, even if they chose to add their name to his, the babe always retain his given name first: Jacob Michael McBride.

~~~

"Jacob. He was my father's father." The awe was strong in Abigail's voice.

Nicholas nodded, "Yes."

"Did you see him often?"

"Yes."

Trying to filter the fact that her husband had cradled her infant grandfather in his arms, Abbey stated, "Nicholas, you're going to have to give me more than one word answers,"

Nicholas smiled at the fine memory her flailing thoughts brought him, but he waited for her to speak and purposely blocked himself from her mind until she did—it didn't take long. "Was he a vampire?"

With a negative shake of his head, Nicholas informed, "No, but he *was* strongly gifted."

"Like me?"

"More so." Nicholas gathered his thoughts. "You see, Malcolm was an old and powerful being. Since Jacob had half of his characteristics, he also shared his power."

"Did Rebecca know that Malcolm was a vampire?"

He forced steadiness into his words. "Yes, she knew."

"*Before* the pregnancy?"

Sadness filled Nicholas' dark eyes. "No."

Realization covered Abigail's features. "*That's* why it was so important for you to tell me first— *before* we were married, *before* we made love."

Nicholas nodded affirmatively. "Watching the strain that Malcolm's omission put on their relationship taught me the value of honesty. I did not want our love to suffer after I had touched you."

"Thank you." Abbey whispered and leaned close to kiss Nicholas softly. Easing back again, she requested, "Will you tell me more?"

Nicholas touched her cheek. "Of course."

~~~

Nicholas had kept his word to the McBride family for over fifty years. Throughout those decades, Rebecca's reasoning for his safeguard had always been clear – Malcolm's ulterior motive wasn't as obvious until the youngest of the McBride's was seventeen years old.

From the shadows of her life, Nicholas had watched Abigail grow. The day she was born. Her first steps in the backyard on a warm spring day and her first day of school.

And throughout all of her life, the only struggle Nicholas had with his role as protector were the times when he wanted to, but couldn't make his presence known. To comfort her when she fell from her bike. To console her after a bully's words made her cry. To cradle her when she was ill.

To cherish her beauty on the night she attended prom – the exact moment Nicholas completely realized the depth of his devotion for Abigail McBride.

At seventeen-years-old, Abbey was a vision of pure beauty. The gown she had chosen to wear was sleeveless, showing the porcelain skin of her rounded shoulders and sleek arms outside its Kelly-green satin. The design clung to each curve and at her knees, flared out with white crinolines beneath. Her glorious red curls were upswept, with a few swirling tendrils left to grace her neck and shoulders. A single string of pearls with matching earrings was her only added adornment – Nicholas doubted their necessity.

The child he had watched grow was a woman now and in that instant Nicholas Adamouras knew what secret Malcolm had kept from him on the day of his death – Abigail McBride was Nicholas' destiny – his Beloved.

As the protective creature watched in the dark shadows, a bright red 1987 Trans Am pulled up to the curb. The teenage boy walked to the front door to collect his date and put on a mannerly greeting for Abigail's parents. Nicholas wasn't fooled and chose to read the young man's true thoughts. As expected, the vehicle the boy had borrowed from his older brother wasn't the only thing revving tonight.

Nicholas battled the urge to step forward and tell this young man that if he tried any of the vulgar ideas floating through his mind, his overestimating and perverse head would be severed from his unsatisfied body.

Yet, on the other hand, Nicholas could completely understand the young man's desires.

Abigail kissed each parent lightly on the cheek and turned to walk down the porch steps toward the waiting car. Once, Nicholas saw the boy – Greg he had heard her introduce him – try to take Abigail's hand. His light touch brought brewing-nausea to Abbey and she let go of his friendly offering as soon as she could – Nicholas grinned, insanely happy that she had inherited this gift.

As the flashy car pulled out, Nicholas followed. Over roof and treetops, Nicholas had trailed them to the prom location, just a few miles east. Once they were in the crowded hotel ballroom, Nicholas had a more difficult time staying in tuned to what was happening with Abigail – so many minds, meant extra interference.

After three hours of filtering through the teenage thoughts inside, Abigail and Greg stepped out with a small group of couples. They discussed where their best party option was and soon were on the road again.

The house they traveled to wasn't far, less than five miles – just outside Funksville and bordering the portion of the Antietam Creek that ran through the small town.

The nearly two acre wooded lot was perfect for Nicholas' camouflage. Unfortunately, it was also ideal for Remington's hunting and Greg's exceedingly hopeful plans.

There were teens everywhere and the sound of music floated out of the brightly lit, large two-story house. Some of the cars near where Greg parked had windows already steamy from within. When Abigail placed her hand on the door handle to exit the uncomfortable scene, Greg reached across to stop her.

Stealing a haphazard kiss he asked, "What's your hurry, Abbey?"

She didn't' reply – doing so would have been difficult anyway since Greg now rammed his tongue into her mouth. The sound she made was one of pure disgust, which her date either chose to ignore or mistook for excitement since he kissed her harder and promptly shoved his hand down the front of her gown.

Abbey's senses whirled – first she smelled body odor, strong like a locker room. Then came a burning smell, mixed with something sweet . . . was it flowers? No matter what it was, Abbey couldn't concentrate – she had to stop Greg who was now running his lips over her throat and eagerly pulling the front of her gown further down.

"Greg, you need to stop this."

His words were intermittent with panting, "Come on, Abbey. Don't be a tease."

The door on Greg's side of the car opened quickly and a masculine voice spoke, "I think the lady said no."

"What the – ?" Greg's question halted.

The strikingly handsome blonde man responded, "Watch your language and consider me, border patrol."

The smell that had assaulted Abbey earlier was overwhelming her now. "No wonder Mike's parents agreed to this party, they sent guards."

The impatient looking man said nothing – simply waited for Greg to get out or leave.

Abbey made the choice for them. "Greg, just take me home."

"What?" The disappointed teen turned back toward Abbey at the same instant she vomited.

"Damn it, Abbey, Chris is gonna be pissed *if his car smells like puke. Why didn't you tell me you were sick?"*

Abbey just held up a silencing hand. "Get me home before it happens again."

Ignoring the man standing outside his car, Greg closed the door and started the engine. He was pulling down the drive when Abbey noticed the unpleasant smells were finally fading. Her head hurt now, but around it's throbbing, she swore she heard someone whisper, Hurry home, Abigail.

Then again, she thought she heard a car crash in the yard from which they had just departed.

Neither possibility seemed conceivable, so she put them immediately out of her mind and concentrated on not being sick again.

~~~

Abbey cringed at the rehashed memories. "I *meant* something I didn't already *know* about."

He smiled, "Did you know I was there, watching over you?"

"Not exactly, but I guess I always felt safe—does that mean anything?"

"To me, a great deal." Nicholas admitted.

Abbey smiled, "I should have remembered your voice."

Nicholas thought of his own opportunity to hear Abbey speak before knowing her, "Not necessarily."

"So it wasn't just Greg's lust that I smelled that night, it was Remington too." Abbey shuddered, "I can't believe he was that close."

"I was close too." Nicholas reminded her softly.

"Thank you." She kissed him sweetly.

"You are very welcome, *aatria*." Nicholas would have deepened his touch, but Abbey halted him.

"None of that yet. I want another bedtime story."

"Exactly like you used to say to your father."

Abbey shot him an odd look, pointedly considering their state of dress and corrected, "Thankfully not *exactly*."

Nicholas chuckled, "Suffice it to say that it is James' fault you are so needy for my stories."

"Needy isn't a very nice word," Abbey pouted.

"What word would you prefer?"

"Curious or interested," she kissed him again—teasing with her touch, her voice turning husky as she added, "Longing or *yearning*."

Nicholas' eyes began to change, but Abbey knew the difference now and this was definitely a good transformation. With his full-power charm leading, Nicholas requested, "Give me what I want and then I'll give you what you want."

Abbey laughed, pulling her husband closer. "Sounds like a win-win situation for me."

~~~~~~~

Rebecca was moving into her second month of pregnancy. When she stood sideways in front of her full-length mirror – as she did now – she wondered how big she would be at full-term. Since her size compared closer to a woman carrying for three months longer than she had, the outlook wasn't good.

Still perusing her form, Rebecca pulled the thin robe she wore taunt against her swollen midsection. She really didn't care if she were as big as a house – carrying Malcolm's child inside her was a blessing.

Turning toward her wardrobe for clothes, Rebecca let loose a startled squeak – Remington stood no more than three feet behind her.

Immediately, she turned back to the mirror and he disappeared from her view again.

Rebecca's head swiveled once more – Remington was still there.

"Don't scream, Becca. It will only cause trouble and a very messy clean up."

Rebecca's face was pale, though likely not as much so as Remington's handsome features. "What is wrong with you, Rem?"

Her voice was barely above a whisper, but he had no trouble hearing her. The truth was, he could hear her, the cook working in the kitchen below and the maid willingly giving herself to Malcolm's valet in the attic room's two-floors above – all at the same time.

His answer was short, "Ask your husband."

Rebecca's eyes narrowed – she knew her brother's tone, and dislike for Malcolm, well. "No, I'm asking you."

Lazily, Remington moved to the ladies chair in front of Rebecca's vanity and sat in it. Picking up a bauble, he turned it between his hands slowly. "Why do you think it is that your belly grows so quick-

ly?"

She was silent – almost defiantly so. Remington smiled, she was his twin, and they were well connected – he could read her every thought and respond to it as he did now. "It is my damn business."

"How did you – ?"

His eyes darkened, "Because I have abilities now that you can't even imagine, Becca."

She subconsciously took a step back, but her body met with the coolness of the mirror – her blue eyes widened. "I couldn't see you in the reflection with me." She forced herself to swallow. "You were right there; I should have seen you Remington."

The movement of his hands stopped, his fingers tightened and the bauble disintegrated to dust. "Yes, you should have." His eyes – more silver and blood now than blue -- rose to meet his sister's horrified gaze. "You also should have heeded my warnings about Malcolm McBride."

"I need no protection from my husband."

"Your husband is not what you think."

"He is my love, my life." She met his stare with clear meaning, "His is my everything."

"Your family should be your everything, Rebecca."

"Malcolm McBride is my family."

"You have no idea what you are in for, what this lust you have allowed yourself will do to you."

"Then tell me wise brother."

"Malcolm is a demon, just as his friend, Nicholas, just as me."

Rebecca stood in silence.

"You doubt me? Think of him." Remington smiled, "Have you seen his reflection in your mirror?"

She made no verbal reply, but Remington heard her just the same – his laughter proved as much.

"I'm sure I have seen it, I just never noticed since most people do have a reflection."

"Well, if you're sure." Remington patronized.

"Why are you here?"

"To show you the truth." Immediately following his words, Rebecca felt Remington overtake her thoughts.

Like a movie screen, pictures flashed through her mind – Malcolm and Nicholas seeming to speak without words. Nicholas, always knowing her thoughts before she spoke them, and Malcolm, always loving her, and protecting her, as though anticipating danger. Malcolm and Nicholas' subdued happiness when learning of the child. Her subsequent physical changes and the accelerated pace at which they were occurring.

Finally, Rebecca thought of how Malcolm's eyes changed every time they made love. Her gaze swiveled to her brother's again and she saw the coloring there – and the horrid possibility solidified in Rebecca's mind.

Fighting the onset of nausea, she questioned, "How?"

"Malcolm and Nicholas?"

She nodded.

"I don't know. For me it was by choice. I followed you here and one night saw Malcolm and Nicholas as they fed at the harbor."

"What do you mean, fed?"

Remington glared, "I mean they drank the blood from a living creature."

Rebecca's stomach heaved. "A person?"

A harsh laugh sounded, "No, they are too good for such as that. Apparently they prefer the taste of scavengers."

Rebecca's relief was short-lived, "What do you prefer?"

"Your lady's maid."

Tears fell immediately from her eyes – tears of sorrow, tears of anger and tears of fear. "I thought Meg had run off with her lover."

"She had." Carefully, Rebecca edged away from the mirror and closer to the door. "There is no need for you to fear me, Becca."

Tears still rolled and somewhat insane laughter joined. "Why should I believe you? The brother I loved would never choose to live like this."

"The brother you loved did this to avenge you."

"I need no avenging."

"Tell me that after the thing growing inside you rips you open and drinks your blood for its first meal."

Bile rose in her throat, the baby moved and Rebecca whimpered, "You lie."

Remington shrugged. "On occasion."

"You cannot know that what you say will happen."

"No, but I can make an educated guess." His eyes grew bloodier still. "Why don't you watch me feed and then decide for yourself if this demon-child can resist the life-blood you give it?"

"I'll do nothing of the kind." Anger was forcing its way up from the other emotions drowning it. With certainty, Rebecca declared, "Remington, I want you to leave and never come back."

His voice began to change and Rebecca sobbed at the sound – his speech had always been so perfectly southern. None of that remained. "I damned myself to defend you against the monster you so stupidly gave yourself to and this is the thanks I receive?"

Rebecca's speech was condescending. "I'll not take responsibility for this change. You damned yourself for your pride. You couldn't abide that I might love someone more than you or the rest of my family."

Though he made no verbal reply, Remington was directly in front of Rebecca in a flash of movement too sudden for her to see – his stance clearly a threatening one.

Rebecca didn't falter. The bit of Remington that showed through the demon before her, gave her the bravery to stand her ground. If her brother truly loved her as he claimed, he would never harm her. "Leave, Remington."

Rather than lose complete control, Remington decided it was better to do as she said, but first he promised, "I'll go, but know that when I return, it will be to rid the earth of any creatures you and McBride create. I vow that I'll spend my life hunting them, generation after generation."

Rebecca slapped his face soundly. Then she cried out and grimaced at the feel of cold stone colliding with her soft palm.

Remington laughed and when Rebecca's eyes opened again, he was gone.

~ *Chapter Eleven* ~

"Even though I was angry that night when you turned me away—when I learned the truth about you, I'm glad that you told me first. I can't imagine finding out the way Rebecca did."

"To be honest, I thought that Remington would have told you sooner. Maybe he didn't realize the extent of our feelings for one another."

"I doubt it." Abbey intoned dryly. "There doesn't seem to be a thing that he misses."

Nicholas looked to the clock and shifted so that he could see Abbey better. "You need to rest."

"But I want to be with you and hear more."

"Abigail, I can't think of anymore to tell you. You are like a sponge."

"Just one more question."

"Really?"

She ignored his doubt, "When did Rebecca confront Malcolm?"

"That very afternoon, when we returned to the house."

"You lived with them?"

"More or less." Nicholas took a breath and settled in for another tale. "Since I was a bachelor and Malcolm was well off, most people assumed that I was some relative of his."

"Did you and Rebecca get along well?"

"I loved her as I loved my own sister."

"What did she say that day when you came home?"

"I think it was, 'go to sleep'."

Abigail laughed softly and swatted his chest playfully. "I doubt it." She kissed his chest where her head rested. "Tell me please."

"Then no more for a few days. I need my rest too."

"I doubt that as well." Abbey informed, and then said no more as Nicholas began to speak again.

~~~

Rebecca dismissed all of the staff early. No one argued – who wouldn't enjoy time free from labor while still obtaining the benefits of employment?

The table was set, just as any other evening mealtime. Platters were covered with rounded silver lids, the finest china, and crystal waiting to be filled by the diners.

As usual, Nicholas and Malcolm walked through the door together. Their cheerful discussion was interrupted by Rebecca's greeting from the room to their left. "Supper is ready early. Come and sit with me."

She deliberately kept her mind clear – actually focused on taking a mental inventory of her favorite gowns, jewelry, and cosmetics. When that was finished, she sorted through the items in Malcolm's dressing room. The effect must have worked, because as Nicholas followed her husband into the room, the curiosity in his eyes slid to humor.

"How are you this evening, Rebecca?" Nicholas questioned with a little more than automatic politeness.

"Tired," Rebecca admitted and a tiny smile of self-satisfaction graced her beautiful lips. "Why, do I look ill?"

Nicholas tripped over his own tongue – something unusual for him. "No . . . not . . . I didn't mean . . ." he cleared his throat lightly. "You are lovely as always, Becca."

Her attractive appearance aside, Malcolm was immediately alert to Rebecca's needs. "Should we skip supper?"

Rebecca waved their worries aside. "I will probably feel better if we don't." Sky blue evening gown with capped sleeves and shimmering dangles, matching pumps and handbag, which looked fabulous with her short white fur cape on cool evenings.

Taking his seat at the table, Malcolm squeezed her hand. Nicholas sat directly across from her and to Malcolm's right – the younger man's brow furrowing slightly as he did so.

This time Rebecca hid her triumphant smile by glancing down at her hand interlocked with her husbands now.

Just as any other night, Nicholas asked a blessing upon the meal.

Three pairs of eyes raised and as he reached for the covered dish closest to him, Malcolm asked, "Where are the servers?"

"I gave them the evening off."

Her husband was just about to inquire why when he saw the entrée.

In the middle of their perfectly set table, resting on the silver platter Rebecca had been so happy to purchase was a chicken – completely raw, feathers still attached and blood oozing from its severed head, eyes bulging and its beak hanging grotesquely open. Encircling the disgusting sight was a perfectly placed garnish of parsley leaves and four scoops of cheerful red cranberry/citrus jelly.

"I thought perhaps something more to your tastes this evening?" Rebecca nodded her head toward the smaller platters, reserved for side dishes, "If you'd be so kind, Nicholas?"

Nicholas glanced quickly at Malcolm who still sat in stunned silence. Rebecca interrupted their silent conversation. "Don't ask him, do as I've requested."

"Yes, Rebecca," Nicholas intoned, sounding much like a child who had been caught in a great prank.

Separately, Nicholas lifted the three other domes, and revealed fish heads surrounded by damp and foul-smelling harbor grass, a rat – captured by the kitchen cat – cleverly wreathed with cheese and crackers and – almost odd in their normality – steaming hot biscuits with cooled-butter cut into individual leaf shapes. "I thought perhaps you'd like to sop up any of the blood that drips onto your plate."

The silence was deafening.

Rebecca was waiting.

Nicholas was ashamed and uncomfortable.

Malcolm was hurt and livid.

"How dare you mock me like this?" His Scottish accent was thick, his words deep and soft.

"How dare I?" Rebecca wasn't so mild in her manner as he. "How dare I confront you for hiding this dark truth?"

His eyes were changing of their own accord – green to gold to red – fury filled every part of Malcolm. "When did you learn?"

"Today."

Malcolm thought back over his day. He and Nicholas had fed just minutes before returning home. It was impossible that Rebecca would have seen them and still had time to prepare the crass scene before them.

His glowing eyes narrowed. "How?"

"Remington."

Nicholas growled and that was all the longer it took him to change forms. Rebecca's eyes flitted to her surrogate brother. "You'd best watch your tongue, too, Mr. Adamouras. I've no great happiness for your part in this either."

"I could tell you nothing. It wasn't my place."

Her blue eyes flashed – for a moment, Nicholas wondered if Remington had Embraced her. "I have opened my home and my heart to you. It most certainly was your place."

"Leave Nicholas out of this." Malcolm fought for vocal control. The shift in his eyes was enough – he didn't want Rebecca to hear his demon speech too.

"Fine, I'll let him out." Her eyes swiveled to Nicholas, "Pack your belongings and leave."

Nicholas' pain was palpable – he moved to do her bidding just the same.

"You would turn my oldest friend out? Maybe you are more like your brother than I thought."

"And exactly how well do you know my brother, Malcolm? Are you the one that made him what he is or was it Nicholas?" Her cold gaze slid to the man now standing in the doorway. His back was to them, but upon hearing his name, he had stopped moving. "I have been more than fair with your relationship. Do you know how many friends of mine find it odd that I allow my husband to have such a close comrade?" Her voice lowered nearly an octave. "Some think it's immoral the way you act together."

Nicholas turned toward her. "And now you know how correct they are. Nevertheless, the people whose tongues wag in their empty heads are wrong in the manner of which they are blaming. My love for Malcolm is no different from my love for my father. The immoral part is that we hunt together." His eyes narrowed and his smile was fierce, "What do we hunt?"

Rebecca jolted, the very thought was in her mind and Nicholas had plucked it out before she could speak.

"You should have stayed with thoughts of your wardrobe." Nicholas taunted, revealing that he now knew Rebecca's discovery of his ability. Quickly, he revealed, "We hunt for animals, scavengers, because unlike your brother, we do not kill humans."

"Perhaps not kill, but do you create more of these demons?"

Nicholas' offense was evident in the glaring of his dark eyes. "No."

Rebecca's skepticism was obvious. "If you did not change him, who did? Moreover, what, in the name of God, is it that you are? What have the three of you become?"

"Vampires."

At the sound of Malcolm's word, Rebecca stopped breathing. In the next moment, the baby protested and kicked with all of its mighty force against the inside of her womb. Rebecca cried out and Malcolm and Nicholas were both at her side in less than a second.

When Rebecca looked up into their faces this time, they were the men that she loved – and in her heart, she knew that was all that mattered.

Gasping until the painful twinges ceased, Rebecca met each gaze separately and stated, "Nicholas, you'll not go anywhere."

"Thank you."

A bit of fire returned to her green gaze as she warned, "Don't thank me yet. You've yet to hear my terms."

"Then tell me." His words were patient to a fault – no wonder, he has all the time in the world, Rebecca thought to herself. Nicholas smiled and Rebecca knew he heard her thoughts.

"Stop that." He nodded his dark head in agreement, but Rebecca still wanted to explain. "I don't know how often or when you've read my thoughts before, but don't do it again without my permission – unless it's to keep me safe."

"I promise, Becca."

Tears filled her eyes now. "And as much as I love you like my own brothers, do not call me Becca anymore."

Rebecca could see from the look on Nicholas' face that she caused him pain. Quickly she explained, "I don't want anyone to call me that now. Remington always did."

A new light came to Nicholas' onyx eyes. "I understand."

Turning toward Malcolm, she took a breath, but before she could speak he asked, "Am I to leave then?"

Her blue eyes narrowed by the slightest degree, "No, you big Scottish oaf. You'll stay and you'll love me just as you always have, but by all that is holy – or evil – if you ever lie to me or keep a secret from me again, I swear I'll drive a stake into your heart myself."

Malcolm's gaze did not waver. "Agreed." He took her face gently between his hands then and whispered, "So long as you say you forgive me."

The words caught in her throat, "Yes, my love, I forgive you." The baby moved and another thought came to her mind. Looking from one man to the other, Rebecca implored, "There is something else, you must each promise me now."

"Yes." They simultaneously agreed.

Rebecca smiled in a way that made her blue eyes shine beautifully – a light for which Nicholas and Malcolm would be eternally grateful. "Guard this child with all that you have. Remington has vowed to kill my baby and any generation that follows in the McBride line."

Rebecca could sense that both of the beings in front of her were fighting for control. "He'll no' harm any of mine."

"Nicholas?" Rebecca prompted.

"For all that you and Malcolm have ever done for me, I promise to protect your family until I am no longer able."

Rebecca smiled and her face looked peacefully accepting of the new life she would be leading. "Then I promise to love you both for the rest of my life as well."

~~~

"Nicholas?"

"Yes, Abigail?"

"I love you."

"I love you too."

"I know you do." At last, Abigail's curiosity was sated enough to sleep.

~~~

Marriage to Malcolm McBride had been just as wonderful during the last eight months as Rebecca had imagined it would be. Their life was filled with much happiness and laughter and the friendship Malcolm and Nicholas had was now extended to include Rebecca. She counted Nicholas as a brother-in-law, if not by blood, then in the ways that mattered most.

Following their elopement, the newlyweds set up a comfortable home in the city of Baltimore in Maryland. Rebecca missed the south, but not much – for a life with Malcolm, the sacrifice was easy to make. This had been his home for a while and Rebecca knew that he had liked his life here – that was enough for her.

There had been no contact from her family. As a result, Rebecca believed that the Standish men had either given up their search or she had hurt them so severely in her deception and disappearance that they simply no longer cared what had become of her.

Such wonderings made Rebecca melancholy and, lately, she'd found that mood descending on her more and more. She did her best to keep that feeling hidden from Malcolm, but eventually, he saw her weariness.

"Do you want to return home to Atlanta now? It has been long enough that even your brothers and father would not deny our need to remain married."

Lying in bed beside him, Rebecca didn't look up, but imagined the worried kindness that surely filled his green eyes. She'd come to know his expressions and moods so well, she felt as though they were connected as much as any two people could be. Laying her hand against his bare abdomen, she replied, "My home is where you are, Malcolm."

"And I will go wherever need be, to make you happy again." He kissed the top of her head lightly.

With a sigh, Rebecca informed, "I am happy, I'll be fine when the weather breaks."

It was late winter now, the trees were bare, and the air carried a constant chill off the harbor water. Sometimes it was hard for Malcolm to remember that people craved the bright sunlight since he so often waited until it was dim to venture outdoors. Though he could manage it, Malcolm was still exhausted afterward.

Since Rebecca remained unaware of her husband's darkest secret, Malcolm did his best to avoid such fatiguing outings whenever possible.

"It won't be long now, just a few more weeks." Rubbing her bare arm, Malcolm suggested, "We could go away for a few days, travel to where the sunshine is."

"Not with the new properties you've just purchased. You have to tend to business. Do not worry over me; I'll be fine soon enough."

"But I do worry, Rebecca. Nicholas can tend to the business arrangements – "

"No, Malcolm; we aren't going to change our lives for this silliness. I've felt this during other winters; it will fade away soon enough."

"Rebecca . . ."

His argument was cut short again. "Not another word about it, Malcolm McBride, else you'll have more than my irritability to concern yourself with."

Rebecca heard the laughter rumble within his chest before it made its way out of his mouth. "Such feisty words from a tiny bit."

"You would not have married a weak woman."

The movement of his hand slowed on her arm. "Aye, you're right about that."

His Scottish accent thickened and Rebecca smiled. So long as her husband wasn't angry, that change in his wording boded well for her and since they were already in bed, the pleasure would not be *far off. Urging him on, she asked coquettishly, "And what* other *reasons did you have for choosing me?"*

"Your father's money." Malcolm responded easily.

Rebecca laughed; the sound coming out husky as her mood changed to match his. "Much good that did you."

Malcolm pulled her upward, her body sliding against his until their lips were nearly touching. "You've proven to have a few other assets as well."

"And what might they be?"

Running the tip of his finger lightly over the swell of her breasts showing from beneath the chemise-style nightgown Rebecca wore, he responded softly, "You've a fair hand at managing my house." His green eyes rose to hers and he added, "And you're pleasant enough to look at."

One brow rose dramatically over her sparkling-blue gaze. "Nicholas says I'm beautiful."

"That's because Nicholas is a dutiful lad that will always say what a lady wishes most to hear. He is a charmer," Malcolm offered the slightest grin, "though every word I've ever heard him speak is true."

"I love you Malcolm."

"Then are you through bringing talk of my dearest friend into our bed?"

The harsh tone Malcolm used was a farce and Rebecca laughed it aside. "As soon as you give me something else to occupy my mind."

"Gladly." Malcolm assured and then promptly began to do as promised.

~~~~~~~~

Nicholas was sitting in the wooden rocking chair beside the bed when Abbey woke. He was watching her and Abbey knew he was worried. She could not change that, especially now. "I dreamed about Malcolm and Rebecca—before the baby, before she knew the truth."

His expression didn't change, but he replied, "Yes, I saw."

Abbey looked mildly confused. "How? Can you read my thoughts while I sleep?"

A small smile appeared on his handsome features and Nicholas informed, "I dreamed of them too. Or I was in *your* dream, because I could see you watching them there."

Abbey rolled to her side and propped her head on the palm of her hand. "Do you hear how strange you sound? What you are saying is crazy."

Nicholas laughed softly, "I'm a vampire. Dream watching is not so far fetched in my world."

"How silly of me to hang on to my human-like tendencies," Abbey recalled sarcastically. "I guess I should be used to all this Creature Feature by now."

Smiling, Nicholas responded, "If I recall correctly, it *does* take a while to adjust."

"So is dream watching another gift?"

"I imagine so, but this is the first time I've ever done it. I didn't try either, it just happened." When a possibility came to his mind, Nicholas asked, "Did you call for me or feel scared?"

Abbey thought back over the dream and answered, "No, it was more like we were supposed to learn something? Do you think they're trying to tell us something or help us in some way?"

Nicholas shook his head. "Abigail, they are dead, it is not possible for them to communicate with us through a dream."

Abbey grasped only one part of his statement—"Malcolm is *dead?*"

His voice was thick with sorrow now, "Yes."

"How?"

With a negative shake of his head, Nicholas simply replied, "Another time." Abbey instinctively knew to back off and allowed a moment of silence for Nicholas to recover from his grieving memories.

Reverting to their previous conversation, she clarified, with a teasing tone, "So let's get this straight: ghosts and speaking from the grave are pretend, but shape shifters and dream watching are real." Not actually waiting for a response, Abbey tagged, "I'll just add that to my notes, dear husband with no heartbeat."

The moment the words passed her lips, Abbey knew that—despite her playfulness—Nicholas had been hurt.

His eyes locked on hers and he informed clearly, "Not *everything* about my situation is available for your entertainment, Abigail."

Reaching her hand out, she touched his arm lightly, "I was only having fun, Nicholas. I'm sorry."

Nicholas said nothing for several moments. Finally, he thought, *My heart beats for you, aatria mou.*

Tears sprung to Abbey's eyes and immediately began to flow down her cheeks. Sliding from the bed she perched herself on his lap and curled tightly against him. With as much sincerity as she could muster, she whispered, "Please, forgive me."

Always Nicholas thought, and then raising her hand to the exact spot on his chest, he pressed her palm firmly against his skin and she felt the slightest flutter beneath her touch.

Abigail gasped, but her hand remained in place even after Nicholas removed his. "How, how is that *possible* when . . ." Abbey's words trailed off and guilt filled her expression—sorrow filled the room.

"When I am not human?" Nicholas finished for her.

Her voice shook, "I would never really feel that way about you Nicholas."

"But it's true." He sighed, "This entire nightmare I have brought you into is true."

"My *ancestors* began this, not you and *nothing* about you will ever be a nightmare."

Do not be so quick to make that claim.

The hissed words yanked Nicholas and Abigail from their tender moment, their heads turning to look at the misted form of Remington hovering outside the window.

~ *Chapter Twelve* ~

"How dare you enter our bedroom?" Abigail was aghast at even Remington's audacity.

I have yet to enter anything. Though my vantage point assures me, the same cannot be said of Nicholas.

"You are crude," Abigail spat over his laughter.

Moreover, my unpleasant presence here would not be necessary had you invited me into your home when I first requested it. All would be complete already, if you'd done as expected.

"Didn't I offer my surrender to you already? Didn't I tell you to end this madness? You declined to do so, yet you continue with this chase." Scoffing in his direction—not without awareness of her husband's close protection—Abbey demeaned, "Perhaps you are really *no* threat at all."

In an instant, Remington changed forms. Though he remained in a half-visible misted shape, his eyes glowed red and his teeth gnashed menacingly. *You insolent diluted, trash-blood whore, I'll show you what my powers can do.* Abbey immediately felt the sensation of a razor blade sliding upward on her inner-thigh. *I'll do away with you and that whelp within you.*

Abbey's gasp of pain brought a smile to Remington's dark-red lips, for it was clearly a double-edged sorrow—physical and emotional. *You didn't know.*

Laughter cruel and sincere filled the room around her.

In an amazing act of speed—Nicholas gently placed Abbey on the bed while using his mind to order, *Close him out, stay on the bed and no matter what you hear, do* not *look at me.*

Nodding, Abbey did as Nicholas instructed and like a child, burrowed beneath the covers as though they formed a barrier that monsters were unable to intrude.

The next sounds that filled Abbey's senses were the most horrific she ever heard. Abbey knew that it was Nicholas speaking, but she prayed to never hear him like this again. Her sweet dear Nicholas—the love of her life—sounded as though he had arrived straight from the bowels of Hell.

Nicholas' voice was a low timbre, nearly vibrating the inner ear of the unfortunate listening to his words. There was a constant hiss rattling up from his chest and as the darkness of anger mingled with the sound, he emanated of a deadly predator—*precisely* what he was.

Though Abbey heard Nicholas and Remington clearly, when they began their fight, she was certain that she did so through her mind since her eardrums did not rupture amid the tumult they issued.

Nicholas' demanding words left no room for an option as he dismissed, *Leave us, Remington!*

I take no orders from the weak. Have you found the strength to kill yet, Nicky Boy?

I'm waiting for the perfect opportunity.

She's lying in your bed with your bastard growing inside her now. I'd wager her blood would be even richer with that brat struggling to survive as you drained them of life together. Remington's cold eyes turned slowly toward Abigail, though the visual effect was only for Nicholas' benefit. *Maybe even as succulent as your* mother *did after she watched your father die. Fear adds just the perfect flavor.*

Abigail tore from the bed without thought to state of undress, without thought to Nicholas' warning, without thought to the fact that she was preparing to attack a vampire. She lunged at the window just as Remington heard the unspoken invitation, *Come and get me, Uncle.*

Window glass shattered inward as Remington dove into the room, Nicholas slammed into him, and Abigail continued forward. "Move, Nicholas!"

"I told you to stay in the bed!" He bellowed back, listening to her words no more than she was his.

She heard his hiss of pain just before she heard Remington's cry and saw him recoil. "You little bitch."

Immediately, Remington pulled the sleeve of his shirt back to reveal the bubbling skin there. Unhindered, Abigail moved forward, wielding a most innocent-looking weapon, her dull, human teeth bared as she vowed, "I will skin you alive if you come near me or those I love again."

"Nicholas tended to his smaller wound, and guessed with a mix of awe and anger, "Wild rose thorn?"

"I told you to move," Abbey self-defended.

In the brief interlude passing between the couple, Remington took advantage of the distraction and wrapped one clawed hand tightly around Nicholas' throat. *See what love does? It makes you weak, causes you to divide your attentions and in the end stumble stupidly to your doom, just as it did my sister.*

Love did not doom her; it is what saved her.

It didn't save her from death.

No, it saved her from an eternity of living Hell.

Remington's grip tightened. *All the more reason for me to ensure my vengeance is completed. Then I'll not have endured my own prison in vain.*

No matter how often you try, you'll never succeed, Nicholas mentally stated with assurance. Then with no more effort than blowing out a candle flame, he took Remington's hand from around his throat and promptly twisted his wrist until the bones within it cracked loudly.

A cry of sheer agony tore from Remington and Nicholas shoved him away in disgust. *If it's a true challenge you want, then come to me in the Brightest Hour when we can see who is most powerful.*

My challenge has nothing to do with power. I'll have the revenge of my sister choosing Malcolm McBride over her family.

"If this is what family was to her, it is no surprise that she fled you—*all* of you." Abigail called out from beneath the sheath of blankets to which she had returned.

Laughing at the bravado of her words from the position of false-safety, Remington flashed to Abbey, hovering just above her on the bed.

She could feel his body pressed against hers and despite the blanket, it was as though no barrier existed between them at all. When he spoke, his breath was hot and his arousal hard against her. *I have no family. Be a good wench and help me change that. I'll kill what's in you and replace it with my own.*

"Wouldn't that defeat your purpose, *Uncle?*" Abbey spat, forcing down the bile of horror-filled disgust he brought forth in her.

Though the blankets remained unmoved, Abigail could feel him hovering; then begin to slide inside her as he spoke, *Perhaps; but your screams of misery would be worth the sacrifice.*

When Abbey felt him tense for a brutal thrust, she did as he had predicted and screamed—in her mind and with her voice—even her soul cried out at what this man-demon was preparing to do to her.

But, it was Remington's scream that drowned out hers and without conscious thought, her eyes flew open just as an expression of pain washed over her attacker's dangerously-beautiful face—visible to her since he dragged the haven of blankets from her as he went.

To Abbey's human mind, the action happened so quickly it was difficult to focus on.

In flashes of fascinated-horror, she watched Nicholas floating over Remington, gouging his claws deep into the shoulders of the other vampire. There was a vision of Remington hissing in pain and anger, snapping his long canines at Nicholas' face and neck like a wild animal. At some point, Nicholas tossed Remington through the air toward the window and Remington rebounded on a graceful air-acrobat to fly toward her husband with teeth and claws bared, red eyes glowing with hatred.

Nicholas flew backward with the force of Remington's assault, flipping through the air while clinging to his attacker and yet again tossing her great-uncle through the air like a rag doll.

With frustrating repetition, Remington rebounded with an easy spin. Feet first he slammed into Nicholas' chest with a blow that would have easily killed a human.

Nicholas simply moved fast enough to grip Remington's leg and twist it brutally. The crunching sound turned Abbey's stomach, though Remington howled, within seconds the pain filled sound ebbed to a grunt.

Still, the moment was long enough for Nicholas to take advantage of as he hurled the wounded creature out the window from which it had come."

It was when Nicholas turned back toward Abigail that all time stood still.

Her gaze locked with the monster she knew to be her husband and with pain, anger, and fear he demanded in all forms, "*Look away!*"

Abigail did as ordered, though not before the picture of Nicholas in his evil form etched into her memory forever.

The second that thought processed through her psyche, she heard Remington's laughter ring cruelly throughout the room and her mind, followed by the satisfied statement, *That will be enough revenge for now, Pet.*

Then, she knew that Remington's main purpose for this night's visit had succeeded—she had seen her husband—her *Beloved*—in his most evil form.

Moreover, she had felt fear.

~~~

It took more than an hour of consoling—soothing whispers in Greek and English, gentle rubbing and kisses on her face and head and, finally, slowly making love to her—before Nicholas calmed Abbey enough that she slept.

They had not conversed in any way about what had transpired—what had *changed*. Nicholas knew that would come soon enough.

For now, cradling his wife's restful body against him, knowing she was at peace—at least for the moment—gave Nicholas the opportunity for his mind to wander to a place he rarely permitted open . . .

~~~~~~~~

Malcolm and Nicholas managed to avoid confrontation with Remington for three days after placing Jacob in safety. Nicholas had just fed – only on three small rabbits, but it would be enough to sustain him. Malcolm, in his depression, was still refusing to hunt.

Offering a kill he had returned with, Nicholas stated, "It will help you to eat, my friend."

Malcolm barely glanced at the animal, before turning away in disgust. "It's better if I don't."

Nicholas tossed the animal at his friend's feet and demanded, "Better for whom? You? Me? Jacob?" He paused, delved into his friend's mind, and then, spat, "Even if you die right now, you won't be with her again."

Malcolm's eyes burned as he turned toward Nicholas. "Will you preach at me even now? In my state of sorrow?"

"What other state do you have anymore?"

"When your *Beloved is dead because of your love for her,* then *you can preach to me."*

"I have no Beloved." The slightest sorrow tinged Nicholas' words.

Malcolm said nothing, but looked at his friend as though debating the wisdom of telling Nicholas a secret. *"We all have a Beloved; it just takes time to find them."*

"Then it is unfortunate for you that time is up."

Both men turned toward the new voice. Nicholas and Malcolm had been so distracted by their argument that they missed Remington's approach.

"You are very persistent." Nicholas intoned, though his voice was far deeper than it had been a second earlier.

"Revenge is a wonderful thing." Remington was already pale, eyes blood thirsty and ready for battle. His muscles quivered with the need to spring and his hands twitched as though already clawing at Malcolm's body.

"You give too much away in your excitement, newborn." Nicholas demeaned openly.

Remington's eyes narrowed. *"It is no secret why I am here."*

"Remember, you will have to get through me first."

"How touching. Did my sister have to obtain the same blessing?"

Nicholas ignored the hissing insult.

Malcolm did not.

In a move so fast that even Nicholas' gifted eyes did not see it, the towering vampire was over his brother-in-law. Teeth bared and eyes blazing he demanded, *"You'll no' insult her memory by tarnishing her love for me."*

Remington showed no fear. *"My sister would never love a monster such as you. It is the evil you put in her that blinded her and made her want you."*

Malcolm roared – a sound Nicholas had never heard in all the time he had known his friend, and prayed that he would never witness again. Even sharing his vampire-state, it sent fear through him.

In one fluid motion, Malcolm was across the small wooded clearing, far from Remington. The larger, older, creatures back was braced against a tree. His long claws tore into the thick bark, keeping his raging power at bay – fighting every one of his instincts. *"I'll no' kill you today."*

Remington laughed, *"I know that already."*

"It's not that I canno' kill you, but that it is no' as my Rebecca would wish."

Remington stopped, eyes flashing brighter with Malcolm's endearment. *"You say* today *as though my sister would want me dead at another time."*

Malcolm said nothing.

"Speak demon."

Remington moved – in his newborn state slower and more awkward than Malcolm had been – Nicholas intervened halfway. *"My turn."* His hand was gripping Remington's neck so tightly that the captured vampire's lips curled involuntarily upward in a silent snarl.

"Let him go, Nicholas." Malcolm ordered firmly. *"This is no' yet your battle."*

Nicholas dropped Remington as much from shock as respect. *"Would you have me stand by and let him attack you to the death?"*

Malcolm glanced at his friend, *"I would have you trust me."*

Nicholas nodded, *"Always."*

"And I would have you watch over what I cannot." Malcolm added.

Nicholas understood this preparation and a picture-memory of Rebecca's pleading sprang to his *mind.* *"Until the day I am no longer able."*

Nicholas heard Remington hiss from beside him – he had seen the vision too.

In the next instant, Malcolm was in the avenging vampire's grasp. Remington flew him up the tree where Malcolm had previously been based and with no hesitation impaled him on a broken branch.

Nicholas saw nothing but the flow of blood seeping around the wound in his friend's chest and the triumphant gleam in the eyes of the creature that had just done the deed.

Instinct took over and the fear that entered Remington's eyes then was completely founded. He flew fast – Nicholas followed.

Branches and leaves scratched at them, neither noticed. If any human had the misfortune of being within earshot, they would never enter the woods again. The growls and squeals of anger, revenge, and pain that sounded from the treetops were a terrifying symphony.

Nicholas gained on Remington. Reaching forward with his pale, withered hand, that looked strange in its monstrous transformation even to his own eyes, he felt the brush of material against his fingertips. Nicholas would have grasped Remington's cloak, pulled him back and easily decapitated him, but for the voice that stopped him. It was the softest whisper, a feminine tone, and he had heard it only in his dreams.

Not yet, Nicholas. Do not kill and break your vow. Do not kill him and keep us apart.

Nicholas was so stunned by the clarity of her voice and the vision of the woman that filled his mind that he stopped all motion and felt his body transform immediately back into its humanistic appearance.

Remington never stopped retreating and in mere seconds, he was too far to hear Nicholas' voice – so instead he used his mind to swear, Run now, Remington, for one day, you will be mine for the kill.

~~~~~~~~

The sickening feeling washed over Abigail again—she felt closed in, heat coursed through her and she needed air. It was that and the sound of rain pelting against the window, the crash of thunder and flashes of lightening bright enough to illuminate their room that woke Abigail.

Glancing toward the clock, the light from the hallway door allowed her to read that it was just after four-thirty in the morning. With automatic dread, her gaze shifted to the window, but there was nothing but the large oak tree on the other side.

Carefully, she slid from the bed and padded toward the bathroom. She was not successful in escaping without Nicholas noticing. "What woke you, the storm or dreams?"

Abigail stopped just inside the bathroom and turned toward him. "I didn't mean to bother you."

Pushing to a sitting position, Nicholas replied softly, "You are no bother to me, Abigail." Nicholas held his hand out toward her, "Come back to bed with me so I can ease your mind."

"You know," she began with light humor in her voice, "when you reach for me like that, I can't seem to resist it. It reminds me of that old vampire movie. All you need is a black cape up over your face and to wave your fingers to entrance me deeper."

Wiggling his dark eyebrows, Nicholas did as directed and said softly, "Come to me bride."

Straightening her arms out in front of her, Abbey closed the remaining few steps between them in a slow walk and mumbled, "Yes, Master."

Nicholas dropped his hand and burst into laughter, "I could get used to hearing *that*."

Raising her knee to climb beneath the covers with him, Abbey said, "Don't count on it," then laughed. "Count, get it? *Count* on it."

Nicholas rolled his eyes then returned his amused gaze back to the lovely face of his wife. "I love you Abigail Adamouras." Abbey smiled and snuggled closer.

Nicholas enjoyed the warmth of her body against his. Though Abbey couldn't feel his coldness, the only time *he* felt complete warmth was when she was touching him. He imagined it was the reason he had learned to sleep again since they had become intimate.

Nicholas leaned over to kiss Abigail, but her expression of surprise stopped his motion. "Nicholas?" "Yes, *aatria*?"

She took his hand, placed hers over it, and lowered them both to rest upon her abdomen.

Misreading her intention, Nicholas soothed in a voice promising pleasure, "There's no need to rush, Abigail."

Then he felt it—the fluttering movement beneath their hands. "Remington was right." Other than, the breathless whisper with which she offered it, Abbey was completely calm about her mixed realization and admission.

Nicholas' expression went from surprise to shock to joy to fear to horror. "That can't be possible, you were sick as a child, remember?"

Abbey's heart thudded in her chest. For the briefest instant, she had been nothing more than a wife, learning with her husband, that they had created life together. Nicholas' reminder proved that such a relationship would never be entirely true for them.

Though she couldn't remember the vivid details of her early childhood illness, Abbey *did* remember the sad day as a teenager when her mother had explained that due to that sickness, Abigail would never be able to bear children.

But, now, all of that had changed in the blink of an eye—as so much of her world had.

The expression holding on her husband's face was not the one Abigail would have chosen and in her emotional wave of the last several minutes, Abbey explained, "I'm learning that being in love with you is not always a pleasure. It is unnerving that you know things about me which I barely remember myself."

"Abigail, you must remember that I have been watching over you since your first breath. When you were sick, I was sick, when you are sad, I am sad and when you are in danger, I feel fear."

Considering their connection, what he said was no exaggeration. "Then I'm betting you know *exactly* what I am feeling *and* thinking *right* now."

A raised dark brow was the only indication he gave that she was right or as a response to her angry and hurt thought-words.

His silence infuriated her even more and tears stung her eyes. "Is *some* small sign of happiness too much to ask for the news I have just given you?"

Nicholas knew—even without her verbal or mental rebukes—that his responses disappointed Abigail. However, right now, his fear for her overrode that problem. With a shake of his head, he replied, "You don't understand, Abigail, you have no idea what is in store for you."

Immediately Abbey's mind shot back to the night Remington last visited her. With heavy sadness, she whispered, "That's what Remington said." Blinking back tears, Abbey's green eyes snapped from sorrow to fury. "I hate that even this which should be thrilling and happy for us has to be tainted by *him*." She dashed the resentful tears roughly away with the back of her hand. "I should have guessed before this—before he ruined this special moment for us." A short, laugh void of humor, escaped over Abbey's trembling lips, "God knows Remington offered me enough clues."

Abigail's emotions triggered Nicholas' and his eyes began to change—the iris outlining in gold as his defensive anger came forth and with a primal growl in his tone, he demanded, "What did he say?"

"Exactly what you did. That I, like Rebecca, have no idea what I'm in for and that our love or lust led us both blindly to it." Nicholas started to speak, but she cut him off. "But I was *not* led blindly; you told me the truth before we were together."

"Yes, I told you what I am, but not what we could create."

"But you just said you didn't think it was possible." Forcing herself to keep her gaze steady with his despite the recent change of his brown eyes, Abbey added, "The truth is, I didn't give pregnancy any thought at all, but if I had, my guess would have been the same as yours—impossible."

"Yes, but *I* should have known better. I know the fertility of a lusting vampire—when one finds their Beloved, then the strength of creation multiplies."

Reaching out, she touched his hand and reflexively, Nicholas entwined his fingers with hers. "Nicholas, why does this have to be negative? This is our child you speak of, created in love. He will be no different than I am."

"What we created will be much stronger than you and your ancestors."

Slow dread and self-uncertainty began to seep through Abbey. "How?"

"Because Rebecca was human and Malcolm was a vampire. Since I am a vampire and you already have partial blood in your veins—"

"There is more power in our child," Abigail finished with complete horrified understanding.

With a nod, Nicholas confirmed, "Yes."

Abbey asked the question with the most dreaded answer of all, "Will the baby kill me?"

Nicholas' grip tightened on her hand. "I do not know."

"What can we do?" Abbey felt the child move within her again, but this time, instead of feeling joyful excitement, she felt a fear of the unknown gripping her. Looking to Nicholas, she saw that his eyes were fading back to the warmth she loved and she admitted, "I don't want to fear this child that I cherish already."

"Then first thing tomorrow, we will begin learning what we can of vampire pregnancy and birth."

Abbey nodded, but said nothing, so Nicholas raised her hand to his mouth and kissed her fingers lightly. "Abigail, I will die before I let any harm come to you. We will find a way to make it through this together and raise our family in happiness."

Looking at him, Abbey felt confidence fill her—she knew it was Nicholas' power of emotional persuasion, but she would use the strength it gave her just the same. Abbey's green eyes were full of trust when she asked, "*Will* you be happy, Nicholas?"

"As happy as I can be, *aatria mou*." Nicholas admitted, and then he kissed her softly. There was no seduction in his touch, only love and together, in the circle of each other's arms they found the peace of rest again.

~ Chapter Thirteen ~

Three weeks had passed since Remington's attack and their confirmation of Abigail's pregnancy. She had done her best to put the picture of Nicholas-the-Vampire out of her mind. For as much as was possible, Nicholas and Abbey continued their steady existence that was their normalcy.

With only a little coercion, Nicholas convinced Abbey to officially give up her job at the radio station. Considering the time she had taken off already, in addition to that she spent researching *How to Raise a Vampire*—as Abbey had laughingly begun referring to it—quitting made the most sense. When she threw impending motherhood into the mix, her decision was even easier.

Nicholas also reminded Abbey that they had no need for her income. The mortgage on their home was already paid, Abigail had enough from her inheritance to live off of and with the fortune Nicholas had acquired throughout his existence—not including his current medical profession—the American Adamouras ' would likely never go without.

Life—as they knew it—was good, and even better, it was a perfect early-spring day outdoors. Nicholas was at the hospital and Abigail was once again sitting at the dining room table conducting research on her physical condition.

The mouse button clicked and Abbey read:

```
Cihuateteo - Skeleton like female vampires who died in childbirth,
subsequently stealing children and feeding off the newborn flesh in
revenge.
```

Abbey quickly exited that one.

```
Manananggal - An older, beautiful female vampire able to sever her
upper torso from the bottom half of her body and fly through the
night with huge bat-like wings. Also having died in childbirth,
the Manananggal would prey on sleeping pregnant women, using elon-
gated proboscis-like tongues to suck the fetus from the pregnant
women.
```

That one did her in and Abigail exited the site entirely.

Her eyes strayed to the window and the inviting sunshine in the sky.

In the last days of her research—bits and pieces filled in with Nicholas' recollections of Rebecca—Abbey learned that her pregnancy would progress much faster than a normal-human one.

Looking down at her already rounding stomach, she was convinced. Despite the fact that she was only in her fourth week of pregnancy, Abbey's physical signs were that of a woman in her twelfth. Her clothes were becoming uncomfortable and her appetite—now that the morning sickness was waning—was increasing rapidly.

A grumbling from her mid-section loudly punctuated her thoughts.

Smoothing her palm over the bump there, she murmured. "You're right; enough of this for now. We need to get outside and find some food." Glancing at the clock on the lower corner of the computer screen, she knew that it was now the Brightest Hour—the only time Nicholas allowed her to go out without him—and *then* only for necessities.

Her stomach protested again and Abbey chuckled, "I agree, this is defiantly a necessity."

Closing the computer top, Abbey grabbed her purse and moved out the door into the inviting fresh air and sunshine.

~~~~~~~~

Nicholas was checking the status of an elderly man that had fallen on a slope in his backyard and broken his hip on impact. The surgery had gone well and following a few weeks of rehabilitation, Mr. Weller would be able to return home to his family.

Jennifer was Nicholas' assisting nurse today and following their last conversation when he had informed her of Abigail's presence in his life, the attractive woman had eased up a bit in her pursuit—but not entirely.

Jennifer Crawly was a prime example—especially today—of actions speaking louder than words.

Throughout the morning, she had done her best to anticipate Nicholas' needs and provide them with ease. Just as she had found numerous opportunities to brush up against him—whether with her hand, arm or entire body—just as she now bumped her hip against his when handing the patient his pain medication. After readjusting the bedridden patient's pillows behind him, Jennifer turned and walked out of the hospital room directly behind Nicholas.

In the partially empty corridor of the post-lunch, semi-quiet the hospital floor was slipping into, she finally took advantage of the days professional pairing. "So tell me, Dr. Adamouras, is that girlfriend of yours still keeping all of your attention for herself?"

Nicholas smiled—anyone who said, they didn't enjoy being seen as attractive by another person was—in Nicholas' opinion—a liar. Simply because someone chased, didn't mean that the action needed to be accepted—which his next words proved. "Did I say Abigail was my girlfriend?"

Hope lit the nurse's eyes, "No, I just assumed . . ."

"She's my wife. We were married just about a month ago."

Jennifer dropped the pen in her hand. "You're kidding?" Bending to retrieve the writing utensil, she asked, "Isn't that a little soon?"

Nicholas shrugged his shoulder, "Some people might think so, but it's like we've known each other forever."

"Of course it is." Jennifer rolled her eyes. "I *really* should have acted sooner."

"Maybe." Nicholas teased back though he knew the woman never stood a chance. "But just the same, I am head over heels in love with my wife and happy to say that we're expecting a child."

A new light came to Jennifer's expression. "Oh, I see."

Nicholas chuckled and wagged a corrective finger in her direction. "Don't jump to any conclusions. We didn't know about the baby until *after* the wedding."

"Oh."

Tuning in more closely to Jennifer's thoughts and feelings, Nicholas questioned, "Are you telling me that a woman as lovely as you is confined to finding romance with co-workers?" Smiling, he held open the door to the employee lounge for her. "I find that hard to believe."

"There are a few prospects, but I was hoping for a kind of stability not usually found in a local dance club." Pushing the appropriate button, a can of diet soda clattered to the bottom of the vending machine and Jennifer finished, "A doctor just seemed like the best direction to go."

Watching as she popped the top of the soda can and took a sip, Nicholas offered, "Well, unless you'll settle for friendship, *this* doctor is out of commission in the single world."

Jennifer rolled her eyes, "The story of my life." With a dramatic smile, she said, "Put me on the shower guest list; I'll buy a pretty outfit, make friends with your lucky wife and keep on searching." With a fresh smile, she added, "Unless you have any available brothers?"

A bit of sadness entered Nicholas' dark eyes, though if Jennifer noticed, she made no comment. "I haven't seen him in years."

"Does your wife have any?" Nicholas chuckled at Jennifer's humorous desperation."

"No, she's an only child."

"What did you say her name is, again?" Jennifer asked, more out of politeness than curiosity.

"Abigail."

The way his features lit with happiness as he turned toward the coffee machine made Jennifer want to scream with indignation—why couldn't she get a guy to think of her and have his expression change like that?

Nicholas spoke in a tone of considerate friendliness when he suggested, "Maybe because you're too eager. Let the man lead."

"*What* did you say?" Jennifer asked, her stunned expression meeting Nicholas' head-on when he turned away from the coffee pot and back toward her.

"I answered your question."

"But I didn't *ask* it."

"Really?" Nicholas stumbled only briefly before adding with extreme charm, "I just must be that in tune to you."

"Yeah . . . *now* that you're *married*."

With light laughter, Nicholas returned, "So what were you going to say about Abigail?"

Shaking off the remainder of her surprise, Jennifer asked, "I was just going to say that she should have a co-ed baby shower."

Nicholas sipped at the hot coffee. "I don't think we'll be doing any of that; neither of us has any family and only a few friends between us."

Looking skeptical, Jennifer stated, "Well, we can't have that. You're friends here will have to throw her a party. Your first baby can't go uncelebrated."

"I don't know; Abigail likes her solitude," Nicholas advised.

"Well *Abbey* will just have to get over it." Tossing her half-full can of soda in the trash, Jennifer headed out of the room. "Now if you'll excuse me, I've got a shower to plan."

~~~

The breeze was cool, but the sunshine that greeted Abigail was warm, the sound of leaves crunching beneath her feet a comforting one for her. Several neighboring yards had piles of nature's end-of-winter debris, clumped at their edges and porches decorated with soon-to-be-budding flowerpots.

The sound of children laughing in backyards and a few sweater-clad elderly individuals calling out greetings from their front porch perches added to her happy mood. Abigail gleefully entered the local dairy/grill that offered sandwiches, soups, subs, and delicious hotdogs—Hershey's ice cream was available for dessert.

After ordering a hotdog with sauerkraut, Swiss cheese, and mustard, Abbey moved back outside and made use of one of the picnic tables the establishment offered for customers. The sunshine was refreshing, though the wind was picking up and had the feel of rain.

Abbey was nearly finished her hotdog when she noticed clouds had rolled in, dimming the earlier brightness of the morning sun. She wasn't scared—but a definite level of concern entered her consciousness. After all, she had more to think of now than her own well-being.

Tossing the last bite of lunch to the waiting birds, Abbey stood, stretched, and began the journey back toward home. Another factor she hadn't considered when she left was that the return trip was primarily uphill. Still, it was a short distance and Abbey was in fairly good shape despite her pregnancy so she pushed onward.

And, the clouds continued to roll in, darkening the sky as they came.

~~~

Nicholas had just stepped through the exit door of the hospital when he felt the first sensation of Abbey's unease. Glancing up at the sky, he immediately joined in the feeling—the clouds were dark gray and full to bursting.

He hurried his steps toward his waiting vehicle.

~~~

In three more minutes, Abigail would be home and in the secluded safety found there. She was passing the neighboring house when its screen door creaked open and an elderly lady called out, "Abigail, won't you ride out the storm in here with me?" With a welcoming smile, she added, "I've got tea steeping and from the looks of you, I'd say you need a rest." Glancing pointedly at Abbey's growing midsection, the woman finished, "I think it's been far too long since we've had one of our afternoon talks."

Mrs. Shank had been her neighbor for as long as Abbey could remember—the funny thing was the woman had seemed eighty for the duration of Abigail's life. She was easy to befriend, the kind of neighbor everyone should have. She never ran out of the items that those living around her needed to borrow and Abigail's parents had been friends of hers from the first day they had moved into the neighborhood.

Abigail felt an instant pang of guilt that she didn't make more of an effort to spend time with the woman. Still, now, Abbey wanted nothing more than the serene comfort of her living room couch and Nicholas' soon-to-be-home arms securely around her. With a sincere smile of regret, Abigail called back, "I've got plans already, Mrs. Shank, I'm sorry."

Nodding in understanding, the elderly woman absently bent—slowly with age—to retrieve a white cat rubbing past her feet at the chance to sprint outside. "I *thought* I'd seen a young man or two spending some time here."

With a light chuckle, Abbey corrected, "Only one; we wouldn't want the neighbors to talk, now would we?"

"Well, I'm not one to gossip," Mrs. Shank began and Abbey didn't have the nerve to say differently, "but I was certain that the gentleman I saw leaving earlier was dark haired."

Abbey nodded and couldn't help the smile that lit her face. "Yes, that's Nicholas, my husband."

"*Husband?*" The exclamation held a hint of reproach that this was how her longtime neighbor had learned of Abigail's recent marriage. Looking down at the animal in her arms, she scratched gently at the furry white neck and questioned, "Then who is the fair gentleman that said you were expecting him?"

When Mrs. Shank looked up again, her face was clear innocence, but Abigail's blood ran cold. "When did you speak to *him?*"

"Just twenty minutes ago; he asked if I could let him in with my spare key since he had supper plans with you and was early."

Supper plans—Abbey cringed.

The hair on the back of her neck stood on end and Abigail immediately smelled sulfur and magnolia. Without looking toward her house again, Abbey turned and headed in the direction of her neighbor's open door. "On second thought, I think I *will* have that tea with you, Mrs. Shank."

Abigail was already passing the older woman and her cats—the other four of which were crowded around her feet behind the barrier of the door—when the confused woman reminded, "But I thought you *had* plans, dear?"

Abigail moved as far into the safety of Mrs. Shank's home as she could and stated, "They've changed."

~~~

Nicholas had never wished for anything about his vampire state before—now he wished he had the gift of tracking. He couldn't sense others of his kind until they were within a mile radius of him. In vampire terms, that was mere seconds of travel time.

He knew Remington was near though—Nicholas's senses were attuned to him. When he stopped his car in front of the house he and Abbey shared, Nicholas knew with sickening certainty that Remington was already inside.

What he was unaware of was if Abigail was with Remington or not. Nicholas considered it odd that he didn't sense her as strongly as he normally did when coming home.

The instant that thought fully processed through his mind, Nicholas felt pain rip through him. Was it possible that he was too late to save Abigail's life from the monster that had been stalking her?

Anger—maddening in its severity—surfaced, and Nicholas flashed inside the house—giving little thought to the witnessing neighborhood families. In all likelihood, their human eyes missed his movement anyway.

The air inside the cloud-dim house was heavy with burnt-magnolia. Nicholas' eyes had no need to adjust to the lighting, he immediately saw Remington seated halfway down the stairs in front of him.

"This is no true invitation, Remington."

The sitting vampire shrugged one shoulder. "A window, a door, a stupid old lady's extra key . . . should it *really* matter? It's all taking too long for me—even *with* the spawn." He looked Nicholas in the eye, making his point abundantly clear. "I've had enough of the rules."

"And if the Sovereign's were to learn of your *adjustment*?"

Remington scarcely reacted to Nicholas' reference to the law-keepers of the vampire realm. "Abigail would be dead before they could arrive and my reason for existence would be done at any rate."

Nicholas' hissed at that reply.

Remington smiled, "All's fair in love and war."

"What do *you* know of love?"

"Rebecca."

"She was your sister; a Beloved is much, *much* different."

"Perhaps I'll sample yours and see for myself."

"Perhaps I'll rip the skin from your body if you try such a thing again."

"Doubtful, but an impressive threat none-the-less," Remington complimented with southern gentility.

"You are an irritating soul, Remington."

"I *have* no soul, Nicholas." Remington pointed out with disdain.

"Not true; your soul is merely trapped. How else do you explain the fact that your charming personality was able to continue on with your vampire body?"

Remington was quiet for a moment. "I think that might be the most intelligent of all the drivel I've ever heard you spout."

"Good, because I hope you remember that I cannot wait to see your soul damned to Hell for *all* eternity."

Rolling his finger in bored rhythm, Remington moaned, "On and on with the *drivel* we go."

"Rebecca had a faithful foundation, where is yours?"

"Damned with her soul." Remington's eyes flashed with the thought, "Just as *any* creature like us is damned."

"Jesus Christ was crucified so that I might have the chance for eternal life." Nicholas spoke with a glimmer of hope, but there was still evident uncertainty in his tone.

Remington caught the hesitancy. With a sneer he taunted, "Are you afraid you'll be left behind, Nicholas?"

Fighting his doubt, Nicholas boldly declared, "Christ's blood covered my sin."

Remington knew this weakness of Nicholas' surely as he knew the sun would rise in the morning. With happiness, he used his adversary's remaining religion against him. "And if you stood at the base of that cross now, your denied instincts would take over and you would lap at the very blood you claim to love so purely."

Nicholas lost a bit of his control with the grotesque picture Remington painted. With teeth bared, he readied for attack. "You blaspheme in matters you do *not* understand."

Remington chuckled at Nicholas' continued paraphrasing of the Bible, even in his state of passionate anger. "Well, I *am* after all a brute beast living by instinct."

Nicholas' eyes were full red and silver-specked now, swimming with the desire to kill Remington and end his mockery of faith. Nicholas continued to cling to the Word of God in order to refrain from lunging. "And so you will be caught and destroyed and perish." Muscles taunt and shaking with the battle to stay clear of murder, he quoted, "'They will be paid back with harm for the harm they have done. For we must all appear before the judgment seat of Christ, that each one may receive what is due him for the things done while in the body, whether good or bad.'"

With forced horror, Remington cringed—then a slow evil smile spread across his lips. His teeth dropped fully down and his face completely transformed into the pale, skeletal features of the vampire-demon he was. "Then I should make certain the crime is comparable to the punishment."

"I only pray that your *punishment* is comparable to your crimes." Nicholas growled in return.

Remington only smiled more. "We shall see."

It was Nicholas' turn to smile fully. "*I* live by faith, not by sight."

"Stupid vampire," Remington seethed.

It was sheer pleasure for Nicholas to realize how his constant use of the Bible—whether in perfect or paraphrased form—irritated Remington. "Return to your vomit, *dog*."

Teeth gnashing, Remington began to morph into the very dog-beast of which Nicholas spoke—the one, which had started this chapter of Nicholas' life with Abigail. "Only after I've dealt with your *clean* sow."

The insult to Abigail finally broke Nicholas' resolve and he lunged at the dog-man on the stairs in front of him.

Nicholas' attack met only air and the fading sound of Remington's laughter. The southern voice with a demonic sense-of-humor whispered tauntingly, *Away from me, Satan.*

~~~

Abbey's phone rang within fifteen minutes of her entering Mrs. Shank's home.

"Where are you?"

The question echoed between both callers.

"I'm at home." Nicholas replied to Abigail.

"I'm next door at Mrs. Shank's. Was he there?"

"Yes."

"Is he gone?"

"For now?"

That answer wasn't the most comforting Abigail could have gotten, but at least it was honest. "How did you know to come home early?" Abbey smiled at the woman, watching her oddly from across the table—a ball of gray, black and white fur cradled in her wrinkled arms now as she obviously tried to decipher Abigail's phone conversation.

"Come home and we'll talk."

"I'll be there in a few minutes." Abigail closed her phone and smiled at Mrs. Shank. "Thank you for the hospitality, Mrs. Shank, but it seems my husband was able to get off work early after all."

Nodding, Mrs. Shank remarked, "I remember those days. Go on and enjoy yourself. We'll talk again," Abigail had her hand on the back door when Mrs. Shank added softly, "*soon.*"

Chills ran over Abbey's arms and down her spine. She turned slowly to see the cat jump down and scurry from the kitchen as the elderly lady began clearing her table. "Mrs. Shank, *what* did you say?"

The kindly woman looked toward Abbey, smiled slowly and informed, "I said, *soon.*"

Without another word, Abbey turned and left the house. From behind, innocently soft laughter sounded. What was once a comforting sound—a source of refuge for Abigail—became tainted by the terror that was her new life.

~ *Chapter Fourteen* ~

They spent the better part of two hours searching the house, but nothing was out of place, nothing was new, nothing was there to prove that Remington had touched any of their belongings while he waited for Abigail to come home. Only his scent, Nicholas' anger, and Abigail's new fear remained behind.

After Nicholas detailed his confrontation with Remington and Abbey had described her eerie exit from Mrs. Shank's house, Abigail suggested, "Maybe we should leave. We could go to Greece. Surely you've no family left there that would remember you."

Nicholas smiled, but not with an expression of joy. "You are right, *aatria mou*, and there's nothing I want more than to share my homeland with you and our child, but first we must deal with this demon. He will follow us to the ends of the earth—it's best to see it through and start fresh."

"Even with all we know and all we've learned, I still feel like I'm fighting blind."

Nicholas pulled Abbey into the security of his arms. "Ask me your questions and what I don't know we'll find answers for together."

"Where does this start?"

"Remington?"

"No, vampires. I've heard your stories—myths, legends of Vlad the Impaler and Count Dracula and even Cain, but which one is right?"

"I don't have that answer for certain. All I really know is to take what those histories tell us and draw our own conclusions."

"I think I'll need a recap. You get the computer—*if* you *need* it—I'll get the drinks." Winking at her husband, Abbey asked, "You want Coke or O-negative?"

"I'm good, thanks," Nicholas replied, watching appreciatively as Abigail headed to the kitchen for her own refreshment.

The laptop rested on the table in front of Nicholas when Abbey returned with a drink in one hand and a plate in the other. Taking inventory of the steaming pepperoni-topped goo Abbey was preparing to eat, Nicholas asked, "What did you eat when you went to *The Dairy Deli?*"

Abbey narrowed her eyes in preparation for his doctoral lecture. "A hot dog with sauerkraut, Swiss and mustard."

Nicholas looked at her a moment longer, then at the plate in front of her and warned with mild reprimand, "*You* are going to have terrible indigestion *and* swollen feet."

Realizing she had dodged the expected scolding, Abbey informed carefully, "I'll drink some milk and be fine." Then blowing on the clump of mozzarella balled on the end of her fork, she decided it had cooled enough to eat, and slid the bite into her mouth. After swallowing, she asked, "What's that?"

"More ancient beliefs and myths that people have handed down over the centuries." Nicholas laughed lightly, "Some of them are more factual than others and some have veered so far from their beginnings, it's hard to believe they are founded in vampire-lore at all."

Finishing another bite, Abbey invited, "That sounds like fun. Read them to me."

Nicholas laughed at his wife's idea of fun and then began reading aloud from the computer display.

```
Tales of supernatural beings consuming the blood or flesh of the
living are found in almost every culture around the world and have
been for many centuries.  Presently, we would associate these enti-
ties with vampires, but in ancient times, that term did not exist.
Blood drinking and/or flesh eating was attributed to demons or spi-
rits—even the Devil was considered synonymous with the vampire.
```

Nicholas glanced in Abbey's direction. "Should I continue?"

She nodded, "I'm okay."

```
The Persians were one of the first civilizations to have tales of
blood-drinking demons.
```

```
Ancient Babylonia had tales of the mythical Lilitu, a she-demon of-
ten depicted as subsisting on the blood of babies.
```

"Whoa, I need a second on that one." Abbey took a drink of water. Closed her eyes, inhaled through her nose and asked, "Is *that* true?"

"Remember the stories we read about Lilith? My guess is that Lilitu is simply based off of her."

"That doesn't exactly answer my question."

"You don't exactly *want* that question *answered*." Nicholas returned, using his intuition to read her feelings closely.

"That's horrible," Abbey opinionated softly. Nicholas didn't speak, so she clarified further, "I mean the fact that such a creature existed and killed babies, *not* that you know me so well."

Nicholas smiled at her unnecessary need to reassure him before stating, "Remember that there still *are* those that would harm babies—vampire and human alike."

Abbey simply nodded—she hated this topic.

Nicholas looked into her tired eyes a moment longer before asking, "Do you want to stop for the night?"

"Not just yet." Clearing her throat, Abbey coaxed, "Read just a little more."

And, Nicholas found that—just as always—he could not resist her desires.

```
In Greece, Empusa was the daughter of the goddess Hecate and was
described as a demonic, bronze-footed creature.  She feasted on
blood by transforming into a young woman and seducing men as they
slept before drinking their blood.
```

"It figures the Greeks would be the ones seducing people to get what they want." Abbey teased with a smile.

"Does that mean you're ready for bed *now*?"

Reaching her hand toward his, Abbey winked, "Almost."

Nicholas' fingers moved back to the keys and he typed again. The screen displayed the results for Nicholas' keyed search: `Blood in the Bible`, and he read aloud:

Christianity is inescapably blood based. Old Testament writers describe blood sacrifices in painstaking details and their New Testament counterparts layer those symbols with theological meanings.

The word "blood" occurs in the Holy Bible three times as often as
the word "cross." In addition, Christians commemorate Christ's
death with a ceremony based on his blood.

"Interesting, but not what I'm looking for." Abbey said, then slid the computer her way to type Cain in the Bible.

"We've been through that already." Nicholas reminded her as he watched her brow furrow in concentration.

"Yes, but we never found out exactly what The Mark of Cain is."

He slowly placed his hand over her flying fingers. "You'll not find your answers there."

Abbey raised her eyes to Nicholas'—knowledge and frustration lining her brow. "*You* know already."

Nicholas nodded. "God did not physically mark Cain. He marked him as I am marked—as all of those that have been damned between us are marked. By our powers, by our thirst and by the near impossible task of killing us."

"So it's a spiritual marking." Abbey verbally clarified, then continued, "But didn't the Bible say that if anyone killed Cain then . . ."

"They will suffer vengeance seven times over," Nicholas quoted from the Bible.

"Right, so . . ." Abbey was incredulous, "*that's* why you wrote that before. You wanted to prepare me for what *you* think is the truth." Even with all the myths that were becoming fact in her life, the very idea of this Biblical person still living—or walking around—was a lot to comprehend.

"You're right about *my* belief, but no, Cain is no longer on earth."

"Then who killed him?"

"Cain died an old man."

Abbey's green eyes narrowed doubtfully. "By *what* cause?"

Nicholas shrugged, "By God's time."

A light of understanding came to Abigail's eyes. "So then Cain *could* die, but only when God said his time was up?" Nicholas would have spoken, but Abbey spouted another thought, "How is that any different than the rest of us?"

"It's not," Nicholas agreed with certainty.

"Are you telling me that there really is *no* exact answer, even for *you*?"

"I am telling you that even *I*—with all the knowledge of legends and myths, experience and learning that I have accumulated in my centuries of existence—am still *nothing* in comparison to the hand of God."

"Then why does He let such horrible things happen?" Abbey took a breath of aggravation and let it out on a sigh, "Why are children hurt by those they trust? Why do strangers hurt them? Why are murders committed and why are vampires created and left to watch those they love age and die?"

"Why are vampires created at all?" Nicholas added to her list.

Abbey's eyes were clear when she responded truthfully, "That one I'm not so concerned about."

Nicholas stood and pulled Abbey into his arms. "Well, for all of your other concerns, I can only say that they happen because where there is good, there is evil."

"I *refuse* to think of you as *evil*."

"But can you think of *Remington* as *good*?"

"No, but then you cannot put me and a child killer in the same category either, simply because we are both human."

Nicholas nodded, "You are right. However, I think it is time for us to stop searching for answers and just start living the life that we have together. If Remington comes, then I will deal with him."

Nicholas could sense the direction of her thoughts, even before she spoke, "And what am *I* to do? Just stand back and watch you fight that demon?"

"No," Nicholas informed with conviction, "*You* are to protect our child."

~~~~~~~~

Nicholas' comment to her days earlier had stayed with Abigail in more ways than he could have anticipated. Protecting her child—*their* child—was a given. It was something Abigail would have done with instinct—no prompting needed. However, as the changes in her body continued, even those Nicholas was unaware of, Abigail knew their child would have no need of defense—at least to the paltry degree his or her mother could ever hope to achieve.

Aside from its amazing growth, Abbey was beginning to notice the feelings of the child within her. At times, she even heard sudden, unexplainable thoughts about basic needs and comforts filter through her mind like static on a radio.

There was no doubt that Abigail and Nicholas had created a gifted child.

But, *how* gifted was yet to be seen.

Another change—an unexpected and surprising change for Abigail—was a growing thirst. This was the change she wanted most to keep hidden from Nicholas. She tried desperately not to dwell on her cravings, not wanting him to read or feel the growing need or the degree to which it was coming.

At first Abbey was able to quench the desire for blood by eating rare meat. The state of preparation grew progressively less cooked, until now—as soon as Nicholas left for work each day—Abigail had begun eating raw steak and sushi as part of her diet.

Normal food continued to sustain Abbey and she found as much flavor and enjoyment in it as ever, but now she felt better—*stronger*—after every uncooked meal, she allowed her child. Moreover, by focusing on the fact that this was the baby's desire, downing the bloody treats was no problem.

As the day of her child's birth approached, Abbey was seriously considering telling Nicholas so that he could bring donated blood home from the hospital for her.

Today that possibility became definite.

Just as she did every morning now, Abigail ventured onto the front porch. The air was refreshing and the opportunity to sweep stubborn leaves and branches off the floorboard, an added incentive. Nothing seemed out of the ordinary—and she would have noticed since her senses were always on high-alert when she was outside.

The sound of a neighboring door closing caught her attention and as Abbey turned to wave at the man departing for work, her senses reeled.

The sound of his heartbeat reached her first.

The rich, briny flavor of his blood tantalized her taste buds through the keen sense of smell she had always had—now intensified by her pregnancy.

Abbey's pulse began to race, her hand to shake and in a flash of thought, —which, was *not* hers— Abigail seriously contemplated how best to take him down and drain him of each delicious drop.

She left the broom to fall against the wooden porch floor and even as the neighbor waved in return of her prior greeting, Abigail abruptly headed back into her house.

Not for her own safety, but that of those near her.

~~~~~~~~

Nicholas was home within forty minutes of Abbey's call. The sound of the door closing behind him heralded Abigail to his presence—though she had smelled him almost as soon as he had left the hospital grounds, three miles away.

The brown-paper bag he carried looked full, almost as heavy as his dark brown eyes as he set it on the floor beside the couch where Abbey sat in a huddled shape.

Without a word, he pulled her into his arms and sat so that she rested against him. After kissing her forehead lightly he stated, "You could have told me sooner."

"I was afraid."

"Of me?" He sounded hurt and surprised.

Abbey's voice shook. "Of your disappointment."

Nicholas pulled her closer to him, and without words promised, *Abigail, nothing about you disappoints me.*

Does our baby disappoint you?

Is the baby not also part of you?

Abbey forced her next response around the lump in her throat. "It is not *my* part I'm afraid you won't like."

Nicholas understood her hesitancy. She knew him so well and could feel the hatred he had for what he was. Tipping her chin up, forcing her to look into his warm onyx eyes, Nicholas whispered, "Any bit of you makes this child perfect in my eyes." He kissed her lightly, pulled back, and assured further, "I will love this child as much as I love you, *aatria mou.*"

Tears of relief and adoration slipped over Abbey's light lashes and she reached up to kiss her husband more fully on the lips. "I am sorry I doubted you."

Nicholas rubbed his thumb along her trembling lower lip and promised, "You are forgiven."

~~~~~~~~

To a creature of the night, time was nothing. Still, Remington was impatient. He had waited for this moment in time since his Embrace almost sixty-five years before. Revenge was his life—it consumed him.

From the shadows, he watched through the front window of the little house. This vantage point was one from which even a human could detect Abigail's pregnancy.

A tremor of anger ran through him at even the slightest possibility of this family line continuing—even worse, with the added blood of another demon.

At that moment, Nicholas' car slid into its parking space in front of the house and Remington faded further into the shadows. Whatever brought the doctor home caused him to be preoccupied enough that Remington's presence went undetected.

Continuing to watch, Remington witnessed the touching scene of Nicholas gathering Abigail in his arms—comfort being an obvious priority.

The sight of that sincere love pushed the spying vampire over the edge and Remington's control fled—his form shifting instinctively. The only unfortunate witness was the drunken man that was walking home from a local bar.

Someone would find his remains soon enough.

~~~~~~~~

Rebecca woke to an empty bed, a pounding head, and a rolling stomach. After her third race down the hall to the bathroom, she called for the maid, and sent for the doctor. Though she was fairly certain of the diagnosis, she would feel better with his confirmation.

While she sat in bed, awaiting Dr. Reichard's arrival, Rebecca went over the calculations in her mind four different times. When he finally entered her room, she was smiling. Fifteen minutes later, she was wondering why it had taken her so long to realize that she was pregnant.

It didn't really matter though – all that was important at this point was telling Malcolm and seeing how happy this news would make him.

~ Chapter Fifteen ~

Nicholas was anxious to get home. Since he and Abbey decided to move forward and away from constant worry, their life and planning for their child was a joy. Even with the onset of Abigail's cravings, the emotional and physical sacrifices she gladly made to appease and strengthen their baby amazed Nicholas.

While human children were miraculous in their own right, watching Abigail grow in half the time—his child coming closer to term inside her—was an astonishment of another level.

Though Nicholas was not an obstetrician, Abbey had persuaded him to oversee her prenatal and delivery care. So far, all was going well. In only four more weeks, the baby would be full-term for its kind—then the *real* challenge would begin for Nicholas. Somehow, Dr. Adamouras would deliver his child, while warding off any possible attack from Remington at such an opportune time. Nicholas would make sure his wife and baby survived the delivery by normal standards, and that the baby didn't kill Abigail with its possible extra-human strength.

All this, while maintaining self-control, around the fresh blood Abigail would be flowing.

Nicholas' wife assured him of her trust.

Abigail's husband wasn't sure he was deserving.

Still, they had no alternative.

Shaking off the worry, Nicholas thought of this evening's plans to finish the nursery and then spend some time pouring over possible names for the baby.

Nicholas was headed to the nurses' station, to sign off from his shift when—deep in thought—he was surprised when Jennifer rounded the corner and offered an overly welcoming smile.

He returned the expression—though with less enthusiasm. Jennifer would certainly delay his arrival home by at least fifteen minutes.

Nicholas was thinking up an excuse for not talking, when his attention slid to her neck—for reasons beyond the norm.

Immediate concern and unease filled him and his question blurted forth without thought or care of who overheard. "Jennifer, did you have an accident?"

Nicholas' unusual bluntness caught the nurse off guard and her hand flew up to cover the side of her neck. "Oh, that? My cat must have scratched me in the night."

Nicholas looked closer at Jennifer's face and into her brown eyes. "You must have some big cat. Why don't you have someone take a look at that?" The moment the suggestion passed his lips, Nicholas realized he was trapped.

"Is that an offer, Doctor?" Her hand moved away from its position over her wound and Nicholas saw that it had reopened. Blood slowly trickled out of wound holes that had become exceedingly familiar to him during the past decades.

"Tell me, Jennifer, have you made any new friends lately?"

A girlish giggle erupted from her. "Okay, so maybe it *wasn't* my cat." The playful voice morphed to the sound of pure seduction as she suggested, "Maybe it was my *dog* or my date . . ." her smile faded, " . . . or *both*."

Nicholas' gaze held hers. "That's one *Hell* of a love bite, Jennifer."

"I don't know that *love* has anything to do with it." Licking her dry lips subconsciously, Jennifer took a deep breath while closing her eyes. Slowly she opened them again—the color was beginning to change. "He seems to have a great deal of interest in your habits, though. Care to tell me how you know him, Nick?"

"No." Nicholas assured and turned immediately to head home—this change did not bode well. Jennifer would have to deal with the consequences of her foolishness on her own—he had Abigail to care for.

Nicholas was halfway down the corridor leading to the staff elevator when he heard Jennifer call out his name—though in reality it was no more than a whisper. He didn't speak, just waited in silent anticipation of her words.

Remington says soon is upon us.

Fear, like nothing Nicholas had ever felt, —either before or after becoming a vampire—filled him entirely.

What Jennifer did next, Nicholas had no idea because he was already moving stealthy through the doorway to his right and down the stairs on the opposite side.

~~~~~~~~

The room was finished. Pale yellow walls, yellow and white gingham bedding, curtains, and accessories completed the nursery. It was bright, happy and suited the baby no matter what gender it was born.

Abbey felt a motherly-contentedness fill her as she stepped back from her survey of the room—the only item it needed now was the baby.

By delivery, it would be a four-month, full-term pregnancy. Abigail guessed that such an outlook would thrill some expectant mothers. However, with dry humor, she wondered what they would think of the steps needed to obtain that short-term gestation.

The soft slide of the bedroom door opening behind her brought a smile to Abbey's lips. "You're early."

From behind, masculine arms wrapped tightly around her pregnant midsection and his face nuzzled her neck. Still, Abigail could feel the smile and his muffled words against her skin when he explained, "That's because I needed to be here with you."

~~~~~~~~

Every one of Nicholas' senses was alert. He knew that Jennifer followed behind him. He knew that no human would see either of them as they ran toward the home he and Abigail had made. He could smell the hunger in the air around him, he could smell the fear around him, and it made Nicholas sick to know that it was Abigail's terror, he sensed.

Racing into the house and up the steps, he knew the worst truth of all—he paid attention to his senses too late.

Abigail was gone.

~~~~~~~~

Abbey woke with the simultaneous sensation of a razor slicing through the side of her neck, and gravel being forced down her throat. She couldn't get a breath around the pain and the dryness of her airway was unbearable.

Worse than that, however, was the feeling that a shredder was tearing along the inside of her womb.

~~~~~~~~~

Nicholas whirled so quickly that Jennifer, even with her new vampire sight, didn't see his action. She was in his grasp, his hold on her upper arms tightening and his eyes darkening as she watched in horror. "Where is she?"

Jennifer was too frightened to bluff. "I don't know."

"Then you're of no use to me." Nicholas' moved one hand to her throat and squeezed.

Tears sprang to Jennifer's dark eyes even as her fangs dropped down in automatic defense. "Nicholas, I *don't know*. He told me to follow you, seduce you, and kill you. Those are my orders."

Nicholas laughed. "And you believed that you would be able to accomplish any *part* of that task?"

Despite her unfavorable position, Jennifer attempted a smile. "At least the part I most wanted to."

Nicholas looked disgusted. "*That* would be the part you would have the *most* difficulty with." Gripping tighter again, he ordered, "Call Remington."

"What?"

Jennifer looked truly lost. Nicholas sighed in frustration and asked, "How long has it been since he first bit you?"

Jennifer's answer came ready, "Five days."

"Call him—an Embracer cannot deny the call of his child for three days after their Birth into Darkness. You've been a full vampire for two days only. Call him and ask him to come to you."

Fear filled her eyes. "He'll *kill* me."

"If he doesn't, I will," Nicholas guaranteed coldly.

There was no hesitation in Jennifer's reply; "I think I'd rather take my chances with you, Nicholas."

All remaining patience left him then and his eyes colored completely over to red, leaving no trace of the prior onyx. His normally olive-toned complexion paled, the handsome skin pulling tightly to the bone. Fangs slid down, and snapped toward Jennifer in blatant anger for the denial of his threat. "Insolent child, you'd do best to rethink that statement."

With immediate obedience, Jennifer called out telepathically, *Remington I need you.*

And, together the two vampires waited for the silence to be filled, with the sound of another evil.

~~~~~~~~~

A sound of terrified anguish tore past Abigail's cracked lips as she drifted on the edge of consciousness. Fear came around fully when she opened her eyes and total darkness greeted her. Her hands were bound tightly, and something rough, like burlap, scraped against the soft skin of her cheeks. She tried not to move—doing so would only alert her captor that she was awake.

It was imperative that she concentrate now, *not* panic. Surely, Nicholas would be coming for her— Abbey needed to buy them both time. The child within her moved—*gouged*—again and Abbey used the pain as a reminder that of all those concerned, the one growing in her was the most important of all.

~~~~~~~~~

"Why doesn't he answer?" Jennifer questioned, not fully understanding her need to have Remington reply.

"Because he is in control." Nicholas supplied shortly.

"I thought you were perfect."

Nicholas continued to stare straight ahead, searching, listening, and praying for any sign of Abigail's location. "You were wrong."

~~~~~~~~

Abbey wasn't sure how much time had passed—it felt like hours. The air she was taking in was becoming hotter by the second, the searing in her throat was worsening, and her head was spinning and throbbing.

Slowly, she pushed against the suffocating fabric with her tied hands. Nothing met her knuckled touch, which either meant there was only air on the other side or if there *was* more, Abigail couldn't reach it.

If her bearings were right—and with the way she was feeling, that was completely questionable— Abbey was lying on her back. Something hard was beneath her. A wood floor, maybe concrete, but not dirt or carpet—the surface was cool and smooth through the material surrounding her.

Keep trying, you'll figure it out.

Abbey stiffened at the sound of his voice speaking in her mind. Too late, she realized that her ramblings would have been completely audible for his entertainment.

And in the next instant, a new barrage became available to him—the memory of the finished nursery, the sound of the door opening behind her, the sweet scent of vanilla-mint, the feel, and sound of Nicholas behind her . . . *You shape shifting bastard, it doesn't really matter what you hear or see from me now, does it?*

Remington laughed, *For the next few hours, a great deal will matter to me.*

"Why?" The one word she chose to speak was sheer agony and Abbey gasped in pain.

Remington chuckled again. "Ah, sweet revenge on so *many* levels."

This was the first time Abigail had ever heard Remington speak in his human voice—she was astounded. The sound was sweet music—warm and southern, smooth and full of graceful charm.

"Thank you," he accepted the silent compliment of her speech before adding, "I'm afraid I can't say the same for yours just yet though."

The pain fresh in her memory, Abbey used the gift of no-speech to ask, *What new riddle is this?*

The chuckle was genuine—almost excited. "How great is your thirst, Abigail?"

Then light—blinding, bright and painful—filled Abbey's eyes as Remington quickly removed her barriers.

Burlap did not bind her, but a burial shroud, and the prison of a wooden casket. Her great-uncle now held the lid open for her, his hand extended to help her out of one Hell and into another.

The truth was all around her.

Abigail screamed beyond the pain of her throat as the full realization of what her surroundings and Remington's words meant for her.

Her horror doubled when the first contraction tore through her midsection and with it, a slow trickle of blood moved down the inside of Abigail's legs.

~~~~~~~~

In his mind, Nicholas heard Abigail's scream and his heart—the one he had for her—raced in his chest. "He's hurting her."

"I think that's always been his plan," Jennifer stated dryly.

With a low growl rumbling in his chest, Nicholas demanded, "Use your senses to track him, I will use mine for Abigail."

He started to move, but Jennifer remained in her spot. "Why should I help you?"

Nicholas turned toward her. "So that I don't kill you."

Jennifer laughed—it wasn't quite the sound of insanity, but it was just on the brink. "Do you think *death* scares me now?"

"It should. Hell is a terrifying place."

"And life like *this* isn't?"

Nicholas relaxed a bit toward his regular physical appearance. "If you will help me help Abigail, then when this is all over, we will help you survive in the best ways we know how."

Jennifer mulled this over.

Nicholas didn't have that kind of time to waste. "It's all I have to offer Jennifer." A certain light came to her eyes and Nicholas rephrased. "It's all I'm *willing* to offer, Jennifer."

With a nod, she agreed, "I'll help, but only because Remington never warned me about all of this. I had no idea what he had planned for me or that I would become this *thing*." With the same semi-disgusted look she had given him before when they had talked about him being in love with Abigail, Jennifer stated, "I bet you explained it *all* to *Abbey*, didn't you."

"Before the wedding."

"You really *are* one of a kind."

Nicholas didn't hear the compliment—he was already using all of his strength to follow the scent and sound of his wife.

~~~~~~~~

Malcolm was insane with worry. Nicholas was the only one that could keep him from changing, barging into the bedroom, and tearing the throat from the doctor that did not put an end to Rebecca's terrified screams.

He could smell the blood — her blood and he knew that there was a lot of it. Too much for her to be surviving the delivery of their child.

Malcolm looked wild again.

"You must be still, my friend."

Frenzied eyes jumped toward the sound of Nicholas' voice. "The waiting is too much. I need to see to her."

"If you go into that blood soaked room, you will give us both away."

Malcolm knew that Nicholas' words were true, but he didn't want to hear them. He didn't want to care about their consequences or act responsibly. He only wanted to be with Rebecca and take care of her as he had always promised her he would.

Then there was a powerful scream from her and the sound of a tiny baby's wail took over the space Rebecca's cries had occupied. The men's eyes met again and Malcolm stood, he took one step toward the door, stopped, stepped again, and stopped once more.

The door opened. The doctor, much blood covering his wrinkled clothing, looked worn and worried from the doorway. Heavy eyes met Malcolm's as he called, "There's not much time, Mr. McBride. You'll need to say your goodbyes."

Nicholas watched as Malcolm accepted these words without argument. If there was no time to waste, he could deny them later, for now, he would give all that he was able to his Beloved Rebecca.

~~~~~~~~

Abigail did not take Remington's outstretched hand in acceptance of her situation. She did so because of the pain that washed over her, tore through her, took every thought, sensibility and breath, from her body. She did so because all rational thought fled and she grasped at anything for support.

It was that pain, pure and simple, that clenched her fingers around her great uncle's hand.

Labor pains she had expected—but this *had* to be more. Abigail couldn't move; her skin felt as though it were dry to the point of cracking open. As soon as the first contraction wrenched her midsection, they continued to roll over her without pause. Her finger dug into Remington's wrists—he felt no pain. In fact, a slow smile of satisfaction came to his fair-handsome face. "Is your love and lust for Nicholas still worth the price you'll pay?"

Pain-filled eyes rose to meet Remington's satisfied gaze. Gasping for breath, Abbey managed between clenched teeth, "I'll pay with my life if I have to."

Remington rolled his eyes in boredom. "How very sacrificial."

Abbey cried out as a new contraction tore through her abdomen. This one took the muscle spasms down into her thighs.

As though they were conversing over lunch, Remington informed congenially, "In case you've not figured it out, I've decided *not* to kill you."

Even if she had wanted to, Abigail could not have responded to his comment, so he continued in the same manner. "In fact, I think it will serve my purpose better to keep you alive for as long as I can."

"I don't care," she closed her eyes and inhaled deeply through another contraction, "what you do to me."

Remington whirled his free hand through the air. "I know, just don't hurt Nicholas or my baby." The eeriest part of his statement was that when Remington spoke, it was Abbey's voice sounding from him.

Again, she couldn't respond.

"To be honest, I haven't decided about the child yet. I think I'll wait and see what powers it has."

The next contraction brought a scream of terror and pain as fluid gushed from Abigail. With pure disgust, Remington added, "And it looks as though I won't have to wait long at all."

Abbey fell to her knees. Looking up at her great uncle, she asked, "Have you no mercy?"

Remington's conscience was as clear as his answer. "No."

~~~~~~~~

Jennifer was doing as much as she could to keep up with Nicholas, but even her new-vampire energy was no match in comparison to his thirst for revenge, and need to rescue Abbey. "Nicholas, I don't have a scent in this direction. Are you concentrating or wandering?"

Nicholas spun as though shocked by her presence, teeth bared, and a snarl dying as soon as he realized his mistake. "*What?*"

"I think you're wasting time."

He stopped all movement. Closed his eyes and concentrated. It had been nearing half an hour since he had heard Abigail scream, but the sound of it still echoed through his mind.

Now he heard only silence.

Was he too late?

Was that cry he had heard, the last sound she made before Remington killed her?

Just the thought of it had Nicholas changing forms without plan.

Come to me now.

Nicholas turned to Jennifer. She had heard the call as well. Remington had not denied her new-vampire call; he had simply answered it in his own time.

Jennifer barely glanced in Nicholas' direction before—in a sudden trancelike movement—she began moving in the same direction they had been traveling.

Nicholas followed close behind, feeling helpless, but having no other choice than to trust the enemy's creation.

~~~~~~~~

Abbey was only half-conscious when she heard Remington speak. "Who are you calling?"

"Assistance."

Abbey was still on her knees—though now she was gripping the edges of the pine coffin instead of her great uncle's cold hands. The contractions had eased since the one that caused her water to break—she didn't know if that was a good or a bad thing.

When the next contraction hit her, she still wasn't certain of how to judge its magnitude, but she *did* know that there was no going back now. From the front of her abdomen, around her back, down over her hips and thighs, tearing, pushing, pulling pain washed over her in torrents unending. Abbey felt the pressure and dropped her hand—already she could feel the head of her baby crowning.

She looked up, "Remington?"

He was across the room, watching, and his eyes blood rimmed, but unchanged other than that. "I won't come closer. Help will be here soon."

A new contraction came.

"Help is too late." Abbey gasped, as she felt her baby slide out into her waiting hands.

~~~~~~~~

Jennifer scaled the eight-foot-high chain-link fence surrounding the darkened building as though it were no more than a stepping-stone. Nicholas moved quickly behind her, assuring that any humans occupying the nearby intersection would be unable to see him with their normal eyesight.

The abandoned electric-company building stood only a mile from Abigail's house. For years, the factory had been used as a shelter for scavenging animals, the homeless and partying teenagers. Even without its numerous broken windows, the scent of fresh blood would have been strong to both vampires.

Once inside, Nicholas could hear small whimpers. The sounds wavered between Jennifer's newborn lust for blood and Abigail's fear—both caused Nicholas' pace to hasten.

"We're close now," Jennifer panted. Rounding a long forgotten piece of machinery, candlelight suddenly cast a dim light over the dank and dusty room.

Remington stood against the far wall—halfway into vampire feeding mode—but he was obviously fighting the urge. Abigail lay inside a coffin in the middle of the dirty concrete floor. Her moans and pants the only proof that she lived.

Nicholas forgot his adversary for the moment and flashed to Abigail's side. He knelt and turned her face to his; tender love filled him instantly, "*Aatria mou.*"

"Nicholas, you're here." Abbey's voice was weak and tired and he could smell blood, but for the first time, he noticed the difference.

"You're not bleeding."

"She has no blood in her." Remington smirked from behind.

"Then where is the blood coming from that I smell?" Jennifer pleaded for an answer.

Remington chuckled, "From the birth sack."

Jennifer recoiled at the extent of her own bloodlust. "The baby?"

"They are fine." Abbey murmured.

"They?" Nicholas questioned immediately.

A tear slipped out of the corner of Abigail's eye. "Nicholas, they are beautiful. I won't be able to help you save them. Remington bit me, made me weak and then the twins came and now I can't sit up to defend them and he'll kill us all."

Nicholas kissed her lips and whispered silently, *Ye of little faith.*

Not missing one syllable of their reuniting conversation, Remington interrupted, "Do not be over-confident, Nicholas."

Nicholas' eyes did not leave Abigail's face as he replied, "I have what is just and true on *my* side."

"Do not put the Lord your God to the test." Remington's voice sounded different to Abigail as he quoted the Biblical text—it was oddly calm and held an accent that Abigail could not place.

Her confusion did not last long—instantly a picture of Jesus hanging on the cross, crucified for all who would believe in him, filled her mind.

Abbey's disgusted eyes clashed with Remington's bloody ones. The smile that graced his once-handsome features was the worst she had witnessed. The accent was Aramaic and Remington was mocking God and Jesus very much—by using his shape shifting ability to call on the voice of Jesus Christ.

Any doubt Abigail had held onto concerning God's love for her or His desertion in the time of her parent's death fled. God had nothing to do with their massacre—the creature in front of her did. The evil that had been haunting her all her life was responsible for her pain the same as he was responsible for taking her Embrace from her Beloved.

Remington laughed at her assessments, and, final-conclusion. "Now *that* sweet thought will make Him happy. Remember that Matthew wrote that Your Father in heaven is not willing that any of His little ones should be lost." Remington sneered, "I'm assuming he meant even to the likes of *me.*"

Nicholas growled in warning.

Remington ignored the sound. The laughter he had been issuing ceased and his eyes darkened with his tone and words. "Pity for you, that your realization of what is myth and reality came too late, you soulless whore."

Abbey's eyes rose from the floor and as she righted her posture to face her fears, what he had made her began to surface.

She fought the instinct to kill—Nicholas could manage it, than so would she. Instead, she used her words to wound.

Pulling on her childhood memories of church and Nicholas' constant support she growled—not hesitating at the sound of her new demonic voice, "Worship the Lord your God, and serve him only. *I've* not knelt before any others."

"One without a soul cannot worship."

She felt Nicholas' raw pain as the nagging doubt filled him again. She sent her support to him and saw the surprise that covered his face when he looked to her, realizing what she had done and how strong her powers were already.

Then her Nicholas turned and she could tell from the set of his shoulders that he was no longer the man she loved, but the monster she had prayed to never see again.

"Let's end this once and for all," Nicholas growled in his darkest voice.

"Gladly," Remington responded with glee.

All Hell broke loose.

Nicholas launched himself through the air and Remington lunged from his place by the wall. They met in the middle; their connecting bodies sounding like metal crushing together.

Abbey wanted to sit up, to see what was going on, but the babies were lying against her and though she now felt pain only in her neck, throat and head—she couldn't deny her fear. She couldn't watch Nicholas fight Remington—the worry over the outcome was too much. Her entire world hung in the balance—Nicholas was her hero, the father of her children, her lover, her husband, her friend, he was her Beloved. Now that she was like him, now that Remington had made her a vampire, she would be eternally Nicholas'—his in *all* ways—not just in promise.

The clash was still sounding around Abigail when her daughter started to cry. Soothing sounds automatically came from Abbey's throat as though she were in the calmness of the nursery she had so recently decorated. She jumped when Jennifer's face suddenly hovered over hers. "Shall I help you calm them?"

The way assistance was offered, left Abigail feeling less than comfortable. "No, I'm fine."

Before Abbey's weakened senses could respond, Jennifer's long-nailed hand swooped down and scooped Abigail's sleeping son from beside her. "Oh, but I insist." Floating over the casket now, Jennifer smiled, revealing her teeth as they dropped down for the feed. "I've always loved the smell of babies, but I've got to say, he's the most *delicious* ever."

Abigail was on her feet without even trying. "You'll not harm my child, demon."

"Do not throw names that can be returned to you."

"Touch my baby and you'll pray for mere demons to end your torment."

"I could empty him before your weakened body could take him from me."

"Are you willing to take that risk?"

Jennifer raised the boy so that his tiny chest rested against her lips, Abigail braced to move, and in a blink, her baby flew back to her arms. Remington stood behind Jennifer's now decapitated form. In a delayed reaction, her body slumped downward, echoing the sickening thud of her head hitting the floor only seconds before.

Remington grinned at Abigail, "I couldn't let her take my fun away, now could I?"

Abigail had no time to answer the question that was most likely rhetorical anyway before the scent of sunshine and leather ushered a new roar into the room.

"Your fun is over, Remington."

If possible, Remington's already pale features whitened further and he hissed in anger and horror combined. "This is *not* possible."

~ *Chapter Sixteen* ~

From the corner of her eye, Abigail saw a flash of movement, and Nicholas was there, at her side, pulling her away from Remington, before his sure wrath could be unleashed on her, or the child she held.

"Aye, 'tis me for sure." Malcolm stood in the most powerful form Nicholas had seen him in since first they met in Baltimore centuries earlier. His size was as intimidating as ever and in the black suit, long black coat, and cane he brandished at his side, Nicholas was ecstatic that this powerful vampire was *his* comrade.

A thousand questions leapt to his mind, but Nicholas would have to wait for the answers.

"I *killed* you." Remington's gaze—as equally unsure as his tone—swung to Nicholas, "You were there to second that."

"You both saw me wounded. The conclusion of death was your own and, my good fortune—though at the time I would have preferred death."

"Allow me to grant your wish this time," Remington stated and stepped toward Malcolm—unaware or uncaring that he kicked Jennifer's unseeing head out of the way to clear his path.

"Not this time," Malcolm secured. "Today victory will be mine and rest assured that I'll not leave the job half-finished as you did."

"I will admit that the odds *are* in your favor." Remington pointed out with a glance in Nicholas and Abigail's direction.

Malcolm shook his auburn-topped head. "They'll not interfere. Abigail is too new and I'm here to assure that Nicholas keeps his vow of no murder."

"I'd gladly break it for my family." Nicholas promised from his place beside Abigail.

Malcolm nodded. "This is another reason I am here. We are family now in the truest sense. I'll protect you and yours as I would Rebecca."

Remington growled, "It is *always* about my sister."

"As it should be," Malcolm agreed.

"I'll end your torment and send you to her then," Remington promised—his threat ending with his charge.

It was over as quickly as it had begun and both Nicholas and Abigail stared in amazed, horrified silence, stunned by the sudden and thoroughness with which Malcolm ended the century old battle. The cane he carried was obviously a farce, the end broken off the second Remington moved. Its revealed point was directed upward so that Remington ultimately impaled himself upon the weapon Malcolm held tightly in his hand. There was not even time for the cry of indignation and pain to cross his bared lips before Remington was dead.

His rigid body went limp on the stake and fell heavily against Malcolm who pushed his deceased brother-in-law to the side like an errant piece of rubbish.

"My father looked *exactly* like you and *what* on God's earth is that cane made of . . . *garlic*?"

Malcolm laughed, the sound of it was rich and happy, —it was free. "Lass, you sound like you've been holding that outburst back for hours."

His voice still raspy with emotion, Nicholas guaranteed, "Just since you entered the room." With a shaky smile to his wife, he added, "Which in Abbey's vocal world is pretty much the same."

"Well, I didn't exactly have the opportunity for small talk." She returned smartly, indicating the violence around them.

Malcolm nodded, "She's right at that." Allowing another calming moment to completely return him to human form, Malcolm added, "But you'll have to learn to hold those thoughts and words at bay *and* that there's more to us than garlic can scare off."

"The thoughts you needn't worry about, Malcolm; she can hold me out."

"You know that already?" His Scottish lilt was slightly skeptical.

"No, she did so before her . . . *Embrace*." The way he forced the word over his lips left no one questioning how Nicholas felt about Abigail's change.

Pride filled Malcolm's eyes, but before he could comment, Abbey informed, "So, you see, I've figured out some safety measures even before your entrance, grandfather." The flow of the words felt natural to Abigail. She could see from his momentary jolt that it was an unexpected honor for Malcolm, however.

He inclined his head slightly. "You do me proud, Abigail McBride Adamouras."

"Thanks, but I really *do* want to know what that cane was made of."

"You'll understand now, it's the *words* that will get her in the most trouble." Nicholas asserted unnecessarily.

"Aye," Malcolm agreed. His hearty laugh sounded again and he answered for Abbey, "The cane is wood of ash, hawthorn and oak. Each was wetted and then wrapped decoratively around a center post of a steel-iron mixture."

"Sounds heavy," Abbey observed needlessly.

Malcolm smiled and the room seemed brighter. "And it would be—for a man."

Nicholas spoke now, his voice thick with many emotions. "What of the handle?"

Reaching down, Malcolm unceremoniously yanked the stake from Remington's now shriveled body and held the sparkling-handle end upward. "This is a crystal ball with holy water inside."

"A bit risky isn't it?" Abbey asked, automatically swaying from side to side as her son began to whimper in her arms.

"I've learned to be careful, lass."

Glancing around the room, Abbey stated in her witty manner, "Yes, I can *see* that."

Nicholas smiled, some of his energy slowly returning as the layers of shock began to ebb. "She's got a good deal of you in her."

"And what of my Rebecca?"

Nicholas' smile switched to melancholy. "She shows herself from time to time as well." Pulling Abbey against his side, he stated, "But mostly she is my Beloved Abigail."

"Your Beloved?" Malcolm questioned with mild surprise.

"Are you insinuating that you didn't know?" Nicholas questioned his mentor-friend, with obvious doubt lacing his tone.

Malcolm shrugged as Nicholas had seen him do hundreds of times before. "I'd hoped."

"Then that must have been enough."

Indicating the children, one now cradled in his mother's arms and the other by her father's, Malcolm stated, "But even *thi*s was more than I'd dare dream." With arms outstretched, he asked, "May I?"

Abigail responded first, "Always." Handing her son off to his great-great-grandfather, she introduced, "Meet Malcolm Nicholas."

The older Malcolm's hazel eyes darted to her face, and filled with awe. "Truly?"

Abigail smiled, "Truly." Touching the top of her daughter's downy head, she added, "And this is Zoë Rebecca."

"So you've chosen the names without me?" Nicholas asked without insult.

Abigail's hand moved from Rebecca to her husband's face. "I knew you would love the names as much as I do." When Rebecca nestled into her father's chest, searching for sustenance he couldn't supply, Nicholas chuckled and started to hand her to her mother. Abigail shook her head and stepped back. "You'll have to get formula for her."

Malcolm's eyes lifted from studying his namesake to look toward Abigail. Nicholas knew the answer before the thought completely crossed Abbey's mind. "I know you love her. It is because you want to keep her safe that you can't feed her." He pulled his wife close—to both comfort her and keep her from seeing the sadness that entered his eyes.

Though he knew beyond doubt that he was welcome, Malcolm suddenly felt like an intruder in Nicholas and Abigail's need for privacy. Handing the now-sleeping child back to his mother, Malcolm stated, "See to your family. Nicholas will tend to your remaining changes and I'll be back to help as soon as I can."

"You're leaving? I have so much I want to ask." Abbey's anxiousness transferred to the younger Malcolm and his eyes—already bright green like those of his mother and his namesake—flew wide and alert.

Malcolm spoke in a foreign tongue Abigail did not recognize and within seconds, the child slept again. Looking to Abbey, he explained, "I must dispose of Remington properly. I'll take no chances with my family again."

"And you'll return to us as soon as you're able?" She urged.

"Not even Lucifer himself could keep me away," Malcolm promised.

Abbey shuddered visibly, "Let's not offer that challenge too many times." The men laughed at her thoughts and words, but honored her wishes anyway.

Looking to Nicholas then, Malcolm added, "I know that when I return, I have much to explain to you."

Nicholas nodded silently.

"Just know that all I did was for your safety and that of my family."

"I understand." Nicholas allowed.

Watching his only remaining family, Malcolm replied, "Aye, I know you do, my brother." With a growing smile he corrected, "My *son*."

~~~~~~~~

There were some days, during the following weeks, when Abigail wished that Remington *had* killed her.

She hated the need for feast and having to deny her new instincts for the prepackaged blood-bank-meal Nicholas smuggled home for her from the hospital was maddening. Nicholas empathized offering Abbey the same explanation Malcolm had once given him—"You'll get used to it, Abigail. For now you are dissatisfied because it's like ordering baklava, but being forced to eat a dry biscuit in its place."

Abigail also disliked the lack of control she had—anything could set her off for the change to vampire mode. She also hated that when she ate, Malcolm sensed it. He grew frenzied, demanding a feeding, and only satisfied when the nourishment came from his mother. He wanted to be as close to her blood feeding as he could possibly be.

However, worse than that, was the sadness that lit Nicholas' eyes, every time he opened a new bag of blood for his wife to consume. Abigail realized that though her husband's love had not diminished for her—that it never would—he hated that she had become a monster.

Though Remington was dead, and could cause them no more harm or terrorism, his revenge was extracted on Nicholas in this one way—he had damned Abigail with the lot of them.

However, watching her as she was now, with the early-morning light seeping in through the nursery window, casting a glow over her and their son, cradled against her breast, Nicholas saw her as he first had—as he always did—*his* Abigail.

His voice was soft when he spoke, "Even as a doctor, it still amazes me that you produce milk for them. I would not have thought it possible."

Abbey smiled down at the dark haired child she fed now. "I guess no matter the animal, a mother is a mother first."

Nicholas nodded in acceptance of that explanation, but added, "So long as the instinct to love and nurture is there to begin with."

Looking at her husband, Abbey admitted, "What surprises *me*, is that he is so gentle in his feeding, considering the way he acts when he is hungry."

"He'll learn to control the frenzy in time. He is too young to understand regular hunger pains yet." Nicholas leaned over the crib and looked in on the angelic sleeping form of their daughter. Zoë had bands around him even tighter than her mother did.

"I heard that," Abbey teased from across the room. Adjusting their son to burp him on her shoulder, she smiled when Nicholas turned in her direction. "And I wouldn't have it any other way."

With a raised brow, Nicholas questioned, "Are you going to tell me you feel differently about *Cole*?" Nicholas emphasized the nickname Abigail had bestowed upon their son. He didn't mind; her attempt to honor *both* of Malcolm Nicholas' namesakes amused the infant's father. Abbey claimed that with the *chol* of Nicholas and the *col* of Malcolm she was able to derive the combination of Cole.

Pulling their daughter up, Nicholas took his place in the rocking chair, a full bottle of pre-mixed baby formula in hand and whispered, "Come *Zecca*, it's time to eat."

Abbey returned Cole to the crib so that he could sleep in stretched-out comfort. Turning back to face her husband, she asked sincerely, "Are you *trying* to instigate fights for our children?"

Nicholas looked amused. "No, why?"

As though she had given the matter great thought, Abbey opinionated, "Only that since I didn't miss your little twist-combination of her name, I couldn't help but imagine all the kids on the block and playground teasing *Zecca* for being part of the Addams Family." Abbey gave a soft, but dramatic sigh before continuing, "*Naturally*, she would defend herself and Cole will step in as her gallant big brother." Her eyes met his with meaning, "If he's as much like his father as I think he is . . .."

"But let's remember, that if *Zoë* is as you *claim* you were—quiet and self-entertaining—we'll have nothing to worry about."

Noting his use of their daughter's given name, Abbey knew that she had won this small battle; still, just for fun, she rose to the bait of Nicholas' teasing. "It is *not* just a *claim* that I was quiet before I met you. And since you've been plaguing me all my life, you know that already."

"*Plaguing* you?" With evident sarcasm, Nicholas added, "Clearly I've been mistaken about your flair for the dramatic."

Abbey scrunched up her nose and stuck out her tongue at Nicholas.

In the next instant, she nearly bit it off when Malcolm appeared unexpectedly in the window behind Nicholas, causing her to jump.

May I come in?

Fear vanishing with recognition, Abigail asked, "Is there something *wrong* with the front door?" Her mock-irritated words were hollow as she moved to allow her great-grandfather entry.

"You are always welcome." Nicholas formally stated, without moving from his position with Zoë.

Trying not to laugh as her large ancestor twisted and maneuvered his body to fit through the entrance space the window allowed, Abbey asked, "Are you *sure* you don't want me to open the front door? You'll have to do the threshold-thing eventually anyway."

"This will do," Malcolm replied. Once inside, he stretched to his full over-six-foot-height and the size of him, and the fact that he was *there*, amazed Abbey again.

"Is everything taken care of?" Nicholas asked, now doing as Abigail had done with Cole, by moving Zoë to his shoulder for burping.

"Aye."

Not wanting to be shunned, Abbey delved into her husband's mind just enough to decipher the conversations meaning.

She didn't supress her shock well.

"It took you *three* months to rid the world of Remington?" Abbey asked; her incredulous tone high enough that Cole stirred in the crib behind her.

Moving to pat Cole's agitated form, Nicholas suggested, "Let's move this conversation downstairs. There is much to discuss and I don't want to wake the children."

Abbey was already moving toward the door when she heard Malcolm agree softly behind her, "Aye, the bairns need their rest."

~~~

Abigail took the time to change from her nightgown and robe into jeans and tee shirt. By the time she got downstairs, Nicholas was waiting on the loveseat and Malcolm was stretched out comfortably in the overstuffed chair across from him. Abbey took the open space beside her husband and cuddled into the warmth they provided each other even as she asked, "Okay, one more time, *why* does it take four months to rid us of a vampire?"

Malcolm smiled. "I see why Nicholas loves you, this precociousness is very addictive."

"And I see why Rebecca loved you. You are a very dominating presence, Malcolm McBride. That thick Scottish accent of yours is almost as charming as your smile *and* ability to distract one from an unpleasant discussion." Abbey raised a red brow—very much like the ones on the man, at which she directed her expression. "My answer please."

Malcolm's proportionally-equal-to-his-size grin remained in place. "As I told you before I left, I will take *no* chances with my family again. Loosing Rebecca was the hardest thing I've endured in *any* lifetime and I don't want to face such agony again." There was a brief silence while Malcolm regained his thoughts to their intended track. "Nicholas has told me of your great research."

"Wild goose chase you mean?" Abigail inserted, promptly elbowing her husband lightly in the side as she spoke.

Nicholas grunted and Malcolm chuckled. "However you term it, it was a good thing for you to endure. You needed to learn what you were facing in Remington. You also *must* be clear about *what* you love in Nicholas and are part of in your own heritage. Maybe even most important of all is learning about what you are raising as a family."

Abigail took this information in as it came. "I never thought of it that way."

"Because that would have made *me* right," Nicholas intoned dryly beside her.

She turned her head to look at her husband. "You've been right before and I've told you so."

"Not in ways you'd wish to discuss in front of Malcolm."

The meal she had partaken of that morning allowed Abbey's face to flame. "Not in ways you should be expecting any time soon."

Malcolm roared in laughter, a sound Abbey was quickly coming to realize was as natural as breathing to him. "Are you wanting me to continue now?"

"Yes, please, since we'll be having nothing more to pass our time with for a while."
We'll see about that later, Nicholas intoned silently.
Much later, Abigail returned.
I can still hear you, Malcolm reminded, and Abigail flamed again.
Clearing his throat, Malcolm continued his tale. "In your learning's you certainly came across ways to dissuade and kill vampires." He didn't wait for an answer and the only response was a nod of Abbey's head, anyway. "I used them all."
"I beg your pardon?"
"All." Malcolm repeated.
"Would you mind if I ask you to be a little more descriptive?"
"Believe it or not, I already expect it of you." Malcolm said with a smile that showed he minded appeasing her interest, no more than Nicholas minded bending to every one of Zoë's demands.
"First, I used the cane made of all documented means of killing or harming a vampire, to stake Remington's heart."
"Well done, by the way," Abbey inserted pleasantly.
Malcolm nodded in acceptance of her words, explaining further, "Mind you, *that* had to be done with just one thrust for safe measure. I discovered that the earliest beliefs claimed that *two* thrusts would reinsert the "life" of the vampire and empower him with raging-revenge for the one trying to kill him."
"I hadn't heard that one." Abigail said, breathless as a child, hearing a ghost story for the first time.
"Neither had I." Nicholas added, though his tone was more of interest than awe.
"It was new to me as well, but worth the effort."
"I completely agree," Abbey concurred.
"Remington's need to kill me helped since he was so focused on tearing my head off, that he never noticed my hand lifting the spear until he impaled himself on it."
"Does that make a difference?" Abigail asked, her nervous gaze automatically shifting to the window where she had first seen her great uncle's evil form.
"Does *what* make a difference?" Malcolm asked, using a soothing tone since he had noticed the shift in her nerves the moment they changed.
"The fact that Remington impaled *himself* and you didn't actually drive the stake into him."
Malcolm shook his head negatively. "I think not. In addition, just to be safe, I decapitated his remains, burned the body in one place, the head in another until both were no more than dust. Making sure the two did not touch again; I mixed his ash with holy water, garlic and lemon."
"Is that *all*?" Nicholas questioned, his smirk giving away what sarcasm his tone didn't.
Malcolm merely looked at the younger man without breaking a smile, and then stated, "No."
"What *else* was there to *do*?" Abigail asked in amazement.
Nicholas provided this answer. "He sprinkled his remains separately on four different continents to ensure that they never connect again." Awe, thanks, and surprise filled each word he spoke.
"And then I went to visit Rebecca's grave and tell her of our new family."
Instant tears rolled down Abbey's cheeks. "She knows already, grandfather."
"Aye, but not from *my* mouth."
Nicholas' arm tightened around her and Abigail understood exactly what Malcolm meant. If something wasn't shared with your Beloved, then it meant nothing at all.
Nicholas spoke softly, holding on to the tender moment, while moving forward with his own questions. "I thought you were dead in the woods. Do you know how I mourned the loss of my dearest friend?"
Malcolm looked up and sorrow lit his green eyes. "I do because just as you fulfilled your promise and watched over my family, *I* watched over *you*."

"Why?" Abbey wondered aloud.

"Because with Remington following me, none of you would be safe. He was so obsessed with his hunts that nothing else entered his realm of thought. If he were intent on Nicholas, then I was free to watch over him."

"What about the powers I took from you?" Nicholas asked with full curiosity.

Malcolm smiled—this time with fatherly pride. "They were *yours* all along."

"Not possible." Nicholas argued.

"Completely true." Malcolm confirmed. "I always told you that you held back too much and never used your full potential."

"Now I see where Abigail gets her confidence from." Nicholas stated dryly.

"I think some of that comes from you as well." Malcolm returned.

Looking down into his wife's face, beaming with love and pride as she looked back at him, Nicholas agreed, "You may be right about that."

"I know he is," she whispered and then kissed her husband. Abbey was completely uncaring that Malcolm was present and that she was breaking her earlier threat to abstain from Nicholas' touch.

~ *Epilogue* ~

Abigail had never felt as impatient in the last five years as she did now. She paced in front of the kitchen window, glancing out to the clear view of the graveled drive beyond.

"Wearing a hole in the floorboards won't bring them home any faster." Malcolm teased with a smile on his face and in his voice—as was his norm.

"Today is special." Abbey reminded, though there was no need.

Nicholas stood from the wooden kitchen table gracing the kitchen of the eighteenth-century farmhouse in which they now made their home. Wrapping his arms around Abbey, he positioned her so that they could both see out the window. "Five minutes later than you think they should be, does not mean they are in trouble, *aatria mou*."

"I know that," Abbey replied in mild defense.

"Nor will it wipe away their memories of the first day of school."

That reminder had Abbey striding toward the side-door. "The lane is too long for them to walk alone. I should never have let you two talk me into waiting here for them. God only knows what could happen in the distance from the bus stop to our yard."

Malcolm blocked her way in a flash. "You'll wound their pride."

"I'll wound more than that if you don't get out of my way, Papa," Abbey stated. Her threats sounded empty with her use of the endearment the children called their "grandfather."

"They're here Abbey." Nicholas' whisper drew his wife's attention from the battle she was preparing to wage. "Listen."

There was laughter and whispers. "What are they up to?" Abigail had made it a point not to eavesdrop in on her children's minds unless she thought they were in grave danger. Worrying about the eighth-of-a-mile distance they had to walk back their wooded lane didn't really constitute such prying—even by Abbey's motherly standards.

She didn't have to wonder about their antics for long.

"Mama, Dad, Papa, come see what Zoë has done."

It was not odd to hear Cole boast of his sister— Zoë had him as befuddled as any of the other men in her life. What was surprising was the singsong, tattletale tone, in Cole's voice; a role his sister usually played toward him.

Opening the door with expectant smiles of childhood pranks, each of the welcoming adults gasped in shock at the sight that met their eyes.

On their first day of kindergarten, Abigail had sent Cole to school in dark blue denims and a white polo-style shirt. His dark curly hair was kept neatly trimmed, but there was no styling the mass—it tumbled at will, no matter the amount of gel his mother used on it.

Zoë—as one would expect of a princess—usually preferred to wear dresses. Today's choice had been a dark blue denim skirt and white ruffled shirt with a matching dark denim vest over it. Her curls of auburn hair had previously been caught back from her face by a denim headband.

Abigail was grateful that she had taken pictures in the morning, for the outfit Zoë wore would never look the same again.

Malcolm was the first to recover from his shock and find the ability to speak. "Zoë, sweetheart, what have you got there?"

Zoë shrugged, "Cole said I couldn't catch it, that I was too slow."

Cole laughed, "Boy was I *wrong*." Glancing toward his sister, he appeased his wounded pride by declaring, "But she sure was messy."

Abbey reached for and grasped Nicholas' hand without taking her eyes off her children. "I can see that."

Zoë looked back and forth from her mother and father, to her grandfather, worry etching her fair brow. "Mama, have I done a bad choice?"

Nicholas loosened his grip on Abbey and moved toward Zoë. "No sweet, we just want to know what happened."

"And I won't be in trouble?"

"No, you'll not be in trouble." Nicholas responded with a calming smile.

"Cole teased me that I couldn't catch the deer," she repeated, "so I started running and, when I jumped on it—"

"You should have seen her Papa, Zoë jumped *right* over the fence like the deer did. It was *so* cool."

"I bet it was," Abigail laughed nervously, "But where did all the blood come from?"

Zoe seemed afraid to answer, so Malcolm encouraged her, his voice soft and soothing. "What happened when you jumped on the deer, lass?"

Zoë's reply was a conspiratorial whisper. "It smelled so good that I wanted to taste it."

A small sob slipped past Abbey's lips before she could stop it. Zoë looked toward her mother. "Mama, if it makes you sad, I won't ever do it again."

Abbey shook her head and reached out to her daughter. The bond between them had been a difficult one to bridge. For so long, Abbey had feared the humanness of Zoë put her at risk—primarily from Abigail herself. Blessedly, time had shown Abbey that her love for her child, was stronger than her thirst. Now, she took every opportunity to make up for lost time, showing her Zoë how much she was loved.

Glancing down at the mutilated doe-carcass in her arms, Zoë looked quickly back up—she was unsure what to do about the mess, how to get rid of it, so that she could take advantage of the desperately needed comfort, of her mother's open arms.

Nicholas stepped to her rescue, removing the mass from Zoë's grip, he assured, "Go with mama, clean up so we can celebrate your first day of school."

"We get a party too?"

Malcolm smiled down at his namesake. "Aye, with cake and potato chips and ice cream."

His boyish youth keeping him oblivious to the major change in family dynamic, Cole ran into the house ahead of everyone, hollering, "Wow, this is the best day ever!"

~~~

The trio of adults waited until the children were tucked into bed and sleeping before meeting in the kitchen to talk. They entered the room together and Abigail asked immediately, "Papa, how can her tendencies just be coming out now?"

Malcolm took a seat before answering. "I've never heard or seen anything like it. Usually if a child is born of a vampire union, then they are gifted from birth like Cole."

Nicholas nodded, "Just as he has the hunger, the tracker ability and strength."

"Should we assume that Zoë has the same traits?" Abigail asked, concern lacing her words more than curiosity.

Malcolm shook his head negatively. "I don't think it's safe to assume anything. Cole's powers are already matured to the point a vampire of your age. His strength is amazing."

Each of them toyed with that thought as well as a few others that entered their individual wonderings. Finally, Abbey suggested, "Maybe it's time for me to listen to her."

She waited for a reply. Nicholas was the one to give it. "I think you're right. This is definitely for her good."

Abigail took a seat and closed her eyes. Since her Embrace, Abbey's ability to hear the thoughts of others had multiplied incredibly. It was now necessary for her to block *out* thoughts from flowing to her rather than force concentration to read their flow. Abigail was also now able to feel a person's emotional state simply by looking at them. Like Malcolm, she had the ability to sooth—though her capability was not as deep as his was.

In this moment, all Abbey had to do was focus on the picture of Zoë that came to her mind. The dream-like state took over her and she could see the scene from earlier in the day unravel just as her children had described it.

Nevertheless, her vision gave more detail than their words had.

The detail of Zoë's unhindered speed was breathtaking.

The detail of Zoë's quick hunt and capture of the unsuspecting doe feeding in the woods was mesmerizing.

The detail of Zoë's warm brown eyes, filling with blood from the outer rims inward as she held to the squirming animal as it squealed its last protest of life draining from it was terrifying.

Abigail broke the trance with a gasp. "She's a full vampire, just like Cole is."

"That can't be. She's never shown us the signs." Nicholas argued, though he knew better than to doubt his wife's ability to see clearly.

"She's got Remington." Malcolm whispered with pained certainty.

"What do you mean she's *got* Remington?" Abigail demanded steadily, her narrowed eyes swinging toward Malcolm. "That is not something you say as though remarking that she has inherited your red hair or Nicholas' smile. This is *Remington* you are discussing in relationship to my daughter."

"I understand that, Abigail, and I don't want to frighten you."

"Too late," Abbey interceded bluntly.

"Remington had the ability to hide. He watched Nicholas and me before trying to kill me, and many times we didn't know he was near until he made an appearance."

"It was the same with Abigail and me," Nicholas agreed. "Though I never thought about why it was, I just assumed that we were so preoccupied by the rest of our lives that we missed the signals of his arrival."

"No. Remington was a shape shifter, so he could shift his emotions, his physical appearance and even his needs to suit the situations as they came."

"So you're saying that Zoë can hide the fact that she is a vampire?" When Malcolm nodded, Abbey asked further, "Shouldn't that be considered a good thing?"

"As long as she uses that ability for keeping us and humans safe, yes."

"But Remington used his gift for the hunt," Nicholas stated in conclusion.

"Aye."

"Is she a shape shifter?" Abbey whispered with dread.

"My guess would be yes."

Abbey's eyes shifted automatically to her husband with Malcolm's answer. "Do you think she knows?" Abbey asked, only partially wanting a reply to her question.

"I do," Malcolm opinionated without hesitation.

"Malcolm, what you are suggesting is at best, hard to imagine," Nicholas stated in a last stand of denial.

Malcolm's response was calm. "Why? We've already said that Cole is matured beyond his years as a vampire, why is it so hard to believe that Zoë is as well? Can you not fathom that she has figured out our family secret and she simply held back until her wants and needs caught up with her?"

"Like they did today," Nicholas murmured, lost in the suggestive thoughts his great-grandfather-in-law was planting in his mind.

"Then if it weren't for the mess she made in her feeding frenzy, we still wouldn't know," Abbey realized aloud.

"Not unless she wanted us to," Malcolm replied in turn.

"Which means we have in our house—with the responsibility of raising—two of the most powerful vampire-human mixes ever to be created," Nicholas stated for clarification.

"Exactly," Malcolm confirmed.

"God help us all," Abigail whispered, fully praying that God, in His infinite wisdom and grace, would see fit to do just that.

Dear Reader,

I must admit that when a friend of mine approached me about writing a vampire romance, I was hesitant to join the frenzy. With trepidation, I half-heartedly began Abigail and Nicholas' story, only to stop a few weeks later—something just felt too forced and ordinary.

I took the time to complete *Second Time Around* and then was grudgingly convinced to read the Twilight Series by Stephenie Meyer—WOW! A few things I learned and/or remembered, while enveloped in this author's imagination:

1. Giving up hope of becoming an author is *not* an option.
2. An unleashed imagination is a wonderful thing.
3. The plans I had for *Embraced* would save it from being just "*another* vampire book."
4. It was time to finish Abigail and Nicholas' story.

I pray that while reading *Embraced*, you found these same points to be true. Thanks for reading!

Sincerely,

Katrina Shelley

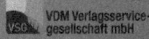

FSC
www.fsc.org
MIX
Papier | Fördert
gute Waldnutzung
FSC® C083411

Zeitfracht Medien GmbH
Ferdinand-Jühlke-Straße 7
99095 Erfurt, Deutschland
produktsicherheit@kolibri360.de

Druck:
CPI Druckdienstleistungen GmbH
im Auftrag der
Zeitfracht Medien GmbH
Ein Unternehmen der Zeitfracht - Gruppe
Ferdinand-Jühlke-Str. 7
99095 Erfurt